THRILL KILL

A Selection of Recent Titles by Don Bruns

The Quentin Archer Mysteries

CASTING BONES *
THRILL KILL *

The Lessor and Moore Mysteries

STUFF TO DIE FOR
STUFF DREAMS ARE MADE OF
STUFF TO SPY FOR
DON'T SWEAT THE SMALL STUFF
TOO MUCH STUFF
HOT STUFF
REEL STUFF

The Caribbean Mysteries

JAMAICA BLUES
BARBADOS HEAT
SOUTH BEACH SHAKEDOWN
ST. BARTS BREAKDOWN
BAHAMA BURNOUT

* available from Severn House

THRILL KILL

Don Bruns

This first world edition published 2017
in Great Britain and the USA by
SEVERN HOUSE PUBLISHERS LTD of
19 Cedar Road, Sutton, Surrey, England, SM2 5DA.
Trade paperback edition first published
in Great Britain and the USA 2017 by
SEVERN HOUSE PUBLISHERS LTD

British Library Cataloguing in Publication Data
A CIP catalogue record for this title is available from the British Library.

ISBN-13: 978-0-7278-8693-4 (cased)
ISBN-13: 978-1-84751-802-6 (trade paper)
ISBN-13: 978-1-78010-865-0 (e-book)

All Severn House titles are printed on acid-free paper.

Severn House Publishers support the Forest Stewardship Council™ [FSC™],
the leading international forest certification organisation.
All our titles that are printed on FSC certified paper carry the FSC logo.

Typeset by Palimpsest Book Production Ltd.,
Falkirk, Stirlingshire, Scotland.
Printed and bound in Great Britain by
TJ International, Padstow, Cornwall.

ONE

Kim Hammond rounded the corner from Barbara's Bridal Boutique, pulling a wool scarf tight around her shoulders and shrugging off the chill. After alterations, the white lace gown would be perfect, and the apricot bridesmaids' dresses had been what she'd dreamed of. The tall thin black man blocking her path was *not* something she'd pictured on this idyllic day.

'Not your lucky day, lady.'

She paused, looking left and right and over her shoulder. *Please, someone drive by. Something.* She saw no one. Her heart raced and she remembered what her father had said. 'When in danger, kick him in the balls.'

The long blade on the knife in his gloved right hand suggested a kick might incite him. If it was money he wanted she didn't have much. There was her engagement ring. She panicked. Oh, God, not the ring. Maybe he'd just take the cash. Please, let her keep the ring.

'I don't have much money.' Her thin voice quivered. 'Maybe forty dollars and it's all yours.' She reached inside her leather purse.

'It's not money, lady.' His left hand was buried in his baggy jeans and she briefly wondered if he had another weapon in there.

'What do you want?'

He was a boy. Staring into his face she realized he was sixteen, seventeen at the most. She kept digging into her purse, finally producing her wallet.

'Everything I've got,' she said. 'Listen, my fiancé is a banker.' Grasping for anything. 'I'm sure I can raise more money.'

The young man nodded and she saw hesitation in his eyes. Hesitation and a sleepy look, almost like he was drugged. Hopefully he was having a change of heart. Dropping his knife hand he frowned.

'I'm truly sorry, but you're the one,' he said.

She side stepped him ready to run. The slender boy stepped in her way.

'Please, my car is just over there,' she pointed to a street spot. 'For God's sake, take the car.'

'You're the first person in five minutes,' he said. 'I've got to do this today. If I don't, there may not be another chance.'

The girl quickly darted to her left. He was there, and when she stepped to her right he again countered.

'What do you want? I'll give you anything,' she cried now, tears rolling down her cheeks.

'I want . . .' He paused, then raised the threatening knife again, 'I need to kill you. It's what I have to do.'

'Oh, God no. No, please no. I'm about to get married. Why? Oh, please.' And instead of screaming she spoke in a soft, little girl voice. She wanted to shout, scare the assailant off but her words came out in pathetic sobs. 'I'll do whatever you . . .'

He grabbed her by the shoulder, squeezing hard. It was crazy but she kept thinking, *He's going to leave a bruise.*

'Nothing personal, lady.' His words were slurred and he lurched at her. 'You just happened to be in the wrong place at the wrong time.'

She watched in horror as he plunged the knife into her chest, again and again. Finally the girl screamed. She screamed as she watched blood flow from the wound but by then it was too late. She closed her eyes and saw no more.

TWO

Detectives Quentin Archer and Josh Levy stood on the corner, a cold mist blowing in their faces. Archer had turned up the collar on his sport coat, but still the chill went bone deep. The owner of the bridal boutique, a frail looking gray-haired lady, leaned against the brick wall, a black umbrella in her right hand. She kept shaking her head back and forth.

A second lady, wearing a yellow windbreaker, stood by her side, wringing her wrinkled hands.

'We didn't hear anything, we didn't see anything,' she said. 'This part of town is very safe. And usually very quiet. Especially in the afternoon. This is just so, so sad. And especially here. These kinds of things just don't happen here.'

Archer knew she was wrong from the start. There *was* no part of this town that was safe.

'Did anyone come in the store shortly before or after she visited you? Someone who might have been stalking her? Asking about her?' Archer asked.

'No. It was a slow day.' The gray-haired lady's gaze shifted to the body bag as two uniformed attendants lifted it up into the ambulance. 'There was no one. She was the only one who visited us today. We usually work by appointment and there was no one else scheduled.'

'Think hard about anything you might have noticed. A car driving by that didn't look right? A motorcycle? Delivery van? Did you have any deliveries today? Any packages or special mail?'

'There was nothing unusual, Detective. It was pretty much a normal day.' She paused, taking a deep breath. 'I imagine this is going to be on the news, right? And they'll mention our shop?'

'I'm certain the press will be here before day's end,' Levy said. 'They tend to gravitate to scenes like this.'

'This can't be good for business,' the lady said.

'It wasn't very good for the victim,' Archer replied.

She nodded. 'I suppose not. She was a sweet young girl. But then they all are, you know? They're getting ready for the most important day in their life. Who will tell the groom?'

'We contact the immediate family,' Levy said. 'Mother, father, husband, wife. It's up to them to tell anyone else.'

A uniformed policeman handed Archer a plastic bag containing a blue aerosol can, the name Chill printed in white on the metal.

'Officer, is this something we should be concerned with?'

'Part of the crime scene, Detective. I thought we should bag it.'

'It was under her body, Q. Could be she just fell on it as she hit the ground,' Levy said.

'Possible. Or maybe the killer placed it there.'

'An aerosol can? Why?'

'I don't know, Detective Levy. It's our job to find out.'

THREE

A TV news anchor had coined the phrase *thrill kills*. The killings appeared to be random murders, possibly committed by someone or multiple someones who killed for the sport. There were three. So far. The young white bride-to-be was a bank teller. She was followed by a black janitor who worked in an office building in the Warehouse District and a gangbanger who was a member of the Nasta Mafia in Little Woods, East New Orleans. One item tied them together. A blue-and-white can at the scene of each murder. Other than that, there were no obvious connections, just three random people who had met untimely deaths. The girl had multiple wounds to the chest; the janitor had been shot at close range; the gangbanger had been stabbed repeatedly. Homicide was feverishly conducting background investigations, looking for connections. And after a week of no leads, no associations, there was just that one item that was identical to all three incidents.

When the department finally released information about finding a can of the pressurized gas named Chill at the scene of each of the three shootings, *The Times Picayune* bold headline read 'The Chill Thrill Kills'.

Quentin Archer had caught the first case. Therefore, the next two were his as well. And he'd never even heard of Chill.

'It's a spray gas, Q,' detective Josh Levy had explained. 'You can get it in some grocery stores or carry-outs. Let's say you've got a six-pack of warm beer, a liter of Coke, or a bottle of white wine and you need to chill it quickly, you spray some of this on the bottle and it chills. Almost instantly. Some chemical called nitroxicetylene.'

'I don't drink white wine.'

'That's why you don't know about Chill. That plus you're not some kid looking for a cheap high.'

'High?'

'The kids like to spray it up their noses. It not only makes the nasal passages get ice cold, but if you breathe enough of this stuff it makes you a little crazy. If it wasn't this shit it would be furniture polish or cleaning fluid. Kids today, they'll huff anything cheap. Chill sells for like three bucks and you can get fifteen, twenty hits.'

One day later they sat in the bullpen, Levy straddling a chair and Archer at his desk. Eighteen desks filled the room and across the hall, in a matching bullpen, were another eighteen desks. Thirty-six places for harried homicide detectives, although only thirty-one were on duty. Thirty-six cops were needed for a full complement but the NOPD homicide division wasn't exactly deluged with resumes, and two detectives had walked out in the last three weeks. Homicide duty in the country's murder capital wasn't everyone's cup of tea. Besides, the pay was lousy.

'So we've decided there's no intention of robbing the victims?' Archer loosened his tie.

Levy shook his head. 'The bank teller, she had her engagement ring on and money in her purse. The janitor had a couple hundred bucks in his wallet and the pay stub from the check he'd just cashed. The banger had bling. A couple thousand dollars in gold hanging around his neck. They all had valuables, Q. You were there. You checked 'em out. Nobody was robbing anyone. It seems like the kill is what's important. Maybe that's all it is. The thrill of the kill.'

'We've been exploring the possibility of a vendetta?'

'We have,' Levy said, 'but the janitor? He was a seventy-five-year-old church-going grandfather. Hardly the model for a gangland slaying. The girl, she was about to get married. Loving family, close friends. Her fiancé was a respected bank executive. Hector Sanchez, now he was a bad ass. Couple of DUIs, did time for selling drugs, rape, a home invasion, and he was only twenty-four. I could see someone cutting him up. But nothing seems to fit together.'

'We need to look at the bank teller again. Jealous ex, or a girlfriend who was in love with her fiancé?'

'We will, Q, but there's nothing in any of their background checks that is a direct link to the others.'

'We keep finding out what doesn't work. What doesn't fit.' He closed his eyes, his fists clenched. 'Eventually,' Archer said, 'the only thing left is what *does* work. What *does* fit. Then we solve the crime.'

He leafed through loose papers on his desk. 'Look at this. We canvassed grocery stores and carry-outs in all the neighborhoods where the bodies were found. Made a list of all of them that carry Chill and viewed video from all the stores that had a camera. We got squat.'

'Problem is, Detective, it's hard to make out the images on some of the videos. The definition isn't that great. And in most of those stores they've got spray cans for dozens of purposes. Everything from whipped cream to spray that will fix a flat tire. You've got insecticides, shoe polish, lubricants, even spray-on cheese. We're studying the video images again, but it's a slow process. We've got maybe twenty stores and we're trying to go back at least a week before the victims were killed. That's a lot of hours of video.'

'And obviously the killers could have purchased the product anywhere. Maybe even online.'

'There's no trace of the chemical on any of the victims,' Levy said. 'The killer didn't use any of the gas on them.'

'And we're just guessing if we think there may be a trace on the killer. No way of knowing.'

'Why does the can show up every time?' Levy laced his fingers together, rocking back and forth. 'What's the purpose? It's a message. Like a graffiti artist who tags his work.'

'Why the can of Chill?' Archer asked. 'What kind of tag is that? Just finding out what purpose the cans have would give us a huge advantage. It's a signature, but there seems to be no reason.'

'The one thing we've kept quiet,' Levy said, 'is that each can has been used. Somebody has sprayed some of the contents. None of the cans is completely full. We measured the content.'

'So the killer, or killers, drink white wine. They chill a bottle then go kill someone.' Q forced a smile.

'Or, the killers want to get high before they murder the vic.'

Archer stood up, pointing a finger at Levy. 'It's a dumb idea, but check the videos for anyone buying white wine.'

'Holy shit, Q, there might be thousands of people. And on a security camera all wine bottles are going to look alike.'

'What if we narrowed it to shoppers who buy white wine *and* Chill? Now that might be interesting. A bottle of wine and an aerosol can.'

'Still, that's going to be a lot of hours.'

'Oh.' Archer frowned, putting on his dark sport coat. 'Of course, you're right. Then we'll explore your idea.'

'I didn't have one.'

'Exactly.'

They walked out of the office, down the hall to the elevator.

'Not one solid lead, Q. By now . . .'

'By now we should have had a concerned citizen giving us a tip. Because somebody besides the killer knows what's happening. Somebody should have called us by now. Somebody who doesn't like the killer, a girlfriend who suspects he's dangerous. A parent or sibling who has noticed strange behavior. Even the crazy people with hare-brained ideas have clammed up. It's too quiet. That I don't understand.'

'Yeah, and you know this isn't going to stop at three. It *will* happen again. No question.'

'It will,' Archer agreed.

'Three murders, Q. All of them looking like the same killer. And for no apparent reason.'

In different situations, in different parts of the city, they'd been killed, and a can of Chill spray had been left at the scene. In a city swarming with tourists, at the peak of Mardi Gras, with hundreds of surveillance cameras mounted everywhere, cops, sheriff deputies and state troopers on every street corner, no one had seen anything.

'Number four is going to bite us in the ass, you know that, right?'

Archer nodded.

'You know, Q, New Orleans has probably the craziest assortment of characters in the country.'

They stepped off the elevator and walked out of the building.

'I give you my former residence, Levy. Detroit, Michigan. I mean, the craziness there is at an all-time high. About fourteen thousand violent crimes per year and ten times the national average of murders. I can't even tell you how many elected officials are in prison. It's staggering.'

'I've got twenty-one thousand violent crimes last year, Archer. We've got politicians in jail, and we've got the highest murder rate of any city in the US.' Levy stopped and folded his hands. 'Well, we trade those figures with Baltimore and Detroit, but still . . .'

'Bragging rights.' Archer shoved his hands in his pockets.

'Finally, Detective Archer, does Detroit have a Chill epidemic? Is there a can of Chill beside your Motor City murder victims?'

Archer was silent for a moment. 'Not that I'm aware of.'

'Then shut up. I've got a city that tops your Mo-Town.'

Archer gave him a grim smile.

'Seriously, Q, New Orleans is an entity all to its own. You can't compare this city to any other.'

Archer nodded. The detective was right. Even though Detroit had been a huge thorn in his side, in his life, there was no comparison.

Archer checked his cell. A six-year-old black girl had been shot in a drug deal gone bad. She was declared dead at University Medical Center on Canal and they wanted him to respond ASAP. Jesus, it never stopped.

FOUR

There was a chill in the air, the temperature never rising above the mid-fifties for the past several days. The throngs that clogged the city streets to see the parades and revel in the debauchery and festivities wore jackets, coats, boots and stocking caps. Only the hardcore tourists and the flamboyant partiers wore shorts and flip-flops or something even more revealing.

Solange Cordray walked briskly, working her way through the crowd that jammed up the French Quarter. From her small shop on Dumaine Street she moved up Barracks and turned left on Dauphine. Grown men and women meandered past her wearing green-and-purple joker hats, green wigs and the occasional sequined bra and thong. Men *and* women. Dozens of brightly colored plastic beads hung from their necks, and many wore half-masks made of glittery fabric and exotic patterns. Beside her a goth-looking woman walked a pig on a leash, the animal painted purple and yellow, and as Solange picked up her pace, a skeleton with a black top hat stepped into her path, a maniacal grin on his face and a green plastic Hand Grenade cup in his hand, filled with gin, whiskey, melon liqueur, rum and vodka. Recipe for a major hangover. The slender black girl dodged the bare-boned character and was immediately confronted by an older woman with fake cloth breasts hanging from the bottom of her T-shirt to her knees. There was no dress code during Mardi Gras. A ragged Dixieland band played 'Rampart Street Parade' in the middle of the street, and a rowdy mix of young people threw quarters at them, the coins bouncing off their wood and shiny brass instruments and covering the street.

'You are one hot mamma.' A glassy-eyed drunk reached out for her and she deftly moved, wondering if she should even be flattered by the compliment.

Water's Edge Care Center loomed on her right, the concrete two-story building stark against the gray Louisiana sky. A hairy gorilla ambled down the street, holding a white poodle sporting a tutu. The beast bumped her as he passed. Walking up the steps she entered the center, nodding to the young black woman with tight black braids behind the counter. Signing the ledger book, she waited while the woman printed her identification tag, then was passed through the security door into the inner sanctum. Kathy Bavely met her on the other side, her blue eyes sparkling and her streaked blond hair hanging just below her ears.

'You're late, Solange.'

'You've seen the crowds. I've got to add ten minutes to my walk,' she said. 'It's literally a zoo out there.'

'I saw Ma earlier,' Bavely said. 'You know I don't believe many of these people who live here have any memory left at all, but half an hour before you arrive I often see your mother glancing down the hall as if she's anticipating your arrival. I think she knows you're coming.'

'I hope that's true.' They walked down the corridor to the coffee shop, first stop of the day.

'I saw Paul last night.'

Solange laughed. 'Hands-On Paul? I thought you were tired of all that physical attention.'

'Yeah, yeah, but I think there's more than just a physical attraction. We actually talked. He may not be as bad as I've painted him. You know he's a journalist and I got him to open up about some of the stories he's worked on. You'd be surprised at what he's writing. He's actually an interesting guy.'

'Well, you told me he was cheap, and you said he's always trying to cop a feel.'

'I'm not saying that didn't happen.' Grinning at her friend she lightly punched her arm.

They poured coffee into paper cups and sat across from each other at one of the twelve cheap plastic tables scattered around the room.

'Any current news on you and the Detroit cop?'

Solange took her first taste of the bitter coffee. 'There was never any old news. I told you that.'

'I thought when you helped solve that murder you two sort of connected.' Kathy Bavely looked into her eyes. 'I didn't just imagine that, did I?'

'He's an interesting man too.' She closed her eyes and took a deep breath. 'But after his wife was killed in Detroit he's not ready to entertain anything else at this moment. Trust me, I know.'

'Pity.'

'Maybe.'

'You need a life, Solange. Look at you. Young, very good looking, great personality.'

'Divorced. You left that out, Kathy. Right, like all I need is another guy in my life. I don't think so.' She ran a hand through her dark untamed hair. 'So tell me, what stories did Paul write?'

'One he sold involved schemes that came out of the big BP oil spill several years ago. It took him several years to document everything in the story. Companies that sprang up from nowhere, making millions of dollars at the expense of commercial fishermen, and then disappearing without compensating anyone.' She sipped her hot beverage. 'One of the articles is about some guy who leased oyster beds in the bay from the state of Louisiana. This guy's territory happened to be in an area where there was some severe damage from the leak. Though his beds were unharmed, he ended up receiving like thirty million dollars from BP. Thirty million dollars. Talk about a windfall. Of course the guy didn't come forward to refuse the money! I've got the transcript and decided I should read some of his stuff. I mean I should probably learn something about this guy Paul, you know?'

'So, a deeper level of your relationship is about to be unveiled.'

'I don't know if there's any future with him. It's still day to day. Some of the stuff he deals in is truly nasty.'

'Like what?'

'He seemed more than anxious to tell me about his work on an article involving sex trafficking.'

'In New Orleans?'

'In New Orleans. In 2013, if you remember, we had a Super Bowl here.'

'I'm well aware,' Solange said. The tourism traffic had been horrific, but her business had gone through the roof. Mostly drunken men who wandered into her shop hoping to have their fortunes told. After they met her, many were hoping to get lucky. She had them pay up front for the read, and then told them that their future did *not* include getting lucky in her shop.

'Almost one hundred people were arrested for sex trafficking. Some underage prostitutes, some of-age prostitutes, but a number of the arrests were of pimps. Men and women who were selling people for sex. Apparently Super Bowls are the largest market for sex trafficking in the United States.'

'I assume some people came here to see the game,' Solange took a swallow of coffee. 'Or am I just naive?'

'Whenever there's a party, like the ones in our fair city, people do things they would never do at home. The drinking, drugs, sex, it's all available at a much higher level. It doesn't surprise, but apparently a lot of tourists, a lot of men, come to these events specifically for those vices. People who live perfectly respectable lives. Paul says that political conventions, Super Bowl and Mardi Gras are like a license to screw around. Mostly with people you shouldn't screw around with. He equates sex trafficking, human trafficking, to modern-day slavery. It's a serious problem here. And maybe Mardi Gras is second to a Super Bowl.'

'So he writes about unseemly topics. I mean, someone has to expose these things, right?'

'I suppose,' Bavely said. 'That doesn't make him a bad person. He was just a little creepy when he told me that story. I think he was going for shock value. But that's what he writes about, investigative stories about manipulators, crooks, perverts and the people they abuse. He's become rather friendly with Senator Marcia LeJeune. Do you know who she is?'

'LeJeune. Sure. She's the lady who is pushing legislation on human trafficking, right? She pops up in the news a lot,' Solange said.

'She was just on local TV last night. Paul has interviewed her several times. I guess she's shared stories with Paul for his investigative piece, but she's very cautious about revealing too much. He complains that she won't divulge names of places that use trafficked people. He wants specifics and apparently she won't share. She did tell Paul that she wants much harsher penalties on the traffickers and wants penalties on the victims relaxed. Did you know that the women who are being sold as sex slaves often go to jail? Like *they're* the criminals.'

'And I would guess their pimps get off a good deal of the time.'

'Paul's invited me to hear a speech by the senator. She's speaking downtown at a fundraiser for a shelter for women and kids. I'm actually excited about going. I'm sure I'll learn a lot more there.'

Solange sipped her coffee. 'Hey, it sounds like you're actually getting interested in Paul's stories. And maybe Paul as well?' She smiled. 'Listen, I hope the senator is successful and I hope Paul does well with the article. It's really unbelievable that in a Western civilized country this could go on.'

'There's an underground in this city that connected people know is there, but they prefer not to talk about it. Telling that story is his job, and he seems to do it very well.' Kathy took a swallow, then leaned forward and in a soft voice said, 'I keep thinking he's probably a great catch, Solange. An intellectual equal, someone I could partner with. But it's early, and what really bothers me is, like I told you, he's just a little . . .'

'Cheap and pushy,' Solange said.

'Exactly,' Bavely said. 'He's intense in everything he does. Very intense. And as I said, at this point in our relationship, much too hands on.'

The two of them laughed.

'I'm going down to see Ma. It's a little chilly so I don't know if I'm taking a group up on the levee to see the river, but I'll talk to you later this afternoon. Let me know what you decide about Paul. I'm curious.'

'I will. And I want you to meet him. You have this ability to read people. I'm sure he'd give you a lot to work with.'

'I'd love to,' she said.

'You need to find a guy, Solange. I keep thinking about who I could fix you up with.'

'Now who's getting intense?' She folded her hands on the table. 'Seriously, I'm not looking, Kathy. Please, just drop it.'

'OK . . .' Bavely reached across the table and touched Solange's hand. 'You're the only person I can talk to about this kind of stuff, and I thank you for listening. Obviously no one here is going to pay any attention. And I don't really have a lot of close girlfriends. I feel better when I talk to you, you know? You're a great listener, Solange. You are seriously a great listener.'

It's what I do, Solange thought. *The same thing my mother did. We listen to other people's problems. It's my job.*

Ma was in an easy chair, staring at the ceiling. She never changed her focus as her daughter walked in the door.

'Ma, Kathy said you were checking the hall to see if I'd arrived?'

There was no sign of recognition.

'It's Mardi Gras, Maman. You used to keep me protected that week before Ash Wednesday. Remember? When I was a little girl, you told me the evil spirits were on high alert, passing through the city on ghostly wings and causing serious mischief. We would play silly games, huddled together, and you would use chants and prayers that no evil would harm me.'

The old lady stayed focused, looking up at the textured plaster.

Solange stood next to her, stroking the silver streaked hair. 'You were my *protectrice*, Maman. You kept me safe. Now, it's my job to keep you safe.'

The lady's eyes lowered. She gazed at Solange, for a brief second connecting, and the girl felt a tremor. The moments were few but she believed she had gotten through.

'The throngs are thick, Ma, and it takes longer to make the journey. Believe me; the most important part of my day is visiting with you. I will leave earlier tomorrow so we can spend more time together.'

Tears sprang to her eyes, and she quickly wiped them away. She never wanted to be weak in her mother's eyes. She needed to be strong during the brief seconds that they shared intimacy.

She sat on the edge of the bed, reaching out to hold her mother's hand and she prayed to Damballa. 'Sky Father, primordial creator of all life, give my mother back her mind, give her peace and tranquility. Give her a voice again so she can help do your work.' She asked the snake god every day. And every day he was silent. Much like the dementia patients at Water's Edge Care Center.

Dementia stole the voices of those affected. But she believed there was a deep-rooted soul that could someday, someway be resurrected. Someday, someway she would see Ma whole again.

FIVE

R oofless houses damaged by the hurricane still dotted the landscape, and corroded remains of the twisting roller coaster that had once been the signature ride of Six Flags Over America were visible from highway ten in East New Orleans. Six Flags had abandoned the one hundred and fifty acre property after Katrina flooded the land, and now urban adventure tourists were among the few visitors who frequented the deserted grounds. Archer surveyed the deteriorating park, a wasteland of decaying amusements and buildings, and a midway of cracked overgrown pavement.

'I was the one who called 911.' The young man in a plaid flannel shirt tugged at his cap. 'We decided to hike out here and see what was left,' he said, clasping his girlfriend's hand. 'They filmed *Jurassic World* out here you know. And I think one of the *Planet of the Apes* movies. This place has some history and we just thought it would be cool to visit and see the remains of the old amusement park.'

'We never expected to find the remains of a person.' The girl shivered, wrapped in a heavy cloth coat with a scarlet scarf draped around her neck. 'One of the worst trips I've ever taken.'

A chilly wind blew across the bleak landscape, and Archer watched as white-coated paramedics placed the victim in a body bag and lifted it into the ambulance. Looking up he saw the curving metal track of the coaster swooping up and down like a giant silver crane. To his right was a small crumbling concrete open-air building with *Cool Spot* painted on the side. A faded Coke sign announced the former sponsor. Ghostly structures stood empty, tall weeds, ivy and scrub trees slowly swallowing them and taking over the grounds.

'What do you want me to do with that, Detective?' The uniformed officer pointed to an object nestled in the ground where the body had been.

Archer stared at the item and shook his head. 'Bag it and we'll check for fingerprints and content at headquarters.'

The officer carefully picked it up with latex gloves and placed it in a plastic bag. Turning to Archer he said, 'Content seems pretty clear, Detective Archer. The spray can is clearly labeled.'

Archer gave him a frown. The can *was* labeled. Chill. But this time things were a little different. The victim hadn't been killed here. Shot twice through the heart, there should have been a lot of blood. There was no blood.

'Have your officers canvas the grounds,' he said.

'The entire park?'

Archer nodded.

'That's a lot of territory.'

'With snakes, boars, alligators . . .' Archer trailed off. The area was far from safe. 'Tell them to be careful, OK?'

'Exactly. What are we looking for?'

'Blood,' Archer said. 'We're looking for a large pool of blood. I want to know if this man was killed within the park area.'

Two hours later he had his answer. The man had been killed somewhere else.

He'd been there before. Too many times in his short New Orleans career. The corner of Earhardt and Clayborn. The coroner's office and the city morgue. A stone's throw from the old train station and a series of rebuilt low-income housing projects.

'Blake Rains,' Marsha Monroe, the coroner, said.

'Should I know the name?' Archer asked.

The petite young lady in the white lab coat shook her head. 'You haven't lived here long enough to remember him, Q. I have.'

'And he was memorable because?'

Smoothing the white smock over her hips, she said, 'A writer named Paul Girard did a story on several city council members about five years ago. He singled Councilman Rains out as someone who abused the Sunshine law, holding illegal meetings behind closed doors. If memory serves, Girard also accused Rains of hiring illegal immigrants to work a remodeling project on his home, supposedly paying them with city funds. And there was a complaint filed by a Guatemalan woman who worked as his maid. She claimed he underpaid her, forced her to work long hours and made sexual advances. There were actually rape charges filed that were eventually dropped. The article got picked up by a syndicate and went national.'

'And you remember all of that about Rains from five years ago?' Archer studied the lady's face.

'First of all, Detective, since August 29, 2005, everything we do in this city is under scrutiny. That hurricane did more than destroy people's homes and lives. It brought out hundreds of journalists who were eager to bury New Orleans. Every news organization in the country wanted a piece of the tragedy we'd gone through. And they uncovered a lot of dirt. Still do.' She nodded. 'Second of all, Blake Rains tried to get me fired.' Color rose in her cheeks. 'The man questioned one of my autopsies involving a drug overdose. The deceased had been his friend. Then the son of a bitch offered a bribe if I fudged the report so I reported *him*. Needless to say, he wasn't too happy about the situation and after threatening me numerous times he went public and called me a liar. The biggest prevaricator in the city. It wasn't a pleasant time, Detective. I will never forget the man. He claimed I was out to destroy his career.' Her words were icy cold and she stared at him.

'She said, he said?'

'It sounds like that, doesn't it? But I'm still here, Detective Archer. Mr Rains was voted out of office three years ago. I think it ends with "she said".'

'I think it ends with a dead body,' Archer said.

'Of course you're right. And I'm right too.'

'How's that?'

'I always maintained that Blake Rains was heartless: the two gun shots destroyed that organ in his chest.'

'I've got victim number four, Levy.' Archer heard the sigh and sensed some pain on the other end of the call. 'Are you OK?'

'I'm sorry, Q. Sometimes it's rough, you know. Rougher than others.' He was quiet for a moment. 'Yeah, *you* know. Look, I just took a call and what I've got here is a dead boyfriend, girl-friend and an ex-lover. Apparently the ex didn't adjust to the current situation. Murder-suicide seemed to be the answer. It's a bloody mess.'

It was Archer's turn to be silent. Finally he spoke.

'I appreciate the help you're giving me on this case, Josh, but in one way you've got it easier on yours, my friend.'

'How's that? How the hell is this easier?'

'You've got your killer. You know who did it. I still don't have a clue.'

He grabbed the streetcar on Canal that would take him to the Quarter. It was easier than fighting traffic with a car, and they'd blocked off half the intersections in town for parades, big and small. A big black lady with an orange wraparound skirt, a flowery top and her hair wrapped up in a matching scarf climbed on at the next stop. She carried a large paper sack in each hand and she glared at him until he got the message and stood up, motioning for her to take his seat.

'Thank you, honey.' She smiled sweetly.

Two teenage boys with tight white T-shirts walked on, jeans rolled up at the ankle, and an old lady with a walker, yellow tennis balls on the bottom of the legs, worked her way up the three steps. A skinny black man, wearing tuxedo pants, a vest and a bowler chatted and laughed with the driver, and a ten-year-old girl in a pink party dress followed her grandma onto the car, never letting go of the older lady's hand. Quite an assortment of characters. As they approached the Quarter, more people jumped on wearing masks, carnival hats and wigs, most headed to party central in the heart of the Big Easy. In Detroit, public transportation was somewhat threatening. *This* was a party.

Archer got off at Bourbon and half the maniacal cast of characters on his streetcar exited as well, following him, whooping, hollering and parading down the street. He dodged those he could and walked down to what was billed as the world's best karaoke bar, the Cat's Meow. Living in a small cottage, a former slave's quarter directly behind the establishment, he could attest that if it wasn't the best, it was probably the world's *loudest* karaoke bar.

He ducked behind the balconied building and walked up the brick path to the cottage. Studying the door, he saw the inch-long piece of Scotch tape halfway up, stretched between the door jamb and the door. If someone entered, they wouldn't notice the tape but it would have separated. As it was, it appeared to be undisturbed.

With one brother in jail and another on the run, Archer was especially careful. He was ultimately responsible for the conviction of them both, and his brother Jason, the fugitive, had shown up several times to threaten him, yet was always able to sneak away undetected. Archer spent every day looking over his shoulder.

What bothered him most was that the ringleader of the drug operation, the leader of the gang that employed his two brothers, was a cop who still patrolled the streets of Detroit. His freedom came down to a simple lack of hard evidence. Bobby Mercer was a decorated, seasoned veteran of the DPD. When Archer turned on him, it was Archer who was forced out of town by not just Mercer's drug ring, but his own brothers, Jason and Brian. The *blue shield* Archer called it. Cops banding together to protect their fellow cops, even when they were committing crimes. The murder of Archer's wife, Denise, was a grim reminder how much certain people wanted him to shut up. Possibly for good. Since then he took care never to let his guard down, never to assume that he was in the clear.

Walking into the small cottage, he hung his jacket on a chair and placed his gun and holster on the bed. Opening the refrigerator, he frowned. It would be nice, just once to be hit with a blast of cold air, but his landlord hadn't gotten around to dealing with the appliance, so he pulled out a tepid beer. Making a note to call the man one more time about the temperature, Archer scrolled his phone for messages.

A voicemail from headquarters got his attention immediately.

'Detective, we've got a report on soil samples from the bottom of Blake Rains's shoes. You were right. It doesn't appear he was murdered at Six Flags.' He smiled. Finally a clue.

He called the lab. 'Samples don't match at all?'

'No. If he'd been walking around Six Flags, we'd have some of the crumbling concrete from the walkways. There's some fill over there that doesn't appear at all on the footwear. We've pretty much narrowed it down. We found samples on the soles of another victim's shoes almost identical to those on this Rains guy's loafers.'

Archer was quiet for a second. 'Are you going to make me guess?'

'I'd bet you'd be wrong.'

Somebody like Blake Rains, a former city government official, he might have been shot in the Warehouse District where the janitor was found. Office buildings, high end restaurants, places Rains might frequent. Or, maybe near the bridal shop where the female teller had been stabbed. Financial area, government buildings, retail stores . . .

'I give up.'

'Same soil as found on Hector Sanchez, the gangbanger in Little Woods up by Lake Ponchartrain.'

Archer took a swallow of the now warm beer. 'What the hell do you suppose he was doing up there?'

'I just report the facts, Q. I don't analyze them.'

SIX

Gangsta Boy sneered at the young black teenager huddled on the worn carpeted floor.

'What, you fifteen, sixteen?' The broad-shouldered twenty-year-old lorded it over the scared kid, five years his junior. 'What the fuck, my man. Simple request was to go out and sell five hundred dollars of street-value H. Now there are kids younger than you that would have jumped straight up to that task. Not you. You come back to me with half the fucking product, you know what I'm sayin'?'

'Sir, I never, never done nothin' like that before.' The boy was crying, tears rolling down his cheeks. 'I can learn, sir. Learn to earn. Please?'

A room air conditioner rattled in the grim hotel room.

'Boy, I don't hold out a lot of hope. Nasta Mafia, we do not, hear me, do not waste time on pieces of shit like you. Prime section of the city, quality horse and you fuck it up. I could give Tigre to a low-life spic and he'd have it gone in half an hour. A street nigger and he'd buy half of it for himself. Product would be gone, son.'

'Give me another chance.'

His cell phone chirped and he pulled it from his baggy low-riding jeans. Listening for a moment, he finally spoke. 'Strippers like H, my man. Makes 'em feel like sex on a stick when they be doin' that pole thing. You make arrangements with Sydney at the club. Get those girls that fix, you hear, and don't go light on the dose. You bring the cash here to the hotel.'

Looking back at the kid on the floor he said, 'Sales is not your fucking forte.' Gangsta Boy spit on the kid's face, once, twice, and then kicked him in the ribs. 'Get up, pussy boy. We gonna put you to work on construction. You be workin' demolition in the Ninth Ward. You don't make much money but you eat and stay in one of the condemned houses out there. It's a roof, nigger. You report tomorrow, six a.m. Outside, in front of the bus. You be there, young man. You got a problem with that, I'll solve it. Put a bullet in your brain, pussy boy. You never forget who you workin' for. After a little rough love, put a bullet in your momma's brain too you ever think about not showin' up. Don't forget, I know where Momma and the kids live. I know Momma very well. Intimate relationship, you understand. Your sisters too. You respect your family, you do what I say.' He smiled down at the boy. 'Now get outta here.'

The phone chirped again. 'Yeah, yeah, this is Gangsta Boy. I can meet you at Chartres and St Louis, twenty minutes. You want snow, I'll make it snow. How much?' He listened for a moment, then whistled between his teeth. 'That much? That's winter snow. I can make that happen, yes I can.'

'The East boys are cuttin' in, Delroy. You'd best do somethin'. Cuttin' up some spic ass in Little Woods ain't exactly sendin' a strong enough signal, you know what I'm sayin'? We gotta do a lot more than kill a couple of bangers from the other side. Tell me I'm wrong.'

Delroy Houston sat on the street corner of Bourbon and Dumaine in the Quarter, flipping a coin, over and over again.

'Dushane, you are right as usual. Warhead Solja don't take second place to some pissant niggers like Nasta Mafia. Turf is turf, brothah. Only so much room for so many gangs.' Squinting his eyes, he looked closely at his lieutenant, proud of the young black man, yet worried about his taste for blood. Dushane White wore the unique badge of a long ugly scar on his cheek, evidence of a vicious knife fight. Dushane sat next to him so it seemed obvious that his man had won that fight.

A group of senior citizens walked by, one limped by with a cane and a woman in the group carried a poodle, dyed in pink, blue and yellow.

The two men shook their heads, arms folded, warding off the chill in the air.

'Heads we go to war, my brother. Tails,' he paused, 'we go to war.' Dushane chuckled. 'What's it gonna be, Delroy?'

Houston flipped the quarter one more time, letting it land on the sidewalk.

'Heads.'

'Like a stacked deck, I knew it all along.' Dushane laughed out loud. 'You say when and where, Delroy.'

'You know,' Houston said in a quiet voice, 'we don't just pick up and start jiving. There are some hurdles to clear, my man. Got to talk to some people, grease the skids, so to speak.'

'You know we'll be waitin' for the word.'

'You like this kill aspect of our gang. A little too much, Dushane. We got to study it first.'

The man reached up and stroked the scar on his cheek with his index finger, an unconscious gesture ever since the violent gang battle where he'd earned it, two years ago. 'War is essential in every civilization, DH. It's the way the world works. Without war we get fat and sloppy. Get rid of the weak and protect your turf. Or, stretch a little and take some of their turf. That's what it's all about.'

'I know,' Houston said. 'I know, but I gotta consult. You know? The play is bigger than just protecting the turf, you understand. Bigger than that. Once we go all out, there'll be hell to pay, my friend. Hell to pay. There are people who depend on what we do, so I got to clear it. Make sure that in the end, no matter what the end may be my friend, that our business is still there. We do answer to a higher authority, Dushane. I'm not even sure who that is, but trust me, there's a higher authority. Don't want to totally piss off the wrong people, you understand?'

There was something in the wind, in the cool air that blew through the quarter that rustled the colorful crinoline dresses of costumed revelers. It reminded Solange of a fine mist. You thought you could feel some moisture, but it wasn't exactly sprinkling. As she walked home, she could almost smell it over the tempting odor of fried oysters and boiled shrimp emanating from the restaurants. A faint odor of sweet jasmine, maybe olive oil and cherries. It was unsettling, like watching a snake that you knew would strike. You just didn't know when. And she thought about Marie Laveau, dancing at her rumored wild orgies with a snake wrapped around her oiled, naked body. The voodoo queen controlled her environment. The snake never struck. And maybe Solange Cordray needed to pay attention to controlling her environment. Not by dancing naked with a snake, but by paying attention to her surroundings. By concentrating on immediate concerns. Maybe Kathy Bavely was right. She needed to start paying attention to her own life, instead of being consumed by the lives of her clients.

She'd read about the Chill thrill kills, and she knew Quentin Archer was lead on the murders. And just the thought of those killings brought goosebumps to her dark skin. She needed to concentrate on the moment at hand. Work on control. She ducked as a woman in a short skirt, tights and feathered wings waved her arms in a crazy menacing dance directly in front of her, the lady's feathered beaked headdress looking like an eagle. Two obese men followed her, wearing Hooters T-shirts and tight orange shorts. Below their cheap wigs of flowing golden locks their guts stuck out like ripe watermelons.

This was her town. Born and raised. She wasn't always proud of it, but New Orleans was in her blood. It was the fabric of her young life, the texture of her soul. The tourists, the crazy people who flew in from everywhere, thought it was Disney World for grown-ups. An adult fantasy paradise. In reality, NOLA was a living, breathing organism. With an unhealthy portion of bad germs. Two girls who could have been twins blocked her path and she moved onto the street, noting they wore nothing but body paint. And the temperature was still in the fifties. Weaving around a guitar player and his Labrador Retriever, the man wailing a blues song, the dog moaning in response, she walked the next short block with no interruptions.

Arriving at her shop she unlocked the door, hoping there would be no customers this late in the afternoon. Her hopes were dashed. A young couple with heavy coats and stocking hats followed her in. She turned, studying the two of them. They looked desperate and it was impossible to turn them away.

'Can you do spells?' the man asked.

'Now is probably not a good time.' She took off her jacket, and rubbed her hands for warmth.

'We can pay you for your trouble. Whatever you want.'

I would hope, she thought. 'Payment is in advance. I guess you are unable to have a child.'

The young woman spun around and stared at the man. 'You've seen her before. You've told her. Right?'

'No, I swear.'

'We've never met,' Solange said, staring at the girl. 'I will cast a spell and make a gris-gris bag for you. If the spirits co-operate, you will be fertile. There are no guarantees, but I do have communication.' And she realized, if she had communication, why was Ma still a wheelchair zombie? She felt connected, but often felt woefully inept, no matter how many successes she'd had.

SEVEN

The streets were filled with cop cars and cops. State troopers, sheriff deputies and NOPD. Several in almost every block. Security during Mardi Gras was paramount. Archer stepped around a green Polaris Task Force vehicle that looked like an army Jeep but only one-quarter the size and greeted the lady manning it. Recognizing a fellow officer, she nodded to him.

'We've got a lot of strange vehicles on our force,' she said. 'You see this crazy Mardi Gras traffic? With this little beauty I can squeeze by on the side of the street. I do it every day. And over there we've got a lift vehicle. It's got a crane. We can be two stories high in a minute. Gives us a broad view.'

Walking by a slim department-issued motorcycle, he passed under a balcony where twenty clean-cut men in dark suits threw plastic medallions to the crowds below. Probably members of one of the Krewes. Men, women and children scrambled to pick up the worthless coins.

Turning down Royal he walked to 801. The restaurant had become one of his favorites. A simple bar, tables and chairs with nothing fancy, but the food was great. Po boys, fried catfish, alligator sausage, fried crawfish tail. Delicious muffaletta on a Leidenheimer Italian bun brushed with garlic-infused olive oil, and filled with Italian salami, provolone cheese and olive salad. He'd memorized the menu item. It was probably the reason he'd put on three or four pounds since he moved here.

'Your regular, sweety?' The waitress handed him a Coke garnished with a slice of lime.

As much as he hated the familiar term 'sweety', it was nice that she knew him.

'Sure.' He forced a smiled.

She walked to the kitchen and he checked his cell phone. Fats Domino sang 'Walking to New Orleans' on the restaurant's sound system as Archer checked his messages again. He glanced up to see an enormous woman, close to four hundred pounds at least, followed by her husband, maybe one fifty, pass by and sit in a booth behind him. They both were garbed in gaudy, green-purple-and-yellow costumes. Jack Spratt and his wife. Someone for everyone. It was meant to be.

Archer faced the door, sipping his Coke as the two strippers walked in. Dressed in street garb, sweats and knee-high boots, they were still definitely strippers. He'd met the blonde before.

'Detective Q!' Alexia Chantel walked over and hugged his neck. 'Sandy, this is the detective I told you about. We met here a couple of weeks ago and I keep hoping he'll stop by the club.'

Sandy nodded. It looked like the word 'detective' scared the hell out of the cute redhead.

'So, you never show up.'

'It's nothing personal.'

'If you were somebody else, not Homicide, not a cop, would you come? Would you check out the show?'

'I'm not somebody else.'

As Sandy moved toward a clean booth, Alexia grabbed him by the arm. She leaned in, looking into his eyes. 'Well, if you knew a certain party was selling heroin,' she said in a hushed tone, 'would you come? Would you send an officer to the club?'

'In the club?'

'To the strippers,' she said softly.

'Who?'

The girl glanced at her friend who had chosen a booth in the back and brushed back her blonde hair. Whispering again, she said, 'I shouldn't say this but there is a very lucrative business selling H to some of the girls on Bourbon Street, OK? Some of the girls even have' – she paused, leaning even closer to his ear – 'handlers. High-class pimps. I could be in trouble for even mentioning it. Now pretend I was just flirting with you.' She cupped his chin in her hand and kissed him full on the lips. The contact was jolting and lasted several seconds.

It was the first time any woman had made an advance since Denise had passed and he felt his heart thumping harder, blood rushing to his face. When she finally broke the lip-lock she smiled and winked. Archer was stunned.

The cute blonde turned to join her friend and, looking back at him, she blew another kiss. She was a stripper. She made her

living teasing guys. Still, she gave him a shock. For a moment
he was still. The information had interested him, but when she
covered with a kiss . . .

The waitress brought him the sandwich, enough food to feed
a Third World country. He ate half of it, she volunteered to offer
the rest of the meal to the homeless, and as usual, he accepted.

Archer walked out of the small restaurant, making a note on his
cell phone to talk to drug enforcement about heroin in the strip
clubs. He was certain they knew the problem existed, but there were
more important crimes to solve. A bunch of strippers who got high?
No big deal. People being killed every day, a little more important.
But the city of vice just got dicier every time he turned around.

Playing the Chill kills over in his head, he still came up empty.
There was a common element, the can of Chill, and nothing
else that seemingly tied the murders together. He flashed on the
attractive voodoo lady, Solange Cordray. She'd helped him on
the murder of a judge. She'd supplied valuable information that
no one else could have known. She offered to help him again if
he needed her. And for reasons he couldn't quite grasp, he was
anxious to talk to her. Something about the kiss at lunch from
Alexia Chantel made him think of Solange. The sun goddess.
For a fleeting moment he wished the kiss had come from
the voodoo queen. That made no sense. None at all.

Passing by a small hotel, he was taken with the sign in the
window. Hand scrawled, it read *Tonight Only: Thrill Kill Plays
Live in the Lounge.* Archer shook his head. It was nice to know
someone was profiting from these insane killings, even if it was
only a local band.

Delroy Houston strolled up Bourbon toward Canal smiling as he
walked past the legendary strip clubs, big guys on the sidewalk
out front shouting at the crowds passing by, promising everyone
a good time.

'Live girls! Come on in.'

Better than dead ones. Delroy knew some of the girls were
having a really good time, higher than kites. With all of the drugs
that Nasta Mafia and Warhead Solja supplied, those special ladies
felt no pain. Some of them were in there literally working their
asses off for the next fix. He'd placed some of the strippers

himself, taking a hefty cut of their pay. Multiple streams of income. Life was good.

Two girls stood outside Woody's, dressed in skimpy lace bras and panties, their stringy hair, thin bodies and pale skin giving them the appearance of emaciated waifs. They shivered in the chilly afternoon air.

Houston kept walking, up to Canal, then left to Magazine Street, with its hip urban aura. Trendy restaurants, art shops, a chili-cheese-and-fries joint, and next to the ink shop where the hipsters went for exotic tattoos was Crescent Employment. The small sign on the door announced the business without drawing major attention. As he walked in, the muscular black man nodded at the thin white receptionist with the white magnolia in her hair and walked past her desk to the stairs. He climbed the two flights to an office facing the street.

'Delroy.' The paunchy balding man struggled to stand, reached over his oak desk and extended his hand. Houston ignored it, pulling up a cloth chair and slouching in it.

'We got a problem, Blount.'

Case Blount wiped at his watery eyes and sneezed into a crusty handkerchief he picked up from his desk. 'We've always got problems. It's the nature of our business. Which specific problem do you refer to?' Fidgeting with his narrow tie he sat back down, mopping his brow.

'We work with you. Warhead Solja finds places to put your people, am I right?'

'You do. You're a very important part of our operation. And, we pay you well for your services.'

'Maybe not well enough,' Houston said, pulling a quarter from his pocket. The black man flipped it once and caught it in his tattooed left hand. A deep purple rose adorned the back and a thorn graced every finger.

'So this is a financial concern?'

Houston watched the heavyset man as he wheezed and sneezed again, and pushed his chair back to escape the germs.

'Stay away from me, old man. I don't need your disease.'

'You want to negotiate a better deal? To tell you the truth, Delroy, there are other organizations that offer similar services. Other organizations that would be happy with what we pay.'

'That's what I'm here to discuss, Blount. We're tired of other organizations interfering. I'm not sure that you're not in bed with some of them right now.'

'What are you insinuating?'

Houston rolled the quarter seamlessly from one finger to the next on his tattooed knuckles.

'Nasta Mafia. They're in our face, taking over turf and cutting into our profits. Time we put the word out. Pretty much time we shut those mothahfuckahs down altogether, you understand?'

Blount wiped at his eyes again, picking up a pair of wire-rimmed reading glasses and setting them on his short stubby nose. He shuffled through a pile of papers on his desk and finally pulled out a sheet covered with notes. Scanning it for a moment, he pointed to the middle of the page.

'This is the name I was looking for. Here, Hector Sanchez. News says he was a member of Nasta Mafia. Think, Delroy. Hector Sanchez. Met a rather unpleasant ending. He's dead.'

'What about the Spanish prick?'

'Somebody cut him up. Like in a butcher shop.'

'Maybe I did see that in the paper.' Houston gave him a deadpan look. 'Lots of murders in NOLA, Case.'

'Can of Chill by his side,' Blount said.

'What that means? Cans be bought at any convenience store, Mr Blount,' he said sarcastically.

Blount blew his nose loudly and gazed around the small room. The picture directly behind Houston caught his eye. It always did. Mounted in the center of the wall, a black-and-white photo of a mousy girl pecking away on a manual typewriter, her horned-rimmed glasses perched on her face and her tongue just peeking through her dark lips. Life was a lot simpler back then.

'If you were in any way responsible, don't you think the word got out? They should have backed off.'

'Assuming we *were* responsible, it didn't do us much good. We're seeing – what's the word – encroachment, Blount. In a number of our endeavors. I would not want you to be involved with this group, because it is my – it is *our* intention to set things straight. If you are dealing with this organization, it might not go well for them, or for you. Is that understood?'

'Boy, if you—'

'Boy?' Houston stood up, all six foot three of him. Now he was loud. Now he was screaming at the cringing white man. 'What the hell, you called me *boy*? Tell me you didn't, mothahfuckah.'

Blount seemed to shrink, becoming smaller in his chair. 'Calm down, Delroy. I meant no disrespect.'

Houston walked to the desk and leaned over, putting his hands on the smooth wood. 'I will not accept disrespect. I came here to consult, little fat man. We are going to have a turf war. Not necessarily conventional, but there will be some bloodshed, there will be some casualties.'

'Jesus, Delroy, not during Mardi Gras. Innocent lives could be at stake.'

'Innocent lives are always at stake. Just a warning. In case you are sleeping with the enemy, and I believe you are' – he placed the quarter on edge, then spun it like a top on Blount's desk. It turned round and round, finally falling on its side – 'then heads, Case. I win. Warhead Solja gets to take down Nasta Mafia.'

'You don't want to do this.'

'You keep sending business to Nasta Mafia, bad things are bound to happen. Let me ask you somethin', Case. A serious question. You know what happens when they bury your fat body?'

Blount shuddered, but kept his mouth shut.

'You become fertilizer, fucker. You get it? Grass grows greener over your dead carcass.'

'What's your point, Delroy?'

'My point, my man, is that you keep fucking with us, your ass is grass. Your ass is grass, mothahfuckah. You dig?'

'Delroy, did you have anything to do with the killing of Blake Rains, the former city councilman?'

Staring into the fat man's beady eyes, Houston said, 'Blount, I am not responsible for every murder in this city. I'm not entirely happy with your insinuation.' Leaning even closer he said, 'You see, when someone is shot, stabbed or poisoned, I am not necessarily the most logical suspect. Maybe I should just give you a list of the ones I am responsible for?' He gave him a grim smile, turned and walked out of the room. He thought the meeting had gone rather well.

EIGHT

A rcher visited the voodoo shop on Dumaine Street, but it was closed. The good thing about the store being closed was he didn't have to breathe in the sweet incense fumes. They gave him a raspy throat and a headache. Archer walked to the French Market, looking out at Decator Street where a blues guitar wailed at the Market Café. He saw Water's Edge Care Center in the distance and continued toward the building. Pausing for a moment, he turned right and walked up to the raised levee of the Mississippi.

Reaching the crest he marveled at the big river curving around the city. A dirty white tug slowly pushed six long barges up the waterway as the *Creole Queen* paddlewheel steamer ran closer to shore, jubilant tourists waving from the top deck. Music from a pavilion nearby featured funky jazz by the New Orleans Swamp Donkeys, their brash horns echoing over the water.

The Detroit River didn't have this romance. It was a working river that froze over in the winter. It was probably clogged with chunks of ice right now. He didn't miss the cold, the river or the ice. And even though the summer months brought recreational boaters and visitors to the islands and parks that dotted it, Archer always thought of the river as just that twenty-four-mile dirty waterway that connected Lake St Clair and Lake Erie. The Mississippi, on the other hand, now this was the granddaddy of all the rivers in the United States. It too was a dirty working body of water, but the river defined New Orleans. Anything to do with Detroit just reminded him of sweet, beautiful Denise and that thought constantly depressed him.

Slowly walking back to the care center, he thought about his wife's murder. His friend Detective Tom Lyons had told him good news, that it appeared beat cop Bobby Mercer had been caught on video camera stealing a car in a deserted parking lot. The same car that ran over his wife. But it was a grainy video and there was still work to be done to prove that the slimeball cop had killed Denise. He wanted to bring down a sledgehammer on Mercer. He wanted to bring down an anvil on the entire corrupt gang of drug dealers that posed as upstanding law enforcement officers.

'She'll be out in a moment, Detective. Please, have a seat.'

The girl at the desk motioned to the chairs in the lobby and went back to her paperwork. Archer stood, pacing across the small room. As soon as he'd sit, she'd arrive. He just knew it. Four minutes later the petite young woman walked through the door.

'Detective Archer, so good to see you.'

Again he was reminded of the kiss. Alexia Chantel had ignited something that he hadn't felt for a long time. Solange Cordray stood her distance, a wry smile on her face as if she knew. It was, of course, his imagination.

'It's been a while since we've talked.'

The last time was at a coffee shop, catching up on a case she'd helped solve. He remembered it well.

'Your mother is doing better? I mean, she's improving?' He'd rehearsed his opening and was blowing it right now.

'No.' She shook her head. 'Not at all.'

It was the wrong intro. 'No?'

'Detective Archer, my mother has dementia. I don't know how much you know about this terrible illness, but I pray for her return and I never give up hope. Modern science has yet to find a cure. Clotille Trouville may never "improve".'

'I'm sorry. I really don't know much about . . .'

'Mr Archer, you came here for a reason?'

Taking a deep breath, he nodded. This wasn't going to be easy.

'Can we go somewhere? For a few minutes and I can explain the situation.'

'Sign in at the desk and meet me down the hall. There's a coffee shop where we can discuss whatever is on your mind.'

Walking down the corridor he was reminded of Henry Ford Hospital where Denise had worked. The institutional look and feel, even the smell of disinfectant lingering in the air. Quiet and sterile. Archer shuddered. Too many memories, too many feelings.

The hospital was named after Henry Ford, head of Ford Motor Company. Only two things worth talking about came out of Detroit: Fords, the Mustang in particular, and Bob Seger. Archer was a big fan.

'Decaf or regular, Detective?' She stood by the coffee pots with paper cups and napkins in her hand.

'Any tea?'

'No, sorry. We're all a little hardcore here.'

'I'll pass.'

'What troubles you?'

Archer paused. 'How do you know anything does? Maybe I just wanted to see you, catch up.' Trying to be glib, funny. It didn't work. He studied her for a moment, the rich coarse dark hair swept up off the soft face, skin like melted milk chocolate. She was more beautiful than he'd remembered.

'That's not why you are here,' she said.

'OK. I wondered if you had heard about the so-called thrill kills.'

'With the Chill cans beside the body?'

'Exactly.'

She poured the steaming beverage into her cup and sat down on a chair, motioning for him to join her. He sat across from her. Archer was strangely attracted to her and for a moment wondered if she was casting a spell over him, although he didn't really believe that was possible.

'Of course. Everyone in town has heard,' she said. 'It's very scary. Kathy, a friend of mine who works here, she and I talked about it just the other day. It seems like there's a killing every other day.'

'It's probably a long shot, but do you have any information? Any ideas?'

She shook her head. 'No. I haven't concerned myself with the matter. However, if I think of anything . . .'

He nodded, standing up. 'I just thought that . . .' Why did he feel so awkward?

'Can you bring me a can?'

'Of Chill?'

'A can found at the scene of one of the murders?'

'Yeah, I guess. They've already been dusted for prints, checked for DNA, so they're clean. Sure. I can bring one. What do you expect to find?'

'You never know, Detective Archer. I'd like to touch one. To see if there is any energy.'

'Energy?' He was confused. It was an aluminum can.

'Even inanimate objects sometimes pick up vibrations, Detective.' Smiling, she looked into his eyes. 'I sense you don't believe me. Or you don't believe what I believe. That doesn't really matter does it? You came here because you have reached the proverbial brick wall. I'm not sure I can break through it, but bring me a can. Today, if possible. Before another killing takes place.'

Nodding he walked to the doorway.

'Wait,' she said. 'There's someone I want you to meet.'

Solange stood and headed down the hallway, Archer close behind. He studied her, the sway of the bright colored cotton dress as she moved gracefully in front of him, her hips in perfect rhythm. She stirred something inside of him, the way her free-flowing black hair swayed and the way her hips and bare legs moved as she walked. They turned a corner and walked half the length of the corridor. She slipped abruptly into a room with an open door.

Motioning for him to enter, she turned and addressed the white-haired older lady in the easy chair.

'Ma, this is Detective Quentin Archer. He's the man I told you about. There have been a number of discussions. We worked with him in the murder of the judge, remember?'

The frail lady with wispy hair looked straight ahead, never acknowledging either of her guests.

'This is the famous Clotille Trouville, Detective. She was the queen of all the voodoo practitioners in her day. In her current state, she still knows more than most, and still strikes fear in the hearts of evil men. Or something like that.' She smiled at Archer. 'Maman is in there somewhere, I'm sure of it, but no one has found the key.'

Solange put her hand on her mother's shoulder, squeezing it affectionately.

'I wanted the two of you to meet. He's an important man in the city, Ma. He's down from Detroit and he's one of the good guys.'

Archer stood still, not sure what to say or do. Finally the lady turned her weathered, sad face and glanced at him. She opened her mouth as if to speak but nothing came out.

'There's no reason for you to stay. You can leave, Detective.' Solange gave him a wistful smile. 'I didn't think she would respond but you never know. I make an attempt to stimulate her whenever there's an opportunity.'

'I'll try to drop off a can of Chill this afternoon,' he said.

'Anything, anything at all would be appreciated.'

'I'll do all I can, Detective. And I'll probably give it to Ma. Let her handle it, feel it. I know deep down that she still has the touch. She still communicates with spirits, quietly, deep inside her mind.'

'Thank you.' Archer turned to leave and heard the soft whisper, a voice he didn't recognize. One word.

'Q.'

He spun around but the old woman had lost her focus and was staring at the ceiling.

NINE

The fifth killing took place on Canal Street that night during one of the biggest parades. Throngs of people lined the street as the lighted floats passed by. A paddle steamer sailed along the designated route, its wheel churning and puffs of white vapor drifting skyward from its smokestack. The boat was followed by a pirate ship complete with billowed sails and pirates with scarved heads and patches over one eye who tossed throws to the assembled rowdies. The next float featured a fire-breathing dragon snorting as flames shot from its nose. As the crowds oohed and awed and dived for the cheap souvenirs that were tossed from the float, someone shoved a knife blade under the breastbone of a bystander, working it under his ribcage and into the heart. The killer caught the lifeless body in his arms and gently laid him on the ground.

There were dozens of law enforcement officers monitoring the parade, thousands of people with cell phone cameras snapping lasting memories, yet no one saw a thing. The victim appeared to be just another drunk passed out on the sidewalk. But when a beat cop almost stumbled over the body, he nudged it with his foot. That's when he saw the blue can of Chill and the thick pool of blood. That's when all hell broke loose.

Krewe Bachus was incensed when two state troopers, sirens wailing and lights flashing on their cars, pulled across Canal Street, stopping the parade dead in its tracks. Members of the organization screamed their protests and a rowdy group stormed the troopers' cars. A large crowd assembled quickly and became unruly, almost riotous, as dozens of uniformed patrolmen surrounded the murder scene. The mob pushed and shoved, screaming for the parade to continue. Some of them tried to get close to the crime scene, throwing beads and doubloons at the officers. The smart ones tried to put as much distance as possible between themselves and the parade. It was evident that whoever committed the murder had moved on, blending in with the group pouring out of the neighborhood.

A belated canvass of those that stayed in the vicinity proved nothing. Was it a copycat murder? Was it one that made no sense, with no correlation to anything else, or was it tied to one of the other victims? Due to the press coverage, everyone in New Orleans knew about the Chill thrill kills, and any killing with the blue can appearing at the site would be counted. Still the question remained, why the can of Chill in the first place?

The can had been fingerprinted. The gas had been sampled and the aluminum swabbed for DNA. The Chill thrill kills were number one on the priority list, in a city where a new priority developed seemingly every two or three hours. They moved fast on this one.

The victim was identified as Trevor Parent, an attorney from the Garden District. He had handled adoptions for people who had the fifteen to twenty-five thousand dollars to spend on finding a US newborn baby to be a part of their family. Foreign kids, forty thousand or more. American kids, foreign kids it made no difference. Parent made a small fortune hooking up babies with couples who felt they couldn't live without a child. The man's name had been in the papers recently regarding his relationship with the Cuban government. Parent was setting up a US facility that handled Cuban children. Now that relationships were normalizing with the southern neighbor, there was a wealth of opportunity. He'd been involved in mediating the adoption of children from Ecuador, and now with US–Cuban relations easing he intended to take full advantage of that prospect. Until tonight. His window of opportunity had slammed shut rather abruptly.

The attorney was a forty-two-year-old scumbag. If he saw an opening he took it. If there was a chance to make a buck at the expense of needy couples or children who were in limbo, he jumped at it. Trevor Parent was a player in the trafficking of humans, and not just a player. He was a game changer. His Cuban connection was extensive, if not exactly legal, and legitimate adoption agencies were crying foul when they found out how his operation worked. All the same, a lot of his connections seemed to be with friendly politicians. Congressmen, senators, commissioners, council members who, it was rumored, possibly shared in his wealth. It was strictly rumor. A Parent who helped other people become parents. A strange twist of fate.

* * *

Levy met Archer at a coffee shop on Severn Street in Metairie. The Morning Call was open twenty-four hours, and being thirty minutes from the Quarter, Levy suggested the location, halfway between his home and Archer's.

'Another Chill kill,' Archer said, checking his watch. Nine p.m. 'This guy made some enemies, but was it random or does it tie into the other murders?'

'How many cases are you handling at this moment?' Levy sipped the dark coffee.

'I'm not even sure. Why?'

'Solve this one, Q, and you won't have another one tomorrow and the next day and the next. At least it won't be a killing with a Chill can involved. This is a serial killer and it doesn't stop till somebody finds the reason why. Why are the murders happening and why is the can showing up?'

'I keep thinking that it's more than one person. The MO isn't the same. Some are shot, some are knifed. And not even knifed or shot in the same way. The gangbanger took multiple stab wounds, so did the bank teller. This guy, a single wound to the heart.'

'The councilman took a knife to the heart.' The low hanging ceiling fan spun lazily over their table and Levy shook powdered sugar over his beignet. He took a bite, slowly chewing it. 'You've been over the backgrounds of each individual. None of them are similar.' Wiping his mouth with his hand, he continued. 'You've looked at the locations of the killings. One is rather puzzling, but the others are in different sectors of the city. First, think about why there would be random killings. There are reasons for murder. A jealous lover, like my case yesterday. Then there's money. Someone either wants the vic's money or thinks the vic wants theirs. Revenge. The killers believe they have been singled out and they want payback, like Columbine. Religious zealots, who think they have been called upon to murder the infidels.'

'And then there are those who are just batshit crazy. The guy dressed like the joker who mowed down a theater crowd. The guy who killed all those partiers at the gay club in Orlando. We've had dozens of those,' Archer said, shaking his head. 'They are breeding a different type of criminal, Levy. There used to be reasons behind murder. Now . . .'

'None of these seems to fit.'

The two were silent for a moment, contemplating the situation. Finally Archer spoke. 'You're right, Josh. There's a common reason. The vics may not be tied together but there's a reason that the Chill can still pops up.'

'Which is?'

Archer sipped his tea, watching a young couple cuddling at a table across the room. The intimacy distracted him. Thinking of Denise, the kiss from Alexia Chantel and his feelings about Solange Cordray.

'Q?'

'Yeah. What if there are two whys?'

'You're losing me.'

'We've alluded to this. Maybe there are two reasons for people being killed.'

'Still with that one common theme? The can of gas?'

'Someone will have a reason to kill random victims. I don't know what it is, but there'll be a reason. Then someone else has a reason to kill people who are connected to each other: maybe they were in a financial scheme together, but whatever it was, this person, to hide the underlying scheme, uses Chill to blend in. Make it look like it was part of the random killings.'

'We've considered that and maybe that's it, they're using the canned gas as a decoy. It's a thought.'

'It's as good as anything else we've got.'

'Why?'

Archer shook his head. 'I don't know why, but we'd better find out in a hurry. You're right. This could happen every day unless we find the answer.'

TEN

She studied the can at a distance, before finally lifting it off the worn, weathered oak table. 'This was found last night?'
'During the parade.'
Brushing back her wiry, coal-black hair, she held the can to her forehead.
'What are you looking for?'
'Inanimate objects absorb energy, Detective Archer. Therefore, they give off energy. It's up to us to detect that energy.'
'And how do you do that?' He studied her figure, her soft shoulders, the swell of her small breasts. He breathed a deep sigh. A major distraction.
She set the can down. 'Right now my room is thick with energy. Radio waves, sound waves, that heater, the light, the undetectable tremor of the earth as it rotates. And we are surrounded with spiritual energy. Finally, there's human energy. Your negative energy when you entered my store.'
'I'm not negative.' He unfolded his arms and pushed back the wooden spindle chair from the table. Gazing down he was aware of the oiled-wood floor and as his eyes rose he noticed, for the first time, the object in the corner. Just to the right of gris-gris bags and a collection of ointments. A small six-inch statue of a figure in robes stood in the middle surrounded by cut glass or tiny crystals. Sweet-smelling incense burned from a stone basket.
'You are skeptical. That comes off as negative energy.'
'I came to you for help,' he said. 'I must have some positive energy to believe you can help me find the killer.'
'It's up to us, to me, to isolate the energy that comes from this can. And believe me, there is energy coming from this can.'
'You can do that?'
'I believe I can. But once that's done, I'm not certain it will give you the answers you are looking for.'
'At this point, I'll take anything.' He gave her a grim smile.

'I sense your frustration, Detective Archer. If I can help in preventing a murder, of course I will.'

'Do you need to keep the can?'

'Yes. For a day.'

'We've taken all the information we needed, fingerprints, DNA samples, but I'll still need it back.'

'I'll have it here for pickup tomorrow.'

'Ms Cordray—'

'You can call me Solange.'

'I can, but it's not entirely comfortable. We don't know each other that—'

'Detective Archer, we know each other better than either of us will admit.'

'So you can call me Quentin. Or Q.'

She studied him, a whimsical smile on her lips. 'And maybe that's a little too familiar as well. After we get to know each other a little more . . .'

'Ms Cordray, I look forward to working with you. I trust there won't be any monetary consideration, because to be frank, the department doesn't have any money. And if they did, I'm not sure your invoice would be looked on favorably by accounting.'

'No, Detective.' She laughed. 'No pay is required.'

'I just saw that sign on your counter, about payment in advance and . . .'

'If you came to me and asked about love advice, financial advice, then I would obviously charge you.'

'I probably could use advice on all those subjects, but . . .'

'If you asked me about your family situation, about your brothers and your departed wife . . .' She hesitated. 'Perhaps I've said too much.'

'No.' He was emphatic. 'What would you say?'

'I would offer free advice.'

'So?'

'Now you're not so skeptical. You are seeking information on how this chapter in your life will play out, am I right?'

'Of course.'

'Here is my advice. Use what you will.'

Archer nodded.

'You are on the verge of bringing a ton of weight down on a large organization, exposing a number of people to serious charges.'

'I've never told you anything about this.'

'No. You said you would like some information on how this will play out. Should I go on, because seriously, you don't need to know all of this.'

'Yes, I do,' Archer said.

'Your life, Detective, is in serious danger. Your family, members of the Detroit police force and prominent figures in the New Orleans City structure are all at odds with what you are attempting to do.'

'So what you're saying is . . .'

'What I am saying is there are people who don't agree with you.'

'Tame words.'

'Yes. They vehemently oppose you. Most of these people are out to get you.'

'How do you know all this?'

Solange smiled. 'Most of it is on the Internet, Detective.'

'The *Detroit Free Press* did run a series,' he said.

'But I've taken it one step further.'

'One step?'

'While I admit to using a Google search, I have done some consulting with my spiritual guides.'

'OK.'

'They agree. On both counts, continue your course. You are on the side of righteousness and you will win in the end.'

'*You* feel that's the best advice?'

She hesitated, again touching the can. 'No.'

Archer looked at her with a puzzled expression on his face. 'I don't understand. You just said . . .'

'It is the opinion of my spiritual guides. Legba is the god of destiny. I sense he feels it is your destiny to fight the good fight.' She paused. 'But I also still feel the negative energy coming back from you, Detective. You're skeptical.'

'So what are your feelings?'

'Back off of everything,' she said. 'You may lose your life if you keep on pursuing these avenues. There is a very good chance.'

They sat for a moment, studying each other's face. Finally Archer stood up.

'Tomorrow morning, then?'

'Maybe tonight,' she said. 'I hope I can be of some help.'

'Whatever you can suggest will be appreciated.'

'Detective, wait.'

She walked to a drawer and pulled out a small burlap bag. The bag was tied at the top with a thin rawhide strand. Solange handed him the tiny sack.

'What's this?'

'Crystals,' she said. 'When you go home tonight, scatter them on the floor.'

'Why?'

'They absorb negative energy. There will be a lot of negative energy at your place during the next several weeks.'

'A warning?'

'Yes. You might say that. And add a houseplant or two. You'll be surprised at the difference it will make. And, Detective, skeptical or not, there's one more thing you should know.'

'What's that?'

'Legba is the god who opens the gate. The gatekeeper.'

'And why do I need to know that?' Archer stood in the doorway, sorry to be leaving but anxious to get rid of the tension.

'Legba transitions you from flesh to spirit. He ushers you into the other side.'

'The other side? You mean . . .'

'He's the guy you probably should listen to.'

ELEVEN

Case Blount shoved down a forkful of spicy red beans and rice, wiping his double chin with the paper napkin on his oversized lap. The hot sauce he'd ladled on the dish made him sweat. The man stared at his buzzing phone, taking a gulp of his NOLA Blond Ale before he answered.

'Charlain, can't it wait until I'm done with lunch?' He'd been in the Magazine Street diner for twenty minutes. Couldn't catch a break. 'I mean, Jesus.'

'Hey, boss, it's Manuel. He needs to talk right now.'

'Shit.' Another swallow of beer. 'Put him off for an hour.'

'He's not taking no for an answer.'

'OK.' Silently he cursed. 'Put the son of a bitch on. But this had better be good. Damned good.'

'Case?'

'Manny, what the hell is so goddamned important?'

'Trevor Parent is important. I just heard down here. You weren't going to call and tell me?'

'Pissant adoption attorney gets stabbed. So what?'

'Hold it, Case. You know damned well what's important. Blake Rains, Trevor Parent, what's going on, my friend? Bodies are starting to stack up and that doesn't look good for the operation. And what's this shit about cans of Chill? You trying to signal there's a tie in?'

Blount took a deep breath. Those two boys, Rains and Parent, in some capacity worked for him. Therefore they worked for the syndicate in Ecuador.

'Case?'

'Look, there's some sort of a turf war going on. Warhead Solja, Nasta Mafia, two of the gangs we rely on for some of our logistics. They run people and supply drugs to some of the girls and—'

'I don't give a shit about a turf war. Don't tell me about shit like that, you understand? I don't like it when our guys get hit. Understand, I don't care that they are dead. I could give a fuck about slimeballs I don't even know. A dime a dozen, those two. But I do care when someone starts to look into those deaths. There are a lot of people here in Quito who depend on us, Case. A lot of people in NOLA as well. You are aware. You got to stop this shit. Your NOLA police start nosing around and pretty soon our pretty little operation gets blown wide open. You got me?'

What was the little spic going to do? Fly in from Ecuador and investigate the murders himself?

'I'll talk to the boys, Manuel. They get a little jealous and want to protect what they've got. Understand?'

'I understand that if we get turned, you are going away for a long time, Blount. Now *you'd* better understand, because my friends down here are very concerned. No more killings.'

'Yeah, yeah. I'll fix things.'

But he wasn't sure he could. He wasn't sure how much control he'd have when the boys got riled up. Holding the phone away from his ear, he picked up the napkin and blew his nose.

'You put out some feelers, Blount. Find out who is working on those murders in the homicide division. Best we know who we're dealing with. Someone we can put in our pocket, if need be, or deal with in other ways. *Precaución*, Blount,' he said in Spanish. In English, he added, 'Don't fuck this up.'

'I'm on it, Manny.'

'I'm talking to some of the big shots in your country, Blount. They're not happy either.'

'Can't we deal one on one with this? Why bring them into it?'

'Because they'll take the biggest hit. Me, I'm insulated. You and your petty gangs, you're pissants. But those players, they put up the bucks. They run the show and they need to know. We're talking world headlines, Blount.'

The call ended and the silence was deafening.

Blount sat in his booth, staring at the phone. He mopped his brow with the damp napkin, took a sip of the beer that had turned warm and bitter, and took a bite of the pasty, red beans and rice that had turned cold. *Next time, don't answer the damned phone. Just let it buzz and buzz and buzz.*

*   *   *

The department called a press conference, asking, begging the media to go public and request that any video be turned over to the police. Any cell phone photos, any professional videos, anything at all. They asked the parade attendants to review any digital content they may have. Check it to see if they had even a glimpse of the murder. While the phones were usually clogged with leads on any outstanding case, this time they were eerily silent. Apparently no one had seen anything. Or the revelers were afraid to come forward. Afraid of paybacks.

'It's the first time we can pinpoint the time and place of these murders with precise accuracy,' Sergeant Chip Beeman said, 'and no one saw anything. It defies logic. There were hundreds of cameras, thousands of people, dozens of law enforcement officials and—'

'You've been over it a dozen times, Sergeant. Sometimes things don't work like they should. We can only push so hard. I've got a lead. Not much promise but it's a contact that's come through before. I'm hoping this person can give me perspective.'

Beeman stood at Archer's desk, his palms flat on the gunmetal-gray top. 'Perspective hell, I'm hoping this person can give you the killer.'

'I'll know when I talk to them.'

'OK, when do we hear from this lead, Archer?'

Archer checked his watch. Nine thirty a.m. 'I'll let you know in an hour, Sarge.' Standing up he walked out the door. He could feel the veteran behind him, and knew he was calling him names under his breath. Negative energy is what Solange called it. Beeman was negative energy. Solange Cordray was positive energy. There was no question she brought tension to the table, her antique oak table, and she brought stress and pressure to the situation, but she kept the narrative alive. Positive. She may not be aware, but she held the answer to why. He knew it.

He drove a department car, a repossessed drug dealer's 2015 gray Nissan Altima, and actually found a parking spot in the Quarter. She hadn't called and he was hoping she was still at her shop.

Even this early in the morning the crazies were out. An obese man in a purple tutu and bra meandered arm and arm with a woman who was dressed like a purple-green-and-yellow jester.

They bumped Archer as they walked by, and he shook his head and kept walking, smelling the sweet odor of marijuana right around the corner.

Arriving at her store he tried the door. Locked. He glanced around, looking for a coffee shop where he could kill some time, and as he took a step back she opened the door.

'Detective.'

There was a broad smile on her face. Either she had something positive to tell him or she was very glad to see him. He briefly hoped for the latter. Then he realized it could be both. Positive energy.

'Ms Cordray.'

'Please, come in.'

He stepped inside. While the incense stick was not burning, the air was heavy with the sickeningly sweet perfume that had permeated the cypress walls, the heart pine wooden floor and the low-hanging chandeliers for fifty years. Lavender, patchouli, orange and cinnamon. They sat at the old oak table and she produced the can of Chill, setting it dead center.

'I told you there was energy emanating from the can.'

Archer nodded. 'Energy absorbed, energy released.'

'Exactly.' She smiled again, and Archer caught himself. Her soft face, the line of her neck. This was a lady who was a lead in one of his cases. He couldn't afford to get foolish about an instinct. He folded his hands on top of the table.

'So did the energy tell you anything?'

'Yes.' Pushing her long hair back, she grasped the can with her other hand. She handed it to Archer. 'Do you feel anything at all?'

He wanted to. Didn't believe but wanted to believe. But nothing resonated. Nothing at all. It was a cool can, maybe two-thirds full of a substance he didn't understand. He so wanted to be on the same page as the voodoo girl, but apparently that wasn't going to happen.

'No.'

'Possibly the energy has been depleted,' she said. 'There was only as much to give as was absorbed.'

'But you felt the energy?'

'I did. And I got some very strong vibrations.'

'Something I can use?'

She nodded. 'You have sent out a message to everyone in the surrounding area that you want pictures, video, cell phone captures of whatever they saw at Bacchus. Am I right?'

'You are.' Apparently the request had been broadcast successfully. At least the voodoo lady was aware of it.

'You will get nothing useful back.'

'That's not exactly helpful,' he said.

'No. But it's not because the footage isn't there. 'This blue can and its owner are front and center in every home. Hundreds of people have witnessed it. But they all focus on something else. You must find the person who filmed the murder but focused on something else. But whether or not they know it is another thing. They have no idea what they filmed. Until that person focuses on what's important instead of the actual celebration, no one will be able to help.'

'So, what? It's been shown on TV? It's gone viral? Is that you mean?'

'I cannot tell you more than I have. Only that it is available to thousands. Find out who was filming that one video. Then concentrate on what is happening beyond what they focused on. The individual viewers you are appealing to are useless. Not one of them captured this murder.'

'Everyone was filming. I'll guarantee you there were camera phones, DLRs, Super-8s everywhere.' He put his hands in the air. 'It's almost impossible in this day and age to do anything in a public place and not be on camera.'

'Only a few were filming for the masses. Somewhere in that statement is the answer. It's the best I can do, Quentin.'

It took him a second, and he started to get up, then smiled. She'd breached formality, and also shared something that, if true, could jump start the investigation. The problem was, he had no idea what she was saying. Find one image, then concentrate on something totally different. Maybe she was on to something. And maybe she was crazy. Probably a little of both. Regardless, he felt an attraction that he hadn't felt in a while. And that bothered him. She'd called him Quentin. It felt right and it felt very wrong.

TWELVE

The French Market on Decatur was half-full, a full hour before lunch time, with customers already peeling red-shelled crawfish and spooning spicy grilled oysters from their shells. Bushy-haired Mike with the big eyes was busy behind the bar, selling specialties and mixing drinks.

'Detective Archer, *mon ami*.' The gregarious bartender smiled and waved. 'What brings you to our humble restaurant?'

'Got a minute?'

'For you, of course.' He put down his towel and signaled to a girl at the other end of the bar to cover. Together Archer and Mike walked outside and stood on the cracked, pitted concrete sidewalk. The bartender crossed his arms, hugging himself against the chill in the air.

'You may have heard. Yesterday an attorney named Trevor Parent was killed up on Canal Street.'

'I know the story, Q. So sorry to hear it. A knife to the heart and no one saw anything.'

'Pretty much the whole story. Except, my voodoo friend—'

'Remember, I know your friend. The lovely Solange Cordray,' Mike interrupted. 'She stops in from time to time. She orders the oysters you like so much. A very bright, friendly lady. I knew her mother as well.'

Past tense, Archer thought. 'Yes. Well, the bright friendly lady seems to think that there was someone who has video of the murder. A someone. One person. And that person doesn't know what they have. Whoever shot the video, their focus was on something else.'

'Could she be a little more *spécifique*?'

'She only says that thousands of people have access to the video. Which I guess means that thousands of people may have seen the murder but they all were focused on something else. She has limited information. You tell me you know every-thing that goes on in the Quarter and—'

'And technically, the murder didn't happen in the Quarter. It happened up on Canal and several blocks away.'

'Mike, you are obviously well connected. You've helped before. I really need to nail this thing down. Any help you can give me would be greatly appreciated.'

The man nodded. 'Give me a day, Detective Q. I want to help. Whoever is committing these hideous acts is disrupting lives and giving my city a bad name.'

Archer gave him a wry look. 'Your city doesn't need much help. I think there's quite a bit of tarnish to go around.'

A pigeon hopped by, pecking at something on the cracked concrete. Mike laughed out loud. 'I think you are correct. We are a tarnished city. Sometimes I wonder if our "bad ass" reputation is the reason we are so successful. So many people flock here hoping some of that bad image wears off on them. Some of our visitors want to be bad-ass coonie, Q. Yet they don't realize the implications. This isn't a *game* we play here, it's deadly serious. It's a strange thought, but there's some truth to it. We are truly a unique city.'

'Ear to the street, Mike.'

'See me tomorrow, my friend.'

His phone rang as the bartender walked back to his restaurant.

'Archer.'

'Home invasion, Detective. Laurel and Peniston, uptown. Man and woman both dead, three-year-old child with injuries on life support. Officers have a suspect in custody. How soon can you be there?'

He cringed. 'On my way.' Archer just wished the pace would slow down.

Case Blount called the cell number. Delroy Houston picked up.

'Blount. You calling to warn me about more murders?'

'Actually I am, Delroy. I got a rather urgent call from one of my suppliers in South America. They're very concerned that the police will find a link between us and some of these killings and that our operation will unravel rather quickly.'

'Your fat ass will end up in prison, Blount. Give me a break. That's the big concern, isn't it?'

'Trevor Parent? Stabbed on Canal Street. Was that you?'

'Hold on, Blount. I don't get my hands dirty. You know me better than that. But, we did find out that Mr Parent was working both sides. You were shipping some of his young mothers over to Nasta Mafia. I told you, man, Warhead Solja can handle the traffic. I've got plenty of places to put them. Too bad about attorney Parent, but concerning all those poor mothers who had to give up their babies, we should have had first pick. You send those women to us, understand? I told you, we don't need no competition. I tried to explain that, Case. You just didn't listen. Be more attentive, my man.'

'So you had him killed? In the afternoon in front of thousands of bystanders.'

'Don't know nothin' about it.'

Blount opened his center desk drawer and pulled out a silver flask. He reached for his side table and picked up a plastic cup, then set it back down. A small pour wasn't going to do it. He leaned back and took a long swallow directly from the shiny container. It burned good all the way down, warming his sizable belly.

'Damn it, don't you understand that the cops are all over this? All they've got to do is tie this murder to Blake Rains and that gangbanger in Little Woods and we are all taking a fall.'

Houston was quiet for a moment. Blount could hear him, his shallow breathing, thinking about his response.

'You think we killed Blake Rains?'

'Didn't you?' Blount asked.

'Did you have him working with Nasta Mafia?'

It was Blount's turn to be quiet.

'How was it, Case? Did you have Rains send people to Nasta for placement? Was that crooked politician in Little Woods working with Nasta Mafia? Bad territory, my friend. I understand his body got moved to Six Flags but make no mistake, we know that mover and shaker was killed in Nasta Mafia territory. Maybe *they* killed him.' He laughed. 'Again, after I told you *we* would handle all the traffic? There is such a simple solution here. Make us your exclusive client and your problems go away. Do I have to hit you upside your white-ass head? We get the business. That's it.'

'Some people, some organizations have connections you may not have.' Blount was developing his own full head of steam. One more deep swallow and his voice got much louder, more aggressive. Damn it, he distributed the money and if this piece of shit gangster didn't appreciate that . . . 'Christ, Delroy, you and the . . . you and your Warhead Solja boys get the lion's share of the business, OK? I shove a lot your way. But you're not the only game in town. We've got to spread it around. It's the safest way to make it work. Just think about it.'

'Not OK.'

'What do you expect from us. You're doing very well. I do the fucking books. I see the statements. You guys are making a shitload of money.'

'We can do better. Listen, Case, and listen very carefully. We can take all the business you can send. Don't know how to be more blunt, Blount.' He chuckled. 'We'll take care of Nasta Mafia. You take care of business.'

'OK, but no more killings. They stop right now. You'll get all the business and we'll see if you can handle it. Does that settle this turf war?'

'We'll see. We'll see.'

'We've got some girls from Ecuador coming into the Sister Louise school tonight. Can you deal with that? Probably twenty teenagers.'

'So you've got leads on their families? Fake IDs showing the older ones are at least twenty-one?'

'That will all be provided. Do you have jobs for them?'

'Damn, Sam, it's Mardi Gras.' Blount heard the man slam his fist on something, apparently his frustration level peaking. 'Case. I got girls workin' major overtime who could use a break. I got plenty of openings. Twenty girls? Shit, I could use one hundred. You get me? Never worry about jobs, my man. And those that fight it, we got their families. You tell a girl that her family is gonna get whacked, you'd be surprised how fast they come around. And we got H, my man. Families and H. Kind of a double threat, you dig?'

'No more killings, Delroy.'

'Never said there were any before,' Houston said. 'We had nothin' to do with them, Mr Blount. Random killings, you know?

But you be sure and tell your friends in South America that we are cooperating in every way. It's so simple a first grader could figure it out. You win, we win. OK?'

It was two sixteen in the afternoon when he remembered. He was sitting at his desk, filling out paperwork on the home invasion double homicide when he thought about the parade. Archer was pretty sure a TV station carried live coverage of a portion of Bacchus. One of them, he couldn't remember which, had promised to live broadcast local coverage. Of course they would record the whole parade as well, in order to play back highlights later. So maybe they had footage of the murder. Obviously they'd have focused only on the parade and the floats, but still there might be some crowd shots.

There were 1,400 parade riders on thirty-one floats. Plus as many as ten thousand bystanders whose attention was glued to the Bacchus parade. WDSU had carried some of the parade on their nightly news. He remembered seeing it, lying in bed in his 600-square-foot cottage where the TV was practically on top of him.

A quick Google search brought up the phone number and a minute later he was talking to a reporter.

'We were at your press conference.' The young reporter, Brooke, sounded very interested. Interviews usually worked in reverse. The reporter would call him, and she was the one who asked the questions.

'And thank you,' he said, 'for getting the word out. But I want to know about your footage. Your digital content.'

'I'm pretty sure you'd have to get a subpoena, Detective. I mean if you wanted all the raw footage,' the girl said. 'We are always happy to cooperate with the authorities, within reason. But it's the way things work here.'

'So you have nothing I could look at?'

'Not without a court order. We own the footage.'

'I have reason to believe you may have footage of a murder.'

'And after learning the facts our camera crew thought that was possible as well,' the girl said.

'Why do you say that?'

'Well, we had two cameras on the ground and we filmed a lot of B roll. B roll is when—'

'I'm well versed in B roll,' he said. Archer had been involved with cases in Detroit where network affiliates' footage had been crucial in solving crimes. He was also well aware of getting a court order.

'OK. So we did a quick review of everything that was shot and it doesn't appear there was anything that would help.'

'We're under the gun here,' Archer said. 'I could use some help. Getting a court order would take time and—'

'But I've got another idea,' she said, the enthusiasm showing in her voice.

'What's that?' Disgust showing in *his* voice.

'We contracted with a guy out of California. He has a team of ten trackers that follow each parade with a GPS, and you could track every parade in town on your computer, phone, or any mobile device just by logging on to our website. All in real time. Pretty cool.'

'How does that work?'

'Detective Archer,' Brooke's voice got very quiet, very serious and very direct, 'if this leads to something, I want first rights. If this leads to an arrest, an investigation, a conviction, you call me once you're ready to go public. I'm the first one to hear it, OK? I want an exclusive for twenty-four hours.'

Archer was scratching it all on a piece of notebook paper. Ten trackers, GPS routing for all Krewe parades, available on all digital devices. He had nothing to lose and possibly something to gain. And he really needed some answers.

'OK, I'm pretty sure I can do this. I will give you my word.' He would do everything possible to honor that request. Still, there was always the possibility of complications.

'OK. And, Detective, I'm seriously counting on you. I scratch your back, you scratch mine. Here's the information. Doug Favor is a software guy out of Van Nuys, California. Last year he mapped every parade for us with a team of trackers. We were able to stream live reports on where the parades were at all times.'

'And people wanted to know that because?'

'You're obviously not from here. It's a big deal.'

'I don't see how a GPS will show me a murder. It's simply a tracking device.'

'Stay with me, Detective. This year, at least two of his trackers with each parade carry a Ricoh Theta S spherical digital camera. It's a very small stick camera that has two fish-eye lenses and films a complete 360-degree image.' She was quiet for a moment, letting the information sink in. 'We ran it live using Wi-Fi but he digitally stored some of it for later use.'

Archer held his phone between his shoulder and neck and did a quick Internet search for the camera. There it was, about five inches tall, maybe two inches wide and less than an inch thick. A spherical lens on the front and back. A 360-degree view. Amazing.

'OK, and how is this going to help me?'

'Call Doug. He owns the footage and I've got his number right here. If anyone has an image of your murder, he does.'

'Brooke, thank you. Seriously. But I'm telling you, if this doesn't work, you'll be getting that court order.'

'I hope it gives you your lead, Detective. I'm serious as well. Because I want first dibs on this story.' She paused. 'Oh, and of course I want you to catch the killer. That goes without saying.'

'I want to write your name down, Brooke.'

'Brooke Waters. You can't forget that. And Detective Archer, I get the news first. We've got a deal. Right?'

Case Blount pushed the buttons on his cell phone.

'Homicide.'

'Can you direct me to the officer who is handling the murder of attorney Trevor Parent?'

'The thrill kills? Of course. That would be Detective Archer. Quentin Archer. Let me ring that extension.'

'No need. I have all the information I could want.'

Blount hung up and made a second call. This time to Mexico.

'Hello.'

'It's Case Blount.'

'I hope this is important, Case. This line is not to be used for—'

'I have the name of the lead cop on the thrill kill murders.'

'I'm aware of them.'

'If these murders tie together, our operation may be exposed.'

There was silence on the other end.

'Are we clear?'

'Yes. And of course, we need to delay that inevitability. At least until we can set up another operation. In two to three weeks we can scrub this one, lay low for a brief time, then start another one.'

'Yes,' Blount said. He slapped his hand on the desk. 'My observation exactly. Things are going well right now, and if we can milk a little more, it gives us time to build another franchise.'

'So, what do you suggest?'

'Killing a cop tends to piss people off,' Blount said.

'Not a solid solution.'

'Maybe someone can talk to this cop. This Detective Archer. Set up a situation where higher officials are in charge. His position in the case is back-burnered while State and Federal officials get involved.'

'Slow down his process?'

'Is that possible?' Blount asked.

'We're talking about thousands of dollars per day. The longer we can drag this out the more we make. And it gives us time to shut your current operation down. Open a new business. Give our friends down south a chance to set up a new channel.'

'So—' Blount reached for his handkerchief, and putting one hand over the phone he loudly blew his nose '—you will talk to the detective? Archer?'

'Someone will. What was that sound? Is there a freight train going down Magazine Street?'

'Keep me informed,' Blount said.

'Here's what I envision, Blount. On my end, we will set up a sting. I'll see to it that the FBI and New Orleans Police are involved. We'll do it slowly, making sure everything is in place. Stretch it as long as we can. Then we take down the gangs, look like the good guys, and we can even say you were part of the solution, that you supplied us with all the information so we could make it all happen. And we'll liberate all these young girls. Heroes, Mr Blount. Heroes.'

'I'd need more than your word on that.'

'We'll move you, get you protection and set up somewhere else in six months.'

'It's time, isn't it?' A little sad, a little relieved.

'It's time, Case. Everything runs its course.'

'For now?'

'Business as usual. Keep the boys from killing each other, do what you have to do. We'll slow down the opposition until we have a plan.'

'I'm following your lead.'

'Again, this line is only for emergencies.'

'I thought this was an emergency.'

'You may be right.'

THIRTEEN

She sat on the levee with her three charges. Ma and two women in their eighties. Bundled in sweaters and scarves, the three ladies stared unfocused at the river as if unaware of the swirling water. Ma's vacant gaze to the other shore was a cold hard lock. As if she had retreated into her mind, condemning anything in her line of vision for interrupting her innermost thoughts.

'Ma, I'm talking to Detective Q. You met him the other day. I've told you about him in the past. I worked with him regarding a murder of a judge, do you remember? This time he's asked for some help on another murder investigation. I was going to show you something that was a part of a murder scene. I was going to have you touch it and see if you felt any energy, but I decided now might not be a good time. Still, I want you to be involved. You always had – have good instincts.'

The dark gray-haired lady never looked up, her eyes continuing to stare across the Mighty Miss.

Solange took a deep breath and let it out slowly. Relaxation techniques. The doctor had suggested that she keep Ma engaged. You never knew what the mind may comprehend. Keep talking, about the weather, about personal issues, about the past and the present. Whatever you could think of. If there was a spark, a moment of recognition, it would come from these conversations, these engagements.

'Ma, I pray every day for you. But I also pray that these murders stop. And then, I get this feeling. Some of these victims aren't innocent citizens who happened to be in the wrong place at the wrong time. Some of these victims were causing huge problems for hundreds of people. So, is it wrong to feel somewhat relieved that the evil in society meets an untimely end? Because I'm not certain I should feel bad about some of these deaths.'

No response. The oldest lady in the trio suddenly pointed toward the water.

'Oh look, sweety, the *Robert E. Lee* is coming around the bend.'

There was no paddle wheeler in sight. The woman's husband had abandoned her years ago.

'Maybe George is finally coming home. He was visiting his sister, you know, in Cincinnati.'

'Maybell, I hope he makes it in time for supper,' Solange interjected.

The lady cackled. 'Chicken and biscuits, potatoes and gravy. But he'll have to cook. I can't boil water, I swear.'

'You've reached the office of Doug Favor. Leave a message and I'll call you back.'

Archer slammed the phone down. Fucking answering machines, voicemail, texting. There was no human contact anymore. Immediately his desk phone rang and he grabbed it.

'This is Doug Favor. You just called here?'

'Yeah, yeah.' He took a deep breath. Relax. 'This is Quentin Archer. I'm a homicide detective with the NOPD. Mr Favor—'

'Doug.'

'Mr Favor, I understand you have footage from the Bacchus Parade.'

'Technically, no, Detective. Footage would denote film. This is all digital. I had a spherical camera on each side of the parade.'

'So you were able to see both sides of the event.'

'Not all of the event. There were thirty some floats and several miles of traveling. But I've got about forty minutes of . . . what is it you're looking for?'

'There was a murder committed on the parade route. Apparently no one saw anything, and I thought just maybe if we reviewed your footage . . . uh, your video . . .'

'I'd be glad to assist. I can download what I have to your computer in the next ten minutes. Would that be helpful?'

Would that be helpful? 'Yes. That would be wonderful.' No court orders. Archer was ecstatic.

'To be clear, Detective, these wonderful cameras were mounted on sticks and show a complete 360 field. Understand that the focus was on the direction of the parade, and the floats and riders.'

'But, you are showing a 360-degree video? That's what we'll see?' Archer pictured the view.

'Yes. You get the peripherals. You get everything.'

'This murder, it seems to have happened maybe no more than ten feet from the actual route. Ten feet from one of the floats.'

'I can't promise anything, Detective, but I will send you all that I have.'

'Ten minutes, right?'

'I'll send you the unedited video right now.'

It was a long shot but worth however much time it took. Archer wondered about Solange Cordray's comments. According to her, the energy of the Chill can revealed that it was featured in a video but obviously no one was focusing on the murder or the blue can. And yet, she'd felt certain the video was available to thousands of people. A can with energy? He wondered what he was even thinking, spending time on the supposed spiritual readings of an inanimate object. And it played in his head how much he wanted to believe. He hoped she was right. If energy forces and the supernatural played a part in the universe, maybe things could work out for the best. Maybe questions would be answered instead of humans constantly interfering. Maybe, just maybe there was a rhythm and sense in nature. Left alone, things might just sort themselves out.

No. That was the pipe dream that the voodoo lady's clients bought into. Gris-gris bags and voodoo dolls, spells and fragments of animal bones tossed on a canvas map. He couldn't totally go there. But the 360-degree view seemed to be as good a place as any to start. Canned energy. Like the compressed gas that was released to chill a bottle of wine. He hoped she was right. It might make his life a whole lot easier.

Beeman, Levy and Archer sat at three adjoining desks, watching the unusual video.

'I synced it so we're all seeing the same thing at the same time. Our assumption is the stabbing took place on the Quarter side of the parade route. If we don't see anything the first thirty-six minutes, we'll either rerun the video or check the camera that filmed on the other side.'

Levy nodded. 'Old school, Q. Filmed?'

Archer smiled. 'OK, Mr Technical, the camera shot *video segments*. No film.'

'It's a new world, Q. Especially for dinosaurs like us. I think that breakouts on these videos are called photo-spherics.'

Beeman stared at his screen. 'Let someone else worry about technical terms. We're looking for a killer. To be clear, we're not looking forward, because that's only where the parade is headed, right?'

'That's correct,' Archer said, 'but as the video rotates, you can't be sure what's the front view and what are the side views so we've got to analyze every scene. Now, since we're all hooked up to the same feed, I'll show you the entire view.' He touched the screen on his laptop, dragging his finger across the plastic and the video slowly swirled around.

'Pretty cool.' Levy watched with fascination.

'We may have to run this a number of times,' Archer said. 'Every time I show you the entire circumference and come back to the starting point, the parade has already moved twenty to fifty feet depending how fast I rotate the film. Sorry, how fast I rotate the *video*.'

'We could be here a long time,' Beeman said.

'We could catch the killer,' Archer shot back.

Case Blount swiveled in his leather desk chair. Sipping dark coffee laced with Irish whiskey he stared out the window at Magazine Street, which stretched out in front of him down below. Tourists paraded with colorful T-shirts advertising local restaurants, questionable slogans like *I'm Not A Gynecologist But I'll Take A Look* or their favorite college logo. He'd done a personal survey, and even though LSU was the local favorite, Ohio State was apparently the most wearable university in the country. If you saw someone with an Ohio State T-shirt, you shouted 'O-H'. The response should be 'I-O'. His nephew had come back from Columbus with that choice chant. He took a swallow of his coffee and contemplated the situation.

Delroy Houston had made it clear he was a hands-off manager. He had people to do his dirty work. It was hard to trace anything back to him, personally. And Blount wished he was a hands-off guy. But he wasn't. He was intimately involved in almost every aspect of the operation. From bringing in the workers to finding them employment. He'd set up quite a network, and the drugs were a nice bonus. He worked deals, spent hours on the phone and computer setting up outlets and dealers. But if this fragile empire he'd developed came undone, if this web of tangled lies suddenly untangled, he was in a world of shit. And even though he could take down some of the high and mighty in this twisted city, probably some of the power brokers in Washington, if this system broke down, Delroy Houston would be right. Case Blount's ass would be grass.

He watched a young couple stroll down the street, holding hands and occasionally staring into each other's eyes. That romantic world was so foreign to him. He dealt in the real world where there were commodities, exchanges, and everything had value. A set worth. Drugs, merchandise, even people. Everything had a price. And Case Blount set that price. If you wanted to play in New Orleans, you paid that price. It was entirely up to you.

Quentin Archer was the officer in charge of the thrill kills. A decorated detective from Detroit, but there was a hint of scandal Blount had found on several social media platforms. A drug ring that involved members of his own family. Would this guy take money or was he a straight, stand-up guy? Nobody knew. If the investigation into these connecting murders had legs, Blount could throw up some serious roadblocks. There were high-powered people in this city and state who called the shots. People who profited off of his little venture. There were people even higher up who would help with a block. However, if Archer was an asshole who refused to cooperate or be put off by the roadblocks, then Blount and his contacts would be forced to make some serious decisions. He hoped that the talk would result in Archer backing off. If it didn't, he'd have to make some decisions. First and foremost was to keep his hands clean but let someone else dirty theirs.

From what he'd read, it seemed that Archer leaned toward the clean-cut, all-American boy. And that was too bad, because unless the detective rolled over on these cases, he might just end up in the same situation as the victims. Dead.

FOURTEEN

Archer pushed back his chair and looked away from the screen. Rubbing his eyes he glanced down the row at his two companions.

'We'll view it a second time. We didn't see everything. Every time we saw the front view, for a few seconds we missed a side view. Every time we saw a side view, we missed a few seconds of a rear view, a front view. Let's take five and run it again. Agreed?'

Beeman and Levy nodded, picking up empty coffee cups and heading for the pot. The two hours had been filled with stops and starts. Going back twenty seconds, advancing ten seconds. Thank God for modern technology. Every movement was analyzed, yet they hadn't really seen everything just yet.

Archer's cell rang and he checked the area code. Detroit. Thank God it wasn't Bobby Mercer with another harassing threat. He recognized the number.

'Hey, Tom.'

'Q, I've got a question. I think I already know the answer.' DPD Detective Tom Lyons was to the point.

'Shoot.'

'Regarding our friend Bobby Mercer, the photos of him heisting a car in a parking lot are, according to our prosecuting attorney, inconclusive. Looks like him stealing the car that killed Denise, but, and sorry, man, the prosecutor doesn't feel we have quite enough. She doesn't seem to think it's that clear. Truthfully, I think if this were the case of some scumbag drug dealer from West Warren and McKinley, it would be a slam dunk. But this is a decorated street cop and they can't afford to fuck this one up, you know what I'm saying?'

Archer knew it was him. Mercer, that son of a bitch, had come up over the sidewalk and run her down. And Denise's death was the warning that drove him from Detroit. If he kept trying to out the drug ring that Mercer, his brothers and a handful of other cops ran under the wire, they'd kill him too.

'You're right. They're going to play this very carefully. Does Mercer know that you guys have the surveillance video of someone stealing that car?'

'We don't think so. But he is so plugged in I just never know. The guy has lookouts everywhere. You found that out. It's why he's still walking the streets. He may have heard we were reviewing a video. I can't be sure. You understand that I've got to be extremely careful with this, Q.'

Tom Lyons was one of his best friends, who'd had his back for years in Detroit. The last thing Archer wanted was Lyons or his two partners to get burned. One person had already been killed because of his drug investigation. He prayed no one else would die, but he knew there was that chance.

'You understand, my friend, the three of us working it, if we get it wrong we are toast, man. Burned. Scorched. Not to be insensitive in any way, buddy, but we need to go very slowly.'

'I appreciate what you're doing, Tom. Thank God you're willing to work it. What's the question?'

'If we get a little closer, are you willing to come up and talk to the prosecutor? You've got your cell and proof that Bobby calls and threatens you from time to time. You've got evidence in that phone that your brother Jason calls and harasses you. And your brother's on the run from the law. Someone may be able to get a lead on his location through your phone. Prosecutor says your testimony and your phone may be what pushes this over the top. After we get evidence on that stolen car.'

Back to Motown, back to the family that wouldn't stand up for him. Back to the town that still held his brother Brian in jail. The town where his father, a former police captain, wouldn't even acknowledge him because he'd put Brian in jail and because Jason was now a fugitive. Back to the city where a handful of cops wanted him dead for ratting out his blue brothers.

'Prosecutor is Maurine Sheldon, Q. You know her. She's straight up. I don't think she'd back off with a threat. I mean, we get the right stuff and she'll be all over this. But it's got to be right.'

He knew her. She *was* a straight shooter. 'If we can get Mercer for Denise's murder, hell yes. Hell yes. I'd be there tomorrow.' Of course that would be impossible the way things stood.

'We'll be in touch, Quentin. Be safe.'

'I worry about you guys, Tom. It means a lot, the time the effort you're putting into this. Thank you for keeping the faith. And *you* be safe. Be safe.'

Five minutes later Archer, Levy and Beeman walked back into the office followed by three more detectives.

'Extra eyes, Q. Can't hurt,' Levy said.

Archer quickly explained how the video worked, then started at the beginning, dragging his finger slowly over the screen, showing everything the camera's two fisheye lenses saw.

'Stop, Archer. Can you back it up a second or two?' Beeman pointed at his screen. 'I saw something.'

He stopped the motion and set it back ten seconds. They watched with rapt attention, the three new observers looking over the trio's shoulders.

'Right there,' Beeman said, 'guy reaches in his jacket pocket . . .'

'And pulls out a pack of cigarettes,' Levy wryly commented.

'And so it goes,' Archer said.

Cueing it up again, Archer continued to direct the action. Twenty minutes later his phone rang again, and he checked the number. A New Orleans area code. Thirty minutes later they took another break.

Archer called the number back, and Mike answered.

'French Market.'

'Mike, this is Quentin Archer. You called?'

'I did. I have some information regarding the murders involving the can of Chill. It's not verified, but . . .'

'I don't care, man. Tell me what you've heard.'

'I put out an APB, Q.'

'Civilians have an all-points bulletin?'

He could hear the smile through the phone. '*I* do. That's why you check in with me, my friend. The man with the plan. Action Jackson.'

'So someone has given you information.'

'They have. The can of frigid gas is used to cool something. White wine, carbonated beverages and anything else that needs to chill. To be honest with you, we sometimes use it here. People expect us to keep all the whites in a chiller, so don't tell anyone, OK? But, you know that this canned gas is also responsible for a certain cheap high, right?'

'You spray it up your nose, don't you?' Nothing new to report. Mike had yesterday's information.

'You do, Detective. It practically freezes the nasal passage, not that I can personally attest to that, and apparently it freezes the brain. It induces a temporary sense of euphoria. As in most cases of drug induced ecstasy, people will step outside their boundaries. They will lose sight of their common principles, their core values, and act stupidly. They are *couillion*.'

Archer wasn't always clear about the Cajun language but he let Mike continue. It must mean stupid.

'So it would make sense to some that with a whiff, or as it's sometimes called a "huff" of this Chill gas, someone's mind, their will, might be compromised.'

'We've considered that possibility, Mike.'

'My contact, a trusted friend and confidant, has told me he believes that is what has happened.'

'That's it?'

'What I am led to believe is that the courage to kill someone at large is helped by huffing the gas. Now hold on. What you may not know is that the *reason* for the killing goes a little deeper.'

'Mike, get to the point.'

'You always like to know why, Q. It's an initiation. To a gang.'

'Initiation? Murdering people?'

'My sources tell me there's a street gang called Warhead Solja that requires new members to kill a random stranger, which they achieve by getting the kids to take a hit of Chill and leave the can by the body. Last but not least, they snap a picture of the body next to the blue can as proof that they did the deed.'

He sat there with the phone frozen to his ear. Archer was stunned. He shouldn't have been. He'd been through a number of gruesome murders, two brutal beheadings, bloodbaths, he'd been through the deliberate, violent murder of his wife, he'd seen children gunned down in drug wars, and even discovered a body hanging from the Ambassador Bridge over the Detroit River. He'd seen a local judge with a bullet in the brain pulled from the Mississippi River, but to randomly kill innocent people simply to get into a gang was hard to grasp. Very hard to grasp.

'Q? You still there?'

'Jesus Christ. Your city may have reached a new low, Mike.'

'I'm thinking you may be right, *mon ami*.'

They were both silent for a moment. Finally Mike spoke.

'It's only a rumor, Detective. I'd like to think it's not true, but then you would have to find another explanation.'

Archer had no other explanation.

'I prefer my job to yours. My mission is to make people happy with food, drink and a sparkling personality. To enhance their unique experience in New Orleans. Your job . . . to deal with the *merde*. I could not do that. Could not.'

'*Merde*?'

'The shit, Q. The shit.'

FIFTEEN

'**N**o shit?' Levy just happened to use the English word, probably not knowing the Cajun one.

'No shit, Levy,' Archer said.

'That's new,' the detective said. 'I know Warhead Solja and this hasn't popped up in the past.'

'What do they do?'

'Christ, what don't they do. Prostitution, drugs . . . they're really big into heroin. And they work some of the strip clubs. Both the people and the drugs.'

'They sell in the clubs?'

'We're pretty sure they supply drugs to some of the girls. Well, they also supply some of the girls, period.'

Archer nodded. Alexia Chantel had given him a heads up, but he hadn't known who was dealing. Now he did.

'Random killings, Levy. Yet maybe there's a deeper connection. What do you think now?'

'Not at my pay level, Detective.'

'I think we need to find out who killed Trevor Parent at the Bacchus parade and why. That may answer some questions. For some reason, I don't believe that he was a random stranger for some punk initiate to earn his wings. Someone is using the Chill cans as a decoy.'

As Beeman and the other three detectives entered the room, Archer filled them in on his phone call. To a one they were silent, shaking their heads.

Finally Detective Boudreau spoke up. 'There are a lot of sick fucks out there, Archer, but this is the kind of stuff we've got to nip in the bud. When these assholes are killing each other, it's one thing. But an initiation that requires murdering innocent people? Not on my watch.'

'Then let's make this video work.'

For the third time Archer started the video. Twenty minutes into the viewing Detective Bellerose asked him to stop it.

'Back it up, Q. Maybe five seconds. When you scanned the far right corner of the screen there's a quick movement that caught my eye. Physical contact with two people. I could be wrong. Maybe it was something else.'

Archer ran the video back then stuttered it forward.

'Right there. Can you freeze it?'

He did. The six men leaned in, studying the still picture. It appeared a man in a gray hooded sweatshirt had his hand up another man's jacket. The picture was somewhat blurry and the man with the hood had it pulled tight over his head.

'Not conclusive,' Archer said with a twinge in his chest. The surveillance camera in Detroit that should have framed Bobby Mercer wasn't conclusive either but he knew it was him. He wished the rat bastard a slow, painful death.

'How long can we keep him in frame?'

'He'll be there another three to four seconds, then the camera has moved on.'

'Damn.' Levy put his finger on his computer screen. 'Let's see the next three to four seconds, then see if we can blow up some of these scenes.'

Archer again stutter-stopped the video. Running it one frame at a time. Although the picture was blurred and out of focus, the man's hand seemed to stay under the jacket for maybe two seconds. When it emerged, it was holding something. All six officers looked intently.

'Blow it up, Q.'

He did. It was a blur. A fuzzy blob of a picture. Each detective stared, feeling like they needed an eye exam. Gradually, the focus got a little better as their eyes adjusted to the pixels. Then the room got louder as each one of them realized what they were seeing.

The hand appeared to hold a knife.

'Damn,' Beeman said. 'Got to be. How many seconds left before the camera leaves that scene?'

'According to what I've seen the last two hours, we've got another two seconds, Sergeant. At that point the camera and the parade continue to move ahead.'

'Well,' Levy studied his screen, 'We're one hundred percent

beyond where we were thanks to Detective Bellerose,' he hesitated, 'but we're still in the dark as to who this is. If we . . .'

Archer stroked the screen as the man in the gray hoody looked up. Up from the knife he had in his hand.

'Clean that picture up, Q, and we've got our killer.'

'Just one killer, Sergeant. It's a great start, but as I told you, my source said there are several.'

'Regardless, send that picture to the lab. Put a priority on it. When and if they can clean that picture up, we've got a clear shot of at least one of the Chill thrill killers. Boys, this may be the break we needed.'

It was after six when he caught the streetcar on Canal. The old black man wearing suspenders and his bowler was busy chatting up the driver as Archer climbed on board. He wondered if the man spent his days riding back and forth on the cars. Three young boys about twelve or thirteen huddled in a seat, giggling and sharing something on a cell phone. He sat in a seat by himself, pondering the events of a long day.

It started with Solange, the voodoo queen, telling him that his can's energy spoke to her. Then there was street-smart wild-haired Mike with his questionable connections, describing a gang initiation that involved the Chill cans, and finally there was a 360-degree camera that might have unveiled one of the killers if the tech department could clean up the image of the man's face. A big if.

Without voodoo, phantom informants and high-tech equipment, none of which he truly understood, this case would still be a total mystery. When he got to his stop he jumped off and walked briskly to his cottage, ignoring the smell of spicy shrimp, Krystal Burgers and the wafting odor of garlic and onions. He also ignored other odors of stale beer and vomit, common smells in the Quarter. He just wanted a hot shower and a beer. The pounding bass pouring out of the Cat's Meow reverberated off the wooden bench and the short brick walk that led to his porch. That same porch where a brown paper package was propped against his door.

No address, no identifying marks. Just a thin, book-size package wrapped in brown paper. Archer hesitated, knowing that his Detroit connections often sent threatening letters and unusual gifts to his New Orleans home. He'd come home to find a dead cat on this same porch, and one night someone had entered his home, smearing rabbit blood on his bed sheets.

He pulled out some latex gloves from his sport coat pocket. Because he was called to crime scenes on a near daily basis Archer kept a pair of the thin gloves on him at all times. It was best to touch nothing with your bare skin during the first stages of a murder investigation. Then he checked the tape on the door, undisturbed, and studied the parcel.

It could be explosive, set to detonate when he moved it. Chances were slim that his brother or whoever had left it would go to such elaborate steps. There was no address, so someone had to have hand delivered it. Throwing caution to the cool breeze, he reached down and picked up the package. Lightweight, thin, very defined. Carefully tearing the brown paper, he watched for any telltale signs. No visible white powder, no ticking time bomb. He realized he should call the department, but they were short-staffed enough. And sending the bomb squad for an innocent package? Another homicide detective had quit today. Manpower was low. No reason to sound the alarm.

He kept removing the paper, layer after layer. And there it was. His heart jumped. A framed wedding photo of Archer and Denise. A silver frame that was engraved at the bottom. She was in her beautiful white wedding gown, her veil thrown back, staring at him with a loving smile on her lips, and he was in his dark tuxedo looking back, brown hair carelessly falling over his forehead. Denise had never looked more beautiful, and Archer's eyes filled with tears.

For a moment time evaporated and he remembered the small wedding. His brother Jason giving the best man toast. 'To my brother and best friend. Quentin Archer. Denise, may you find all the strong characteristics and the decent humanity that lives in this man.' A lot of bridges burned. Things had changed.

Archer closed his eyes. He was aware this was not meant to be a sentimental moment. It was meant to be one more reminder that he should stay out of the Detroit scene. Now he wondered if Mercer knew that they were reviewing security cameras and trying to identify him as a potential thief and killer.

The inscription was simple.

Stay out of this, Archer. More bad things are bound to happen.

SIXTEEN

It was three in the morning when the yellow school bus arrived at the gray stucco building just outside of the Quarter. Congo Square in Treme was unforgiving. A place where slaves had congregated in another century, and a place where any civilized person wouldn't be caught dead at night, or the early morning, or at any other time of the day. Or if they *were* caught here, they probably *would* be caught dead. There were places in New Orleans, like Louis Armstrong Park and right here in Treme that you just plain avoided. At all costs. It was a great place to locate the Sister Anne School of Divinity. Even the cops tried to stay away.

The driver stayed in his seat as three muscle-bound men stepped up into the vehicle. The largest, a bearded man dressed in a camouflage jacket and stocking cap, addressed the tired young girls in Spanish. He first asked who spoke English. Six of them slowly raised their hands. He told them to stand, and when a pretty young dark-complexioned girl stayed seated, one of the men grabbed her by her long black hair and roughly pulled her from the seat then twisted her arm behind her back until she screamed.

'When I tell you to do something, you will obey me,' the leader said.

Walking down the aisle, which smelled of piss and vomit, he scrutinized each of the girls. Then, pointing to four who appeared to be older than the rest, he ushered them off the bus.

As they huddled together, tears streaming down their cheeks, he slapped each of them on their cheek, a stinging reminder of who was in charge.

'You were sent here because your parents couldn't afford to keep you. The harder you work for me the more money you will make. The more money you make the sooner you will be reunited with your family. Do you understand?' He'd given the speech dozens of times.

Two of the girls nodded.

'I'm going to ask you one more time, because if you don't get it now you're dumber than I thought. You don't listen to me, you're fucked. If you think it's been hard, think again. The worst is yet to come. The worst, ladies. You understand? You *comprender*? Do you understand that if you don't follow my instructions, you will never see your family again? Never. Get it? I will slap you silly if you don't answer me.'

This time all four of the girls nodded.

'I'm gonna guess you will not like your new jobs. You will take off your clothes for strange men, and they will take liberties with you. You will learn to deal with it, so that the money they pay you can funnel back to your families. Your poor, struggling mother and father, your sisters and brothers. If you cause problems, if you refuse to cooperate, your families will be in serious danger. You understand? Your mothers will be raped, your fathers will lose whatever income they have and they will be left penniless. They will die in poverty. You are the only salvation they have. It is entirely up to you. Nod if you understand what I am telling you.'

They sobbed as a quartet. The salvation they'd been promised had come to an abrupt halt. A cold wind rustled leaves in the huge oaks towering above them, and they shivered in the thin white blouses and cotton skirts they had worn from Mexico.

The gruff man studied them, wondering how long each of them would last. How long each of them would be productive. He was paid on the delivery, he was paid on the placement. And, if they survived for any length of time, he was paid on the H. These girls needed something to keep them going, and H was the drug of choice.

The bearded man escorted them up the thirty steps to the plain building. Up close they could see the gray paint peeling from the stucco and brown stains twelve inches high from where homeless men urinated against the wall. Pointing to the doorway, he said, 'Take off your clothes and enter. Now.'

The girls stood there, looking at each other, exchanging glances.

'Now,' he shouted.

First one, then another started unbuttoning her white top, realizing there was no other option.

'On your right is a shower. Each of you will be scrubbed down, your pubic hair will be shaved, and you will be given a new wardrobe when you are finished. Disobey this command, and you and your family are dead. Finished.'

One girl collapsed on the crumbling concrete parking lot sobbing hysterically and the bearded man walked up to her and kicked her in the ribs. Then he yanked her to her feet, slapping her face repeatedly. He shook his head in disgust as the rest of the girls were herded off the bus, weeping. He gave them their marching orders, this time in Spanish. Never give the girls time to think. Let them know who's the boss and rush them from assignment to assignment.

The shock value worked well and by tomorrow night they'd be working all across the city. In the Quarter, up on Gentilly at the massage parlors, in a couple of hotels, all twenty of them. He could report back to Delroy that the young girls had arrived safely. That they were assigned positions and by tomorrow would be gainfully employed. Revenue on the rise. The bearded man smiled. His worth would be noted.

Delroy Houston stood half a block away, leaning on a live oak tree watching the activity. He'd gotten through to Case Blount. The fat man was handing over the merchandise and if Nasta Mafia backed off, maybe there could be a little less bloodshed. Maybe. But there were always members of his organization like Dushane White who promoted gang war. White and his ilk lived off violence, tension. There was a place for him, but Houston hoped for a less hostile environment. There were deals to be made, and if things would quiet down, a hefty profit to be realized at the end. He rubbed a worn quarter between his fingers, a 1976 D Bicentennial, worth twenty-five hundred dollars in mint condition. The quarter had been minted twenty years before he was conceived and over the last several years Houston had rubbed half the value off of it.

The voice behind surprised him.

'Don't fuck with me, nigger. I've got a knife and I'll run it up your back and leave you here to bleed to death. Nod if you understand.'

Houston spun around, his right foot kicking out, knocking the leg from under the slender man. The knife-wielding bandit stumbled, then crumpled to the ground, the instrument clattered to the sidewalk as his knife-holding hand was forced open. Immediately Houston's size ten foot was on his throat slowly applying pressure.

'I'm sorry friend, were you going to rob me? Was that your intention?' He stared at the man beneath him. Even in the dim street light he noticed the shaved head, a tight beard and a red rag wrapped around his shiny skull.

'I'm sorry, man,' the man struggled, trying to roll out from under the foot. 'I picked on the wrong guy. You—'

Houston applied more pressure with his steel-toed Dr Martens boot, choking the fucker.

The robber struggled, his heels beating the sidewalk, his hands reaching for Houston's foot. Squealing, he said, 'I am so sorry. It won't happen . . .' He gurgled, the pressure stronger and stronger, his trachea and larynx collapsing. He lost his ability to breathe and Houston could see his eyes bulging from their sockets. Whoever he was, he had ceased to exist. Houston applied his full weight, all 220 pounds, just to make sure.

He thought about adding a can of Chill, confusing the police even further, but that would be overkill. Overkill. Plus, he didn't carry cans of Chill as a rule. That was for the rookies. Instead he reached into his pocket and dropped a quarter on the man's body. At least the guy got something.

Ignoring the body, he smiled as he watched the girls entering the Sister Anne School of Divinity. Tomorrow he would pick up some nice cash. All in a day's work.

SEVENTEEN

Archer couldn't sleep. His mind skipped over segments of the case like a scratched vinyl record. The thrill kills were confusing, and there didn't seem to be any clear reason for the murders. A gang initiation? Maybe. Was that all the Chill cans meant? Chill cans with hidden reservoirs of energy. He couldn't ignore that he had feelings for the voodoo lady who introduced him to the idea of energy in even inanimate objects. She was absolutely nothing like anyone else he'd ever been attracted to. The two of them had nothing in common. And then there was the confusion about his reaction to Alexia Chantel's kiss. Probably just a guy thing. Purely sexual. It had been a long time since he'd explored sexual energy with a different woman. It was almost like cheating on his dead wife.

Tossing, turning, he finally gave up and got out of bed at one a.m. He listened to the cacophony of sounds filtering into his small home. Brassy blues, the downbeat of a rap song from the karaoke bar, the faint roar of voices from the crowd on Bourbon Street. Archer heated water in a Pyrex pot on his hot plate and searched for some green tea. He'd have to put it on his shopping list. The problem was that he never had time for shopping. Denise had done the shopping. She knew exactly what to get.

Scrounging through his kitchen drawers he found a packet of instant powdered coffee and he poured it into the liquid. Walking out onto his small wooden porch in his T-shirt and boxers he felt the chill of the early morning air. Coffee at this hour of the morning enhanced his senses. A brisk morning breeze helped as well.

The framed photo of his wedding saddened him. He wished himself back in Detroit, confronting Bobby Mercer and his brothers. Helping prosecute the people responsible for his wife's murder. There was no question they had planned and executed the killing. No question in his mind at all.

He took a long swallow of the hot beverage and ignored the

bitter, acrid taste. He expected that. It was instant coffee for God's sake. He just needed some caffeine. He also needed some answers. He needed to stop the serial killings that were adding up with cans of Chill. Over a third of his caseload was filled with the Chill thrill kills. Enough was enough.

He'd know tomorrow if the photo of the parade crowd would allow them to identify the killer. He'd know this week if the photo of the car thief in Detroit was clean enough to identify the man as Bobby Mercer. Everything came down to clear photos.

Archer sipped the dark coffee and shivered. One of his *whys* had been answered. If Mike's information was to be believed, the Chill kills were part of an initiation into a violent gang. That was why the can of Chill was present at all the murders. It made sense. And yet it made no sense at all. The janitor? The engaged bank teller? Sanchez the gangbanger, the councilman, and the adoption attorney? Which of them was a thrill kill, which of them taken out to get rid of them?

He walked back into the old slave quarters that comprised his rental cottage and gazed at his bed. He wasn't going to be able to sleep. He knew that. Pulling on a pair of jeans, a long-sleeved shirt and his navy blue sport coat, Archer shoved his Glock into the holster. He had a standing invitation to visit a Bourbon Street club and he was ready to ask some questions.

Stepping through the door, he stretched a piece of tape across the door frame, then headed down the brick path to Bourbon Street. Woody's was two blocks away, less than a minute's walk. He bobbed and weaved, working his way through the crowds of drunken crazy people. Garbage bags were piled on the side of the street. Six feet high. A massive amount of waste each night disappeared by the early morning.

Archer considered the piles of drink cups and beer bottles, rotting cocktail fruit and the rancid remains of thousands of dinners. It was somebody's job to clear the trash and garbage from the streets. It was *his* job to clear another sort of trash and garbage from the streets. He just wasn't doing his job as well.

He thought about flashing the badge, making this call official. If Alexia was there, he could question her. But if she was there and the call took on official status, she would get called out by other strippers and perhaps by the owners as well. He might get her in all kinds of trouble. She didn't need to be hassled by drug dealers, especially if they were members of Warhead Solja.

Walking past the chunky pitchman on the sidewalk, Archer stepped into the club. He pulled out a ten and handed it to the bored brunette behind the counter. She stamped his hand with a red circle and he rounded a corner, coming into full view of the stage. Red, purple and yellow lights played over the surface and a petite girl with a short bob lazily hung onto the stripper pole, swinging around and around. Her small breasts were bare and she wore a sequined G-string. Toplessness was all that was allowed in a town where just about everything else was legal.

A young olive-skinned girl in what appeared to be a short nightgown approached him, a dazzling phony smile on her face.

In broken English, she said, 'Would you be interested in a private room?'

Archer shook his head. They were everywhere. Micro costumes that left little to the imagination.

Sitting down, he ordered a Jax beer from a plump, scantily clad waitress.

'I was looking for a girl who goes by the name of Alexia Chantel? Is she working tonight?'

'Ah, a cute little blonde? Tiny ass? I think I know who you mean. She actually goes by Sexy Lexy, honey.'

'Is she here tonight?'

'Over by the bar, talkin' to the cowboy.'

He glanced in her direction and saw the tall man with the wide-brimmed hat. Like a saloon girl from the Wild West hustling a guy in from a long cattle drive, talking, working her thing, whatever that was. Gone were the sweats. She was dressed in a tiny aqua-blue bikini with a see-through cover-up and her golden hair was longer than last time. Extensions, he presumed.

'If you get a chance, just mention that Quentin Archer is here. When she gets the time.'

'Well,' the pudgy girl smiled, 'I don't see any money changin' hands over there. No bump and grind goin' on so she'll probably be anxious to move it along. We're here for the money, honey.' She plastered a silly smile on her face. 'Private rooms are in the back, and upstairs . . . well, she'll probably tell you all that.'

He watched her give Alexia the message and soon the petite blonde walked back to his table.

'Hey, good looking, going to at least buy me a drink?' She pointed over her shoulder. 'The rodeo king kind of came up short.'

'Sure. What are you having?'

'Cheap overpriced sparkling lemon-flavored water. Probably worth about ten cents. I'll tell you it's champagne, you end up paying fifteen bucks for the glass, and I get a five-dollar cut. Something like that.'

Archer laughed. 'So you're telling a cop this?'

'You've got bigger fish to fry, Detective.' She grinned, showing a row of perfect white teeth. Those lips that had given him a full-mouth kiss were a brighter shade of red, and her makeup a little more pronounced. 'Besides, a little deception in a bar is pretty much standard fare in New Orleans.'

Archer swallowed hard and nodded.

She stared into his eyes for a moment. 'Am I making you uncomfortable, Detective Archer?'

'Yeah. A little. I'm not used to talking to—'

'I get it. The two times we met I had clothes on.'

Without it being ordered, the lemon water drink appeared and Archer put a twenty on the table.

'So I just bought a little of your time?'

'A lap dance would buy even more.'

'I can't even afford the drink, young lady.'

'Write it off, Mr Archer.'

He didn't happen to be a corporate, expense account big spender. Clearing his throat, he said, 'You've been doing this, what you do . . .'

'Stripping?'

'Yeah.' A little awkward. 'You've been doing this for how long?'

'I was in Miami for a year. But here? In the Quarter? Two years off and on. I tended bar at Rita's Tequila House for a while during that time. They had a guitar player over there I had a thing for, but I make a lot more money doing this.'

'Stripping.'

'That's the name of the game.'

'You told me that there were sales going on in some of the clubs.'

She twisted around, surveying the establishment.

'Softly, Detective. I don't need anyone else hearing that.'

'Look, when do you get off?'

'After I get some of the customers off.' Her mischievous eyes flirted with him. 'Shift ends at three.'

'Can we grab a coffee then?'

'Sure. Meet me at Café du Monde on Decator. Three thirty. It won't be too busy that time of the morning.'

'I look forward to it.'

'Aren't you going to stick around and see me dance? A couple of singles in the G-string?'

He felt the blood rush to his face. 'No, but I'll see you at three thirty.'

'Stick around,' she said. 'I put on a pretty good show, and even at my age, I don't look too bad in the altogether.'

He nodded. Twenty-five? Twenty-six? She looked fabulous. 'I'm sure you're very entertaining but, really I . . .'

Alexia took a long swallow of the sparkling lemon water. 'Mm, French champagne. Worth every penny of what you paid.'

Checking his watch he stood up.

'Too bad,' she said. 'You'd be fun to fool around with.'

'I can't, you know.'

'I get it, Detective. I get it.'

'Three thirty?'

'You'll recognize me, Detective. I'll be the one wearing sweats.'

EIGHTEEN

He wandered the streets, marveling at the drunken crowds and the piles and piles of waste. He wasn't sure how people could throw garbage bags that high. He worked his way down to Decator, stopping into several doorways to listen to the blistering sounds coming from blues and jazz clubs. The music was amazing. Thumping bass, spot-on vocals and wailing guitars. Shrill brass sections that sent vibrations through your teeth. As spicy Creole dishes and seafood was to NOLA restaurants, New Orleans blues and jazz was to the clubs. If it wasn't first class, top shelf, it would be gone in a day. New Orleans was nothing if it wasn't great food, drink and music. If you had to be sleepless in a city, this place was better than most.

Invisible, alone and somewhat vulnerable, he wondered what the voodoo lady was doing. Now divorced, did she have a boyfriend? Did she spend her nights with some guy wrapped around her or did she sleep alone, feeling the same void that Archer felt? And then he felt guilty about having thoughts about someone other than Denise. She was still his wife. They were supposed to grow old together. That thought never left him.

He ended up at Café du Monde, recognizing it by the iconic green-and-white-striped awning. A twenty-four-hour coffee shop with beignets supposedly to die for. Probably overrated but still, a top-rated landmark in a city of landmarks.

Too chilly to sit outside, but there were several tables open inside. He sat down and ordered a café au lait, there being no tea option. The other patrons presented a stark contrast to what he'd experienced in Detroit. Maybe it was just his imagination, but Motown seemed uptight by comparison. There, revelers had an agenda. In New Orleans, even at three in the morning, party-goers had a relaxed don't-give-a damn-attitude, ready to kick back and continue till dawn. Or beyond.

He felt the hands massaging his shoulders and he looked up. Gone were the extensions, the heavy eye shadow and rouge, and the red lips. Sexy Lexy had disappeared and Alexia Chantel was smiling down at him.

'What's your real name?'

'Does it matter?'

'No. What you can tell me matters.'

'So what do you need to know?'

She sat down, motioning to a white-jacketed waiter.

'You said someone was selling heroin in the club.'

'I'm offered the drug on a weekly basis. And it's not just heroin. I could have just about anything on the street.'

'Nothing's being done to stop it?'

She shook her head. 'Several years ago some clubs got caught. They got their liquor licenses suspended but business went on as usual.'

It sounded like Detroit. Nobody seemed to be able to stop that drug flow either.

'I'm not in Vice, and I wouldn't know a liquor violation if I saw it, but I do have a major concern. It involves a gang called Warhead Solja.'

Her eyes got wider. 'So you do have a handle on some of this.'

'They're selling, right?'

She nodded. The waiter asked for her order and she smiled at him, asking for café au lait. A little stronger than sparkling lemon water.

'You know the gang?'

'Of course. I'm not surprised you know them. I figured someone was aware of what they're doing.'

'I'm new to New Orleans,' he said. 'I may not know as much as you think I should. Give me some background.'

'Look, Detective Archer, I'm not a snitch. If someone breaks the law and it doesn't hurt anyone I'm not the one going to the authorities. I work on shaky grounds as it is. The sex trade isn't the most honest profession in this city. But I make damned good money. I've got a limited time to make this money before I age out, and I'm working it for all it is worth.'

'Your point is?'

'I chose this life. I do what I need to do to make this business work for me. Do you understand that?'

'No. But I'll accept that.'

'Don't be judgmental. It will make this story much harder to tell and harder for you to hear.'

'You work your business. I get it.'

'There are those of us who willfully work the club. We may swallow some pride but we do damned well. Detective, I can make two hundred thousand a year. Do you get that? Two hundred thousand. It's all cash and I don't have to pay tax on most of it. Who the hell is checking? Now, Mr Archer, what's your salary?'

He was silent. Wondering where he'd gone wrong.

'That said, every other week or so we get the group walk-ins.'

'Group walk-ins?'

'There are two types of walk-ins. Girls or ladies who have worked in other cities. Girls who decide this is an easy way to make big bucks and they deliberately come down here to New Orleans to work the business. Local girls who decide to give it a try. Maybe they're friends with one of the strippers.'

'You were one once, right? A walk-in?' He was still working on the two hundred thousand dollar figure. Forty-some-year-old men didn't have that opportunity. If they did, he needed to do some serious research.

'From Miami, Florida. Yes. We all were walk-ins. But there's a second type. I call them the *group* walk-ins.'

'OK.'

'Every week or so a new batch of girls shows up. A group. Four or five, all at once. Some speak English, most speak a little English, some speak no English. I'm never sure that these groups are totally on board with the biz. I mean they're hesitant. They don't seem to know the rules and I always feel that they are a little shaky as to what goes on in the club. Very few of them last.'

Archer folded his arms, studying the girl. Several hours ago he'd seen her almost naked. Now she was a fresh-faced young thing bundled up in a sweatsuit talking about her seamy business.

'So what does go on in your club?'

'You're serious?'

'Yes.'

'You don't know?'

'Woody's is the first strip club I've ever been in.'

'Wow,' she smiled, reaching over the table and touching his hand. 'I don't believe it. A virgin.'

He closed his eyes for a second and pulled back his hand.

'I'm sorry,' she said.

'Lap dances? Table dances?'

'Oh, Detective Archer, it can go a lot further than that. How much money do you have? I can give you services that will take every last cent you own. Just give me a dollar amount.'

He took a sip of coffee, then another.

'Alexia, I work homicide. You ladies are a little off my beat. As I said before I'm not on the vice patrol, OK?' Sex crimes were on the same floor as homicide and in truth he'd worked several cases with that department, but he only got involved in killings.

'My point is, these young girls, the group walk-ins, don't really know what to expect. I'm certain that many of them have never even been naked in front of a man, and all of a sudden, they're strippers. And they can easily become high-end prostitutes. I watch it on a regular basis.'

'And that has to do with the sale of drugs?'

'Warhead Solja brings these girls in. Nasta Mafia brings them in.'

'Nasta Mafia?'

'It's another gang. I am not in the loop, but I'm not blind. No one seems to try and hide what's happening. Look' – she folded her hands in front of her, almost glaring into his eyes – 'my job is to dance, take your dollar bills, sell you a drink, get you to go to a private room with me and—'

'OK,' Archer said. 'You don't have to go the whole route.'

'These girls, they are glassy eyed, stoned from the day they start. My guess is that the gang, or their pimp, hooks them before they even start their first night. Give them a dose of H then hand them over. And then the salesmen show up.'

Archer kept pushing. Sipping his coffee he gazed at the young woman. 'These salesmen, they sell the drugs?'

'They do. And the girls, the regulars, we're all too afraid to say anything. It's like . . . it's not our problem. And some of the regular dancers, the strippers, are actually the gang's best customers. I think the girls who are hooked, they barely make ends meet because all their money goes for the next fix. And, I don't have first-hand knowledge, but apparently it makes this job a lot easier to be totally fucked up while you do your shift.'

'You don't get fucked up?'

'I probably am fucked up, but no. I don't do the drugs. Once these girls do H, and a number of them do, they are hooked. They'll do anything their pimp tells them to do. And these gangs, they get their claws into them.'

'So here's my question. Do you know anything about initiation into this gang? Warhead Solja?'

'Initiation?'

'I'm trying to tie a gang ritual into some recent murders.'

He didn't want to leak all the information. Not yet. 'I was looking for information on how they get new members.'

'That information I don't have,' she said.

'Where do you think these girls come from? The groups that show up?'

She sipped her coffee, a distant look in her eyes.

'Alexia?'

She finally focused on him. 'I don't know how much to tell you. You see, we're not a close-knit group of people. We compete for men's attention and dollars. Aggressively, I might add. You come in with one hundred dollars to drop in a G-string or for lap dances, I want that one hundred dollars. I'm very jealous if it goes somewhere else, you know what I'm saying?'

He nodded. Not such a sweet, fresh-faced girl after all.

'It breaks down like this. I could make fifteen hundred a night. If I work four nights a week, I pull down over three hundred thousand a year. Personally I don't work that hard, but I still want what walks in that door. If someone is cutting my time, if that girl is more attractive, more interesting, I'm not happy.'

'So there's some serious competition.'

'You think? Listen, Detective, there's some serious shit here. We don't talk that much. About who you are, where you come from. My job from sign on to shift end is to take as much money as I can from this sorry bunch of losers. Buy me another drink,

let me grind your crotch, come into the back room with me. I
could retire when I'm thirty-five, Mr Archer, but I've got to work
the job and keep out of other people's business. So I don't ask
questions. Especially when it comes to the gangs. If I get nosey,
if I act like I'm interested, I could be on one of those trash piles
outside, stuffed in a garbage bag and no one would notice.
Actually, no one would probably care. You see? So it would
be much better if I don't say anything at all, but . . .'

Archer gazed out at the street. Almost four a.m. and the
costumed revelers still passed by, tipsy, loud, partying hard.

'How old are you?'

'Old enough.'

And here he was. Thirty-six and planning on working till he
was ninety-eight.

'You came up to me and suggested someone should look into
drug sales in your strip club.'

She nodded, her silky blond hair softly caressing her face.
'I did.'

'So it seems to me you're conflicted. You don't want to cause
a scene, yet you're concerned that people are going off the deep
end. Getting hooked on drugs, depending on street gangs.'

The girl pushed her coffee cup off to the side of the table.
'OK. Is there anything here like *off the record*. If I say something,
I can't get in trouble and you won't tell anyone where it came
from?'

'Immunity? Sure. Tell me what you want and I'll pretend
it never happened. I can do that.'

A drunken couple with faces grotesquely painted in purple,
green and yellow staggered by them and sat two tables away.
Jagged patterns of bright colors covered every inch of their
exposed flesh. Archer saw a white-jacketed waitress shake her
head in disgust.

'No one checks IDs in the club.'

'OK. So you're telling me you've got underage drinkers. That's
it? It's not that big a deal, Alexia.'

'Oh, I'm sure we do. Underage drinkers are everywhere in
this city. If you carded everyone with a to-go cup . . . but we
have underage dancers, Detective Archer. Underage girls who
are professionally stripping. I know, first hand, some of these

girls that come in are fifteen and sixteen years old. Some probably younger. Much younger. I said I didn't talk to the other dancers, but the other day one of them talked to me. A girl named Fabiana approached me last week and told me that she'd been kidnapped, had been given heroin and was stripping to help her family.'

'And how did that help her family?'

'She's under the impression her pimp was sending money to her family so they didn't lose their home. Somewhere in South America. But my guess is that no money is ever sent south.'

'They're dancing topless at fifteen and sixteen?'

'The club owners say as long as *that's* it they don't see a problem. As long as all they do is dance. But that's not all it is, Detective. I watch them. They go to the booths, the private rooms. This girl, Fabiana, said some of the Spanish girls even have a quota. They've got to interact with a certain number of guys every shift.'

'You're telling me that these girls are engaging in prostitution? And they're under eighteen years of age?'

'Oh, don't act all righteous, Mr Archer.' She removed a colorful elastic ribbon from her wrist and pulled her long hair up into a ponytail. Rolling her eyes, she said, 'I see guys your age every day who slobber over young girls. But from a purely personal standpoint, it cuts into my income. I do this for a living, Detective Archer. But it's sometimes hard to compete. You and I both know a lot of guys prefer younger girls.'

'And a quota?'

'She says, and this isn't me telling the story, *she* says they've got to turn at least twenty-five guys per shift. Lap dance, booth or private room. And their pimps, usually a member of some gang, they check on them. They have to make so much money a day and turn it in. Sometimes these guys will sit at the bar, watching. I guess that puts a little more urgency in the girls' hustle.'

'So where are the cops? Don't we interact here?' He was still relatively new to the city's police force and only involved in homicide. Maybe he was missing something.

'*You* show up when there's a customer complaint. Now you saw our crowd tonight, Detective. You saw the girls. Beautiful,

young, some of them, I'm sure, are under eighteen year of age.
How many of our clients, the fine upstanding men that they
are, how many of them are going to call 911 and register a
complaint? They're getting their joint sucked, a first-class hand
job and some sixteen year old girl is pushing her tits in his face.
They're living a fantasy they don't get at home. Their wives,
their girlfriends, they don't give them that kind of action. No
way. There are no dissatisfied clients that I know of in my club.
No, I don't think 911 is getting very many calls complaining
about what goes on. I would guess there are no calls at all. Zip.'

'And you're saying that according to her, this Fabiana, young
girls are told they are working for their families, helping pay the
rent, and therefore they have to keep pushing their product?'

'You used that phrase, not me.' She gave him a grim smile.
'When their families are threatened I'll guarantee you, these girls
are not going to call in complaints. So as far as you guys are
concerned, everything is fine. No one is calling 911 so there
are no problems.'

Archer nodded, sipping his now cold drink. The drunken
couple had passed out, their brightly painted faces bleeding a
strange mix of purple and orange in a puddle of spilled coffee
on the table.

'One more thing, Detective. It may be important, it may not.'

'What's that?'

'Fabiana, she lasted four days.'

'What happened?'

'It's not unusual. Like I said, a lot of them leave shortly
after they start. This girl, she hated the work. I know she wasn't
making her "quota" because she told me so, and then she never
showed up again.'

'And you think . . .'

'I'd rather not think. Please, don't ask. I told you, I'm better
off when I mind my own business.'

'And I told you, I'm not involving you in any way. What
you've said so far is hearsay, right?'

Alexia took a deep breath and folded her hands in front of
her. 'OK, I'll tell you what I think. Only my thoughts, and,
Detective Archer, I don't pretend to have answers. I don't believe
she got along with these guys and I think there's one of three

things that could have happened to her. They moved her to one of their massage parlors, they beat the crap out of her or they killed her. That's what I think. They don't care what happens to these girls. They're just pieces of meat.'

She stood up, never looking at him, and walked away. It was several minutes later when he glanced down and saw that she'd left a phone number on his napkin. Well, this was one way to get a girl's number. He would have preferred more positive circumstances.

NINETEEN

A s he walked back to his cottage, hundreds of revelers on Bourbon Street were bobbing, weaving, stumbling drunk. Old men, one in a pinstripe suit, young women in tight little black dresses and several in leather pants, and a stocky black girl who hugged him and called him handsome. Slurring her speech, she asked if he would buy her a drink. He shook his head, pushing on. He heard her screaming behind him, 'You just don't like black people!'

Garbage bags were still piled six feet high as far as the eye could see, and the street was no longer a surface of concrete, but a blanket of broken green Hand Grenade drink cups and purple-, yellow- and green-colored beads that crunched with every step.

It was four forty-five in the morning. In another four hours things would appear about normal. Normal for New Orleans. All energy feeds on a fuel. This town ran on high-octane alcohol.

Alexia had mentioned that Nasta Mafia was one of the gangs that sold drugs in the club and possibly provided some of the girls. Archer thought back to Hector Sanchez, one of the first victims of the Chill thrill kills. He was a member of Nasta Mafia. Hector wasn't a bank teller, a Christian janitor, a councilman or an attorney. He was a gangbanger from Little Woods. And Blake Rains, the councilman who'd been found at the amusement park, it appeared he'd been killed in the Little Woods area. It may mean nothing but it was the only link he had. Other than cans of Chill. Did Blake Rains have an association with Nasta Mafia? Was that the reason he was in Little Woods when they killed him? What possible affiliation would that be?

Now he knew a little more about two of the NOLA gangs. No surprise, they both ran drugs. He was from Detroit. Hell, members of his own family ran drugs. His fellow officers ran drugs. Same shit, different city.

Why did two victims get killed in Little Woods, the neighborhood bordering Lake Pontchartrain? And why did someone move one of the bodies to the deserted amusement park? He had some more whys. If he answered those two questions, he would be a lot closer to solving the crimes. It played on his mind as he walked the path to his cottage. He checked the tape on the door. Still in place.

Five o'clock in the morning and he was wide awake. It could be the strong black coffee from Café du Monde. More likely it was the ideas and questions swirling in his head. There were dozens of things he should have asked the young blonde. He hoped for a follow-up interview, but he didn't want to put her at risk. He liked her. A girl who made a living with her body. And apparently a very good living. Two hundred thousand a year?

Archer stripped off his jacket, put his holster and gun on the bed and lay down, his hands behind his head. What could he do with two hundred thousand a year? Two hours later he was still wide awake. It was going to be a miserable day.

At eight ten a.m. Case Blount was sitting on a stool in the Camellia Grill devouring a piece of grilled chocolate pecan pie, a cheese omelet, five strips of bacon and a pot of strong coffee. The gleaming white marble countertops reflected sun coming in the Chartres Street windows and he glanced at the iconic Mickey Mouse clock on the wall. He had another forty minutes to indulge in some of the most decadent food in the Quarter. He wiped at a smudge of chocolate on his shirt and swore to himself that he would lose some weight. Spreading the morning paper in front of him he studied the Metro section of *The Times-Picayune*. The story about the possible removal of Confederate statues honoring General Robert E. Lee, Jefferson Davis and P.G.T. Beauregard was front and center. He shook his head, wondering when this political correctness would finally settle down. The next story involved a killing over a bicycle and below that an article about a murder in Central City followed by a drive-by shooting in the Garden District. Too damn many killings in this town.

The grill in front of him was sizzling with breakfast steaks, sausage, and hash browns. He should have ordered some of those delicious hash browns, damn. Flagging down a white-jacketed waiter with a weathered face and a Richard Roundtree 'Shaft' mustache, he asked for an order of the potatoes. Too many good dishes, and a man couldn't eat everything. But he could try.

Scanning *The Times-Picayune*, he noticed the death of the adoption attorney Trevor Parent had already been relegated to the second page of Metro. In a city where murders were an everyday occurrence, you could only devote so much time per killing to the front page. Still, the story was getting some strong coverage. The paper was conducting a background investigation into the man, apparently hoping to uncover the reason why he was singled out in this violent killing. That couldn't be good.

'You eatin' all that shit? Damn, Case, you know what that does to your arteries? Just make you old before your time.'

Glancing up at the tall bald man, he swallowed hard. William 'Gangsta Boy' Washington stood over him. The gangly man sat down on the adjoining stool and picked up a strip of bacon. He took a bite, then wiped the grease from his hand onto Blount's jacket sleeve.

'Greasy shit gum up your innards. Be healthy, man. And speaking of health, you are asking for some unhealthy solutions. What you think you are solving you are only making worse. What's the word I'm lookin' for? Exacerbating the problem.' He looked the short fat man in his eyes and smiled. 'You didn't expect a word like that comin' from a nigger like me, did you? Shit, you might not know the damned word yourself.'

'William, I'm not sure what you're referring to.' He stared at the greasy smear on his newly dry-cleaned sport coat.

'Listen, slimeball, we can go back and forth all day on this shit. You want to cut us out of the business, we would like a chance to renegotiate.'

Blount buried his head in his hands. There was no solution.

'Excuse me, asshole. I'm talkin' to you. The two of us, we need a solution. Right here and right now.'

'William, what the hell do you want me to do?' In a whisper, he said, 'Delroy wants an exclusive. If I don't deliver that, he kills my people and your people. Do you want more Hector Sanchez stories?'

'Like a brother he was,' Washington said.

'Well? Just like Hector, there will be more brothers killed, trust me. Do you want a summit? You and Delroy? I don't know what else to suggest. We are all making money here. And if this gets fucked up, there are people at the top who will bring shit down on you like you've never seen. You have never seen a bloodbath like this before. To quote a famous line, "Why can't we all just get along?"'

'An LA banger, Rodney King, right? He said that?'

'Among others,' Blount said.

'A summit? What do you have in mind? Like we get all one side of the street, they get the other? A summit? Like you get the drug sales in the Quarter, I get them in the Warehouse District. Or maybe over in Treme? Do you think that this is a good idea? We're practically at war here, Case. I don't see how a summit is going to solve this problem.'

'A summit,' Blount said, dipping his napkin in a glass of water, 'like you guys work it out. No more stabbings, shootings. No more war. No more asserting yourself. A summit where the two gangs make a lot of money and quit fucking up the system. I swear, William' – he dipped his napkin in his water glass and dabbed at the grease smear on his jacket– 'you guys don't come to an agreement, the money stops. The business stops. And the higher ups will, as I promised, kick your ass. Nasta Mafia, Warhead Solja, will cease to exist as you know them. The people who are at the top of this organization, and they are very powerful, believe me, will cut off your balls. Mr Vocabulary, they will *emasculate* you. You probably didn't think a white guy from Baton Rouge, Louisiana, would know a word like that, right?'

Gangsta Boy leaned back, surprised at the response. Pulling a plastic toothpick from his shirt pocket he stuck it in his mouth and stared at Blount.

'So you're saying we, us and Warhead Solja, we need to work it out together? Or the shit gonna hit the fan?'

'Nasty shit. I'll make it happen, William.' Fueled on chocolate and caffeine, he reared back. Voice still soft but intense, he said, 'You guys get a grip. This isn't some fucking terrorist gang where just killing people for the fun of it makes sense. We are a business. A goddamned business. People make their livings on what we do. Families put food on the table. Raise families, pay child support and alimony. Some people buy pussy and wheels and high-end living quarters. My man, we deal in property and commodities. Even though the commodities are sometimes human beings, we do deal in commodities, William. Do you even understand that? I hope you do.'

Washington stood up, towering over the short fat man.

'You threatening me, you white-assed honkey? You fucking cracker. Is that what you are doing?'

'You're goddamned right I am,' he whispered, staring at the gang leader, his gaze focused on the spot between his eyes. The most focal spot on a person's face. Staying on his stool, he was aware that people were staring.

The fire in the dark man's eyes slowly died, and he nodded, lowering himself back to his stool.

'OK,' Washington said in a soft voice. 'Get it set up. We will work this out, Case.' Wiping his hands and lips on a paper napkin he said, 'Obviously we don't want to lose a revenue stream. You know? We're not insensitive to the flow.' Looking down, he read the headline. 'Fuck, what are we? The murder capital of the fucking world? Damn, it just keeps getting worse, don't it?'

Blount shook his head as the bald-headed gangster walked out of the restaurant. Revenue stream? The flow? These gangs were getting far too sophisticated. It could be a good thing. It probably was a very bad thing.

TWENTY

He'd had a short dream. Fifteen minutes maybe and he couldn't remember it. It seemed important. Something about the parade and the Chill cans. Maybe something he was missing and should be able to see.

Today was the day. If they could isolate the killer it was a huge start. If tech could clean up the photo. He was doubtful. This wasn't a television show where everything could be wrapped in forty-five minutes. And while technology was wonderful, it didn't solve nearly as many crimes as it did on *CSI*.

Archer took a quick shower in the tiled bathroom he could barely turn around in. The water only got lukewarm much like his refrigerator only got cool. Shivering, he dried off, put on a clean shirt and khakis then strapped on his shoulder holster. He stepped out onto the porch and put on his jacket as he took a deep breath of bracing air. The putrid smell of rotting garbage and stale beer was gone. Walking to Bourbon he saw no signs of the trash mountains. No signs of stumbling drunks weaving down the street.

The streets and sidewalks actually looked clean. They had been washed down as usual by water-powered high-pressure flusher scrub trucks with a patented deodorizer in the early morning hours. God knew, New Orleans had plenty of water.

On the off chance that Solange Cordray was in her shop he walked to her little store. The door was locked and he didn't really want to knock and bother her if she was in. Still, he'd like to get her take on what had transpired so far. Her reading of the energy from the can had led him to where he was. And maybe living so close to her, he'd hoped she would agree to a short walk and a cup of coffee. He wanted to see her and wasn't sure if that was a good or bad thing.

Finally he knocked. Softly. There was no answer. Disappointed, he turned and walked to PJ's Coffee on Chartres. Three squad cars were parked in front of the establishment. No problem, it was just a popular spot for the local police. Coffee and donuts. A stereotypical cop stop.

A green tea, a brief conversation with two of the patrolmen and he was out the door. Down to Canal, on the streetcar with an early morning crowd of misfits. Walking into headquarters, he felt a twinge in his chest. So hoping he would discover the killer today. So hoping that the world of TV fantasy had come to the New Orleans homicide squad. So hoping the picture would show exactly who had committed the hideous crime. He doubted anything would come of it, but it was one of the few leads they had. He wished he'd asked Solange for a prayer. A spell. A gris-gris bag. Something to clean up this unholy mess.

Josh Levy was at his desk as Archer walked by.

'Morning, Q. PJ's Coffee?' He glanced at the cup. 'I tasted ours this morning. Yours is probably a better bet.'

'Tea,' Archer said. 'Any word on the photo, Josh?'

'They want to see us in half an hour and show us what they have. They assured me there's a rush on it.'

'Half an hour? That's like a week from Thursday.' He was anxious.

'Tech is slow, Detective Archer. I'm certain they're doing everything possible to clean up that picture.'

'Damn.' Archer walked over to his desk. As in most situations, anticipation was the worst thing. OK, sometimes anticipation was the best part of an experience. But not this time. They needed to see that picture.

Sergeant Chip Beeman tapped him on his shoulder.

'Detective Q, they're running a little late on blowing up our photo. Should be ready in an hour.'

An hour? Damn. This was supposed to be priority. They'd had it overnight, since yesterday afternoon, but now they wanted a fucking hour? Might as well be into next week. A killer was on the loose and who knew when he would strike again? And Tech was backed up. So much for the value of a human life.

Kathy Bavely threw her arms around Solange.

'He asked me to meet his father, Solange.'

'Paul? Paul Girard?'

'Of course.'

She had been waiting as usual, right inside the door.

'Kathy, you are all over the place with this guy. One day he's too pushy, the next day he's too cheap and now he's the best thing ever. It sounds serious, meeting one of the parents. Are you ready for this?'

Bavely backed away, squinting her eyes at her friend.

'Didn't you just introduce Detective Quentin Archer to your mother? He was here yesterday and you invited him back to Ma's room. Tell me you didn't. Come on Solange, isn't this kind of hypocritical?'

'Hey, I introduced him because I thought Ma might read something into his case. It was nothing to do about any relationship. I just—'

'Paul wants me to meet his father. The last living member of his immediate family. Come on. Really, Solange, I just thought you'd be happy for me. If you're not, then just tell me.'

'I'm only happy if you're happy. You're hot and cold, girl. Or in this case, cold and hot.'

'OK.' Bavely put her arm around Solange's waist and guided her to the coffee shop. 'Let's talk about this over a *hot* beverage.' Their steps clicked on the cold tile floor, the smell of isopropyl alcohol in the air. 'He's got his faults, girl. God knows he's got faults. But he's substantial. He's smart, got a good job, drives a cool Lexus and lives in a nice place in the Garden District. He's talented, and not just in bed. He's obviously a really good writer.'

Solange smiled. 'Well, even though you say he won't take you anyplace nice, he's got a Lexus and a home in the Garden District. He may be cheap but that's a lot better than Warren Dooper. I never understood you and Warren. The guy across the river with a beat up Volkswagen and sheep dog hair all over his apartment.'

'Yeah. I never understood that relationship either. Warren was a trip. And he wasn't that good in the sack. It was kind of all about him. He had to be satisfied first. I think I was an afterthought. Although I have to admit his blogs were funny.' She laughed. 'His conversations with his dog Garcia? I thought those were a riot, but his blogs just didn't pay the bills. Besides, I think his dog was the smarter of the duo.'

'You always go for the creative types.'

'I do. But the more I know about Paul . . .'

'Well, then go for it. Meet his dad. Marry the guy.'

Bavely poured two cups of coffee and handed one to Solange. The two sat at a table and tasted the brew.

'For some reason it bothers me that he won't spring for a nice night out. Or maybe send flowers on my birthday. Simple things. He's cheap, Solange. Why does that bother me? Am I being shallow?'

'Needs something,' Solange said as she tasted her coffee.

'Creamer? Sugar?'

'A better brand of coffee,' Solange responded.

Bavely laughed. 'Paul got a bite today. *The New Yorker* said they're interested in his story about human trafficking in New Orleans. They are running a story about trafficking in New York and this would be, according to Paul, a companion piece.'

'Congratulations to him.'

'*The New Yorker*. That would be nice. He's got an informant. Somebody who actually is inside the business. There are rival gangs that are involved in the trade, and this guy apparently wants to leak information to help bury the competition.'

Solange sipped her coffee, studying her friend. She closed her eyes for a brief moment and saw fire. She saw frozen cliffs of ice. She saw the bowels of hell.

'Stay out of this, Kathy. This isn't good for you.'

'Oh, I'm not in it.' She laughed. 'I just listen to Paul talk about it. His friend the senator is interested in who is leaking information. Paul said he can't betray the source, but Senator LeJeune keeps insisting. She must call him once a day. The senator wants to nail these guys.' She took a swallow of the black beverage. 'Sometimes I wonder if she and Paul . . .'

'You're taking a pretty serious interest in this story.'

'Well, I'm intrigued. And Marcia LeJeune is speaking at noon tomorrow at Phillips Restaurant and Bar for a fundraising event. The money goes to a shelter for women and children and he asked me to go. I'll get to meet a United States senator. So I thought that was pretty cool. And I can kind of get a feel for the relationship.'

Solange shivered. Fire and ice, not a good combination.

'When you told me you were going to go to this event tomorrow

I got a cold chill, Kathy. I can't explain it, but please, stay away. I can't stress this enough.'

'I'm not . . . I'm just listening, Solange. That's all. It's not like I have anything to do with his project.'

'As a friend, I'm begging you, walk away. I have a very bad feeling about this. You shouldn't insert yourself.'

'You're scaring me.'

'I would hope so. I see this, Kathy. Paul is walking into a buzz saw. You must tell him that.'

'You don't know him,' Bavely said. 'You don't know anything about him or his writing. You don't know anything about the trafficking. Or do you? Do you really see things?'

'I see enough. Right now. Please, don't get involved.'

'Solange.'

'Kathy, you're a good friend. I just don't want you to be hurt.'

Bavely shook her head.

'I share things with you. I don't ask you to pass judgment.'

'Please just listen to me. I don't want anything to happen to you. Please, Kathy. Somehow walk away.'

A chill fell on the room and neither woman spoke. Finally Kathy Bavely stood up and walked out the door. Solange sat for another three minutes, lost in her dark thoughts and wishing as she often did that the burden of her gift would be removed. She knew more than she wanted to know.

TWENTY-ONE

'Detectives, we've done the best we can do using what you gave us to work with. I'll apologize head of time for not being able to give you a clearer image. Without getting technical, this video camera was not designed to give you crystal clear still photos. It's somewhat of a novelty device. Maybe in a couple of years from now we'll be able to hand back a portrait photograph of your suspect. One you could frame and place on the mantel. But not yet.'

Archer took a deep, cleansing breath. He'd secretly pinned so much hope on this discovery, largely because he needed a break, and because Solange Cordray had brought it to his attention and he wanted her input. He wanted the attractive voodoo lady to be a part of this case.

'That said, please direct your attention to the screen in front of you. We will pass out prints of the photo after you've seen the screen image.' There was a moment of silence as the three men waited with baited breath.

A photo flashed on the screen and Beeman, Levy and Archer stared at the image with rapt attention. It was a blur. A defined blur, but still, just a blur. They studied the picture then looked at each other.

'It's a face,' Archer said. 'The outline is there. You can make out his gray hood, and it appears that he is showing his full face. But isn't there any way to define more features? Make things just a little clearer?'

'We used everything we had, Detective. Resolution is a problem. A still shot would have been preferable but you only provided us with video. A video from a camera mounted on a stick, and carried through crowds numbering in the thousands. It's not just the camera. There's motion involved. Not only is the camera moving, but the moving camera is capturing motion and motion blurs the image. I'm sure you'll agree that we don't have the best of conditions.'

'We captured stills from security cameras when I was in Detroit. They were usually much clearer.'

'Security cameras are stationary, Detective. And, we're talking about different types of cameras and a wide variety of variables.'

The three of them stared at the screen, then looked at the glossy prints they were handed. Archer looked up.

'OK, we've already checked security video in the immediate vicinity. Now, let's recheck security cameras looking specifically for a guy with a tight gray hoody. Let's review the shops and restaurants within a block. If we see nothing there, spread it out. We may have to review cameras on the entire route. Pick up any visuals of this guy with a hood. Before, we didn't know what to look for. Maybe this time we get lucky, like the videos of the brothers who bombed the Boston Marathon. There were cameras that caught just about everything.'

Levy nodded. 'I'll get on it, Q.'

'Lots of people, lots of gray hoods. It was chilly that night.' Beeman tapped his fingers on the table. 'Still, we're way ahead of where we were yesterday.'

'We're gonna need to do eight, nine thousand pounds of shrimp per hour, Mr Blount. Peeled, peeled and deveined, heads on, heads off, the works.'

'We can supply the workers, Mr Morris. Untrained of course.' Blount didn't really care what the work entailed. He could supply the manpower, Warhead Solja could supply the muscle and keep things running smoothly. Or Nasta Mafia. Or somebody else who could come down hard on these immigrants. He just wished the warring factions would get along. Work out a truce. It would make his job so much easier.

'Oh, don't you worry.' The tall man with greased down black hair rocked back and forth sitting in the gray cloth chair. He rubbed his large bony hands on his faded jeans as if to wipe the odor of fish from them. 'The grunts you sent before worked out just fine. Sometimes we worked 'em twenty-four hours straight, but the job got done.'

'Sounds like Zandar Packing is doing quite well.'

Whether it was his imagination or a true scent, he could detect the smell of a fishmonger. It turned his stomach.

'Oh, hell, Mr Blount. We're doing great. This is the biggest box chain we've ever worked with. These stores sell a boatload of shrimp, but we need to get up to speed quick. We got one month to start delivering, but it's a shitload of money. A shitload of money.'

He considered upping the price. If there was that much money to be made, a shitload . . . 'I'll put Mr Houston on it right away. He and his' – Blount cleared his throat – 'his staff will deliver the workers, and they'll stop by on a regular basis to make sure they stay in line.' He'd almost said thugs instead of staff. That's what they were. Thugs.

'As usual, you cover any problems?'

'We take their passports and visas as soon as they arrive,' Blount said. 'Somebody tries to walk, they don't have anywhere to go. Once we have their legal documents, we own them. Trust me. You need thirty workers, right?'

'Thirty. For the foreseeable future.'

'Lodging, food?'

'Same as before. We stack 'em in a concrete block warehouse building, two showers and two toilets and give 'em a couple of hot plates. Nothin' fancy. Of course they can cook their own food. Lots of fish, Mr Blount.' He laughed, a high-pitched sound coming from his throat.

Blount chuckled. 'Probably better than what they have at home.' So many avenues for selling bodies. The opportunities never stopped.

'Working conditions are nothin' to write home about, but . . .'

The odor was stronger. Blount nodded. A stinking fish-packing company, twenty-four-hour shifts and two showers and toilets for thirty workers. Men and women. No, it wasn't the most pleasant situation he could think of. But sometimes these really were better conditions than what they had at home. At least he kept telling himself that. He picked up his handkerchief from the desk and held it against his nose to mask the smell.

'OK, Mr Morris. Ten thousand per employee upon delivery. Three hundred thousand for the transaction. If we have to replace any of those, the price goes down to eight thousand for their replacement. I trust that we'll be able to supervise these workers so that they last the duration of their employment.'

'No inspections, Mr Blount. That's part of the agreement. Same as before, am I right?'

Case Blount folded his hands over his protruding stomach. His stained shirt spoke of the omelet he'd had for breakfast, a smear of jelly and a Coke from half an hour ago. He thought back to last year when a Thai worker had been seriously injured at Zandar Packing. A woman operating a canning machine manually pushed some raw fish into the device. The apparatus grabbed her hand, immediately crushing it, then yanked her into the jaws all the way up to her elbow before shutting down, the flesh, tendons and bones of her arm pulverized. Blood and the pulp of her skin sprayed across the rubber conveyer belt. Two workers had rushed her back to the warehouse where an employee who was trained as a nurse tried to stop the bleeding. The trauma and loss of blood was more than the woman could stand and she died two days later.

Blount and company had quietly erased the evidence, and there was no investigation. No one ever missed the young lady. And thankfully, no one ever manually pushed product into the canning machines again.

'No, I can assure you there will be no inspections, Mr Morris. If there is a problem, we will do our best to solve it. You know that.'

'Yes, I remember very well.' The tall, gangly man stood and reached out to shake Blount's hand.

The fat man shook his head. 'I've got a bad cold. Don't want to give it to you.' He picked up his handkerchief and blew his nose long and hard. He didn't want to shake the hand of the shrimp man. Just deliver the workers and take the money.

They worked through lunch hunched over screens, watching grainy images with masses of partying revelers who strained to get a good view of the floats. Jumping high, stooping low, the crowd grabbed for throws tossed by outlandishly clad riders. Yes, there were hooded sweatshirts by the dozens. The weather had been cool, dropping into the low forties and almost everyone was bundled up to keep themselves warm.

'Years ago they actually threw gold pieces,' Beeman said. 'I've got a friend who has dozens of those pieces.'

'So, Q, we're isolating this right now to the block where the body was found.' Levy continued to look at his screen. 'What if this killer took off the hood as soon as he walked away. Then we're screwed.'

'We'll hope that didn't happen. Or let's look for someone who is removing the hood. Just keep a sharp eye.'

They'd been over the videos dozens of times. Three security cameras had caught the parade in the vicinity of the murder, but obviously the crowds had hidden or blocked the actual act because there was nothing to indicate someone had been killed. Only the shots from the camera on a stick showed what appeared to be the murder of the adoption attorney. Those videos were the defining shots.

'He's still got the knife on him at this point,' Beeman said. 'We didn't find it dropped anywhere at the scene.'

'He may have dumped it on a trash pile or dumpster once he got out of the neighborhood.'

'Or maybe,' Levy chimed in, 'one of the bystanders picked it up. Let's hope that didn't happen.'

'But,' Beeman said, 'it's a good bet that he's got it on him right now. Let's assume that he still has the knife. In this view. He wouldn't carry it in his hands. He'd freak out anyone who saw him, so he must have tucked it into his sweatshirt. He's hiding it. Maybe in the belt of his pants. He's still got that knife in this scene.'

'And?' Archer encouraged him. 'We don't know where he is, so how do we tell? What's your idea?'

'Well, this may be a small thing, but remember, it's now a murder weapon. Now it's something that's very important to him. Before it was just a knife. An object that he carried with him. Now it's got a lot more significance. You know how when you walk through the Quarter and even with your gun in a holster, snapped shut, you still reach for it occasionally, just to make sure it's there?'

Archer and Levy stared at him.

'Well,' the frustration rising in his voice, 'damn it, I do. I also check my wallet every once in a while. It might pay you to do that, Q.' He glared at Archer. 'Seems to me you got your wallet lifted down here not too long ago, Detective Archer. Maybe you remember that?'

'So what's your point?' Archer asked.

'This guy doesn't want that knife falling out of his shirt or belt. Fingerprints are on it, maybe some blood, so he's sticking his hand inside the shirt, or checking his belt every so often. He's walking quickly through the crowd, the hood is tight on his head, and he's patting his shirt, his waist. The man is just making sure that knife is still there until he can dispose of it safely.'

'OK,' Archer said, 'let's start over again. Anyone in a gray hoody that walks fast and pats themselves periodically. No perverts please.'

'Guy right there,' Levy said, freezing the screen. 'See, he's doing exactly that. Like he's checking to make sure something is secure.'

'Damn, blow that up,' Beeman said.

The camera caught the side of the face. A dark-skinned man, right hand pressed against the front of his pants. As if he was protecting something. He walked fast. Not too fast, but as a man on a mission.

'I'll be damned,' Beeman leaned in and watched the man.

'It's a long shot, Sergeant,' Levy said.

'And no way to prove it's a knife,' Archer added.

'Can we follow him?' Levy pointed at the screen. 'We've got camera vids on down the street. There's two bars, a souvenir shop and a jewelry store in the next two blocks. They all had cameras outside. We've got their views. Cue those up and we'll see if he shows up in any of those.'

'Good idea. If he stays on the street or the sidewalk we should be able to see him. And blow that photo up as big as possible. Let's see if we can see him a little clearer.'

Archer enlarged the frozen photo, the side of the man's face filling the screen. There was no mistaking a long scar on the suspect's cheek.

TWENTY-TWO

Paul Girard watched the river, phone in his hand, recorder ready to receive. The slight, five foot ten blond-haired man was slightly intimidated by his subject. Easily six foot something, muscular and black as coal. Girard had never been given his name, but running a background on Warhead Solja he knew this man was one of the ringleaders of the drug gang. This interview could be the highlight of his story. An inside look at human trafficking.

'So, no names, no gang names, no accusations, right? You're recording this conversation, and so am I. You have to agree, understand?' The man opened his large tattooed hand showing his cell phone.

Girard nodded. 'You are anonymous. You volunteered to talk to me. If you let me interview you, I promise to keep your identity a secret. I'm personally curious as to why you are willing to be interviewed at all.'

'Competition.' He frowned and Girard saw the long scar on his cheek get even longer. 'But understand, you can't mention that. I'm talkin' to you because I need to bury the competition.'

'I'm sorry.' Girard was genuinely confused.

'No names, man. This information comes from an unknown source. No accusations, right?'

'You have my word,' Girard said. 'You won't be mentioned, OK?'

'But' – the black male took long strides, Girard trying to keep up – 'you can mention the other gang. In fact, that's what you need to do.' He moved even faster along the levee, looking back at Girard and smirking.

'Leave your gang out of the story, but be sure and implicate the competition. That's what you're asking, right?'

'Sounds right.'

'So I give you anonymity, but I can print anything else you tell me.' Already he was breathing heavily. They walked at a rapid pace, and Girard was struggling. 'Any chance you can slow down just a little?'

'Listen to me.' The pace continued. 'Nasta Mafia is trafficking. Feel free to say that, you know? They're bad actors, dig?'

'And you're not?'

'I din't say that. There are a lot of bad actors here. You talk to people, you interview low-life scumbags and you know I'm right. But, I'm tellin' you, Nasta Mafia is. Bad. News. Those bastards traffic twenty-four/seven. You can print that. Do your homework. Man, Abe Lincoln never saw slaves like this group has. Nasta Mafia, some serious bad dudes. You put that in your story and you won't be wrong.'

They paused for a moment and Girard studied him. He'd picked up the vibe immediately. Get the authorities to cover Nasta Mafia and this guy's gang was home free. No competition. And Paul Girard was sworn to secrecy. He couldn't turn the black man or his gang. But the journalistic coup would be fabulous for his career. If this gangster told the truth, there was a story worth its weight in gold. Even if he only came down on Nasta Mafia. There would be one gang out of business. If he could tell half the story it was better than no story at all. He wondered if he should call the senator. Marcia LeJeune. Tell her what he suspected, what he heard tonight. Wait till he'd fleshed out the story. Wait until he had all the facts. Wait until he broke the story in *The New Yorker*. Then let LeJeune bring the weight of Washington down on these bastards.

'So, I've promised not to use your name . . . hell, I don't even know your name. And I've given you my word that I won't mention your affiliation.'

'My what?'

'Look, the less I know about you and the organization you represent the better we both are, right?'

The black man nodded. 'I'll tell you what you want to know. But no matter what you find, you don't bring me up, or my what you called it, eflition?'

Power of the pen. He could really break the story open if he had no ethics. Dig a little deeper and expose both gangs for human trafficking.

'Tell me how this works. Tell me how these people are recruited, where they come from.'

The man scratched at his cheek, tracing the long ugly scar that ran from his eye down to his jaw. 'You give me up, I'll put a hit on you, muthah fuckah. I truly will.'

Girard had been threatened before. But never by a gangster and never over his life. The last thing he wanted to happen was to be on the wrong end of a gun. He had no doubt that this man was sincere.

'Tell me everything.'

'Day after tomorrow,' the imposing man said, towering over the reporter. 'I will tell you some serious shit that will make your hair stand on end.'

'Anyone recognize this guy?' Archer surveyed five other detectives, three he'd recruited from their desks.

'That hood is pulled tight. Very few of his features are clear.'

'The scar,' another said, 'I'm trying to remember. Seems like he's a gangbanger, but I'm not sure.'

'There are a lot of battles out there, a lot of scars,' Levy said.

'OK, we're going to try and follow him with some security cameras in the next couple blocks. If we can track him, we need you to keep an eye on his hands. We believe he may have a knife, the murder weapon, under his shirt or in his pants. There's a good chance he'll try to ditch it. Maybe in a pile of trash, or in a dumpster. If we're lucky enough for a follow, watch for any quick movements where he tries to throw it away. Here we go.'

The view from the second camera was to the right of the first and initially there was no sign of the man.

'If we pick him up, it will be in three, two, one . . .'

And there he was. Head up, dodging the bystanders, hand over his crotch, pressed tightly against his pants. The detectives watched for maybe twelve seconds and he disappeared from view. All that was left was the throng of people and the beer cans, crushed drink cups and beads thrown on the sidewalk and in the street.

'Let's get him on the next camera.' Archer turned on the screen and immediately saw the figure.

'Crossing the street and headed toward the palms and bushes

in the median.' He pointed to the palm trees and thick bushes that divided Canal Street, and bordered the two streetcar tracks. 'If he crosses all the way over to the other side, we may lose him and,' Beeman stopped. 'Oh, shit, is he doing what I think he's doing?'

'The row of bushes.'

As they watched, the man appeared to expose himself and stand there by the bushes for two or three seconds.

'The guy is relieving himself. Damn. That's why he was pressing his hand on his crotch. Christ, he had to pee. And there . . .'

'That's not his unit he just pulled out,' Levy said. 'He's dropping something in the bushes. In that one bush in particular.'

Archer froze the picture. The detectives stared at the photo, smiles on all of their faces.

Detective Josh Levy finally broke the silence. 'Boys, I believe we've just found our murder weapon.'

'I'm sorry about this morning.' Solange nodded to Kathy Bavely as she put on her jacket ready to leave the care center. 'There are times when I have these premonitions.'

'Like your mother used to.'

'Yes. Kathy, you know what I do for a living.'

Bavely was pulling on a sweater and her leather boots. With the temperature in the low fifties she got ready to brave the chilly weather for her ride home.

'I do. Of course I do.'

'You've never asked, never mentioned that you wanted to discuss it. Of course that's quite all right, but it's part of who I am.'

'Well, you scared me this morning. I mean, all I'm doing is listening to this guy. I'm definitely not involved in his story. I mean, I am going to see one of his confidants, the senator, but I don't think it's going to affect me.' She paused. 'Is it?'

'I don't think we should visit this morning again. Sometimes it's better not to tell someone how you feel. That's true in all walks of life.'

'If what you know – what you think you know – involves harm, then maybe I should be aware.'

'I can't explain my process to you. You don't want to know the thoughts that come to me or where they come from. You wouldn't understand them.' She paused and looked away. 'I don't understand them most of the time.'

'Your point is?'

'I would like to suggest something you might do to protect yourself. But if you don't want to hear it—'

'What? Buy a gun?'

'That may not be a bad idea,' Solange said. 'Seriously.'

'You're really serious about this. OK, what else?'

'You're still going to Senator LeJeune's talk?'

'I am. I've got the day off.'

'I wish you would cancel, but that's not going to happen, is it?' Bavely shook her head.

'Promise me you won't laugh. Because much of what I do, of what I suggest, sounds, I don't know, somewhat mad to people. But there is centuries old magic that proves the point. I think you may be in danger. Largely because of Paul Girard and his human trafficking project.'

'Why do you even involve yourself?' Bavely asked.

'I have no choice, Kathy. That's the hard part of this.' She clenched her fists, shaking her head. Staring into her friend's eyes, she quietly said, 'I don't choose to know these things. The spirits send the visions, the feelings, to me. It isn't something I can control. Please, try and understand.'

The two of them stood at the exit, Bavely ready to walk to her car, Solange ready to walk to her home at the rear of her shop. The craziness was right outside the door, the late-afternoon crowd already drunk and revved up. And the craziness was right in front of them, staring in their faces. The voodoo lady hesitated.

'It's your choice, Kathy. Do what I suggest or don't. In the morning what I suggest should be in the past. Either you did or you didn't. I don't want it to interfere with our relationship. Please. This is your decision but I'm asking you not to judge me for what I say or do, or ask you to do.'

'Solange, damn girl, just tell me.'

'Go home tonight and take a piece of paper. I want you to write in pencil because ink may run.'

'Write what?'

'Simply write *Bad Vibrations*.'

'Oh, Solange, let's stop right now. You're making this awkward.'

'Soak the paper in rum. Any rum will do.'

'I can't do that. Now you're having fun at my expense, I know.'

'Never. Never,' the voodoo lady said. 'I know this seems weird, but I never kid around about something like this. Put the paper in a bowl and light a match. Burn the message.'

'Solange, please.' Kathy was shaking her head wildly from side to side. 'You know I feel really uncomfortable with all this.'

'Sprinkle the ashes outside your entrance.'

'You're really serious. Jesus, you're really serious. This is crazy. You are just plain crazy.'

'Do this and no harm will come to you. I feel certain.'

'Look, I'll see you the day after tomorrow. Let's pretend this never happened, OK? I mean I can't do that.'

'This has happened. And you're right, it seems very strange telling you this. But it should never color our friendship. I care about you, Kathy. And by extension, care about those you are involved with.'

Kathy took a deep breath, her cheeks red and her limbs trembling. 'Thank you for that. I'm just very uncomfortable talking about these things. Like, religion or politics, I'd rather avoid the conversation. I hope you understand.'

'I understand. I'll say a prayer for you tonight, and we'll talk in a couple of days. About something else.'

A couple of days seemed a long way off. The afternoon sun threw haunting shadows across her path as Solange trudged down the streets in the Quarter, as familiar to her as the canvas map where she cast bones and told people's fortunes, yet as foreign as an unfamiliar land she had never visited. Kathy Bavely was in the middle of some serious trouble. What kind of trouble Solange didn't know, but serious trouble. And all Solange could do was offer advice. Strange as it may be, she was positive her solution would take care of her friend's imminent danger. A message dipped in rum and burned in a bowl, then sprinkled where the spirits would enter. That should stop any threat. And she was certain there was a very serious threat.

TWENTY-THREE

Three patrol cars, blue and red lights flashing, lined up in front of the bushes and palms on Canal. Uniformed officers, guns drawn, surrounded one bush. They'd driven stakes into the ground and stretched yellow tape around the area. As Archer pulled up he wondered if this wasn't overkill. No one except the killer was likely to traipse through bushes that were simply decorative landscaping. The murder had already happened. Now the officers were just watching over the spot where the killer may have dropped the weapon. Or urinated. Overkill. He smiled in spite of himself.

Flashing his badge, he stepped over the tape and looked down into the dense foliage. Levy walked up and nodded at the bushes, which stood about three feet high.

'That's the bush, Q. Strange place to dump the weapon.'

'If it's in there.'

Pulling on a latex glove and taking off his sport coat, Archer spread the tight branches. Levy pulled the branches from the other side until there was an opening that Archer could reach through. He lowered his hand and began gently feeling for an object. If the knife was there, it would be well covered.

A crowd of tourists stood on the sidewalk across the street, straining to see what the commotion was about.

'I'm looking for something on the ground, right?'

Levy nodded. 'I would think. He dropped it, and either it's in the branches or on the ground.'

'We can cut the damned thing down, but I would think I can find it like this.'

Archer kept feeling.

'Whoa.'

'What, you found it?'

'Feels like a stump where someone may have cut another . . .'

'Another what? Bush? Branch?'

'No.' Archer grimly smiled. 'He stuck the blade in the dirt.

It's the knife handle, I'm sure of it.' The detective pulled the weapon from the ground, a four-and-a-half-inch-blade Elkridge sheath knife, and proudly displayed it to Levy and the other officers. Dirt covered the blade.

'Gentlemen, may I present to you the knife that killed Trevor Parent.'

There was a light round of applause.

'And the city of New Orleans thanks you,' Levy said, 'for not destroying their lovely landscaping.' He let the branches go back together and handed Archer a plastic bag. The detective dropped the knife into the bag and smiled at the uniformed men.

'Thank you, officers. There's nothing left to see. You can all go back to your regular assigned duties.'

There were some chuckles and laughs and in sixty seconds the yellow crime tape was gone and the vehicles had dispersed. There was a multitude of crimes that needed tending to.

'The lab is going to have their work cut out,' Levy said.

'The killer, scar-face, was hoping the dirt would destroy the evidence. Blood, fingerprints . . .' Archer stripped the glove from his right hand.

'We've got a pretty good lab.' Levy looked at the knife. There may be blood still on that blade.

'We'll see,' Archer said.

Delroy Houston rubbed a quarter for luck. Normally he made his own luck, but he could use a little help this time. Getting rid of a rival gang was tricky business. Sitting at the bar, 'You Shook Me All Night Long' by AC/DC rocking the room, he watched the stripper Mysty swirl on the pole, grinding her G-stringed crotch into the metal. Those brown deep penetrating eyes with their long lashes looked out from the stage and stared into his. Her tiny five-foot body coiled around the chrome phallic symbol like a snake and the nipples on her small breasts stood out like hard diamonds. Houston had a fondness for those nipples. They'd spent quite a bit of time in his mouth.

The name Jeffy Arbaca definitely wasn't a stripper's name. Mysty was a much better choice. He'd suggested that she take that name. The large black man put a hand in his pocket, feeling the glassine bag of dark heroin. In a couple of hours she'd be chasing the dragon, and for that luxury Delroy would get his cock sucked and then have his choice of orifices.

His cell phone buzzed and he checked the number. Case Blount.

'I'm a little tied up at the moment, Case.'

'So am I, Delroy. But there are two things we need to discuss.'

The music was loud, lead singer Brian Johnson's voice blasting through the large room, telling him the walls were shaking and the earth was quaking. He could almost feel it. And the last thing he wanted to deal with was Blount. The fucking employment counselor.

'What do you want to talk about?'

'Word is, this afternoon police found a knife on Canal Street.'

Houston ducked outside to get away from the loud music. He was hit with a blast of chilled air and the blare of a Dixieland band playing just up the street. He thought about Blount up in his cozy office, while he was down here on the street.

'Why should that interest me?'

'Good question. It seems it may be the knife used to murder Trevor Parent, the adoption attorney.'

'You had Nasta Mafia placin' some of those unwed mothers of his, if I remember right.'

'Delroy, we can go back and forth on this but you need to know. If that knife is identified, the blowback could be bad for both of us.'

'What's the second thing you want to discuss?'

'I hear things, you know?'

'From your ivory tower? What do you hear?'

'Things,' Blount said. Houston could detect Blount taking a long swallow of something. Must be that whiskey in his desk.

'I gotta come through this phone, grab you by your chubby neck and choke it out of you, fat man?'

'You're taking the turf war to a new level.'

'What are you talking about?'

'Word on the street is you're handing over Nasta Mafia to a reporter. Somebody from your organization set a little meeting up a couple of days ago and Warhead Solja is set to spill some secrets about our employment opportunities. We've been over this, Delroy. It's not healthy to have your group talking.'

'Real simple. Cut the mothahfuckahs out,' Houston said. This lily-white bastard seemed to have a connection to everything.

'Can we have a powwow?'

'Powwow? You gotta bring race into it?'

'I didn't know you had Indian in your blood,' Blount said.

'So what are you suggesting?'

'A face-to-face talk. Talk about what's fair. Talk about how we might divide some of the responsibilities.'

'I don't like it, Case.' Houston looked back at Woody's, picturing the former Jeffy Arbaca straddling some poor sucker's lap and grinding her pussy on his crotch. When she'd notice an erection, she would jump up sticking her hand out, and with a heavy Spanish accent she'd say, 'Job well done, eh?' More often than not she got an extra ten or twenty. *Bien hecho.*

'What if we negotiated your role in this business. What if we moved you and your lieutenants up to management level?'

Houston shivered as a gust of wind caught his jacket.

'So, Nasta would work for me?'

'I said we could discuss it. You'd get a cut of their dealings and we'd have peace. No more murders, no more talking to reporters.'

'Let me think about it, Blount. It might be worth discussing.'

'Great. Let's just hope the knife doesn't lead to anything.'

'Don't know what you're talking about, man.'

'One more thing. I think you need to pull your guy as that reporter's contact. Stop the story until we have a chance to talk to Nasta Mafia. If one of your guys spills too much and we have to shut down operations, we're all out of a job, Delroy.'

Houston held the phone to his ear with his shoulder while he lit a cigarette. Point well taken. If he was going to be management, then he'd have to start acting like management. He took a deep lung-full of smoke.

'I'll pull him off, and we'll make sure the reporter doesn't go anywhere with the story, OK?'

'Thanks, Delroy. Whatever it takes. I mean, within reason.'

'Now, when do you want to have this powwow? The one where we have some authority and we start getting a cut?'

'I'll be back to you. By tomorrow, latest. And, Delroy, we're just negotiating. I can't make promises before we have that meeting, understand?'

'Better than you can imagine, cracker.'

Houston walked inside but Mysty had disappeared. Maybe she was in a private room, giving a tourist the tour he'd come for, or maybe she was in the dressing room getting ready for her next performance.

The blonde with long extensions and an ass to die for walked by and he reached out and grabbed her by the shoulder.

'Alexia Chantel, right? Sexy Lexy.'

She removed his hand from her body, squinting, looking him straight in the eyes.

'Asshole who touched me without my permission, right?'

'Hey, bitch, be respectful.'

'Why? Everybody else here pays for the privilege. What makes you so fucking important?'

Cocky little bitch. He'd be happy to teach her how to be a little more mellow. She could use some toning down.

'I can hook you up with some top-grade H, little girl. Smooth you out a little bit. You could use some smoothing out.'

'I can point to some of the girls you've smoothed out,' the stripper said. 'I don't think there's much future in that.'

'I think we need to work together, little girl. You see I can make things easy for you, or I can make things rough. Do you really want to go there?'

The girl gritted her teeth. 'I'm a stripper on Bourbon Street in New Orleans. Not the most glamorous job in this city. I dance for assholes like you and give lap dances to married johns from Hoboken, New Jersey, for forty or fifty bucks a pop. If they pop, maybe more. They try to force oral and they tend to get a little rough. One even burned me with a cigarette.' She shot fire from her eyes. 'This is my present and my future, you bastard. It's what I've got to look forward to. So tell me, how are you going to make things rougher for me? What the hell are you going to do?'

'Do you know who I am?'

'Oh, I know who you are. I know what you do to your customers, your little girls. I'm not one of them, Mr Houston.'

He smiled. She did know who he was. As confident as she sounded he detected a little tremor in her voice. He'd like bending her over a table and . . .

'Now if you'll excuse me, I've got work to do.' She motioned toward the stage. 'And, don't touch me again unless you're willing to pay the going—on second thought, Mr Houston, don't ever touch me again.'

'Sweetheart, you're fuckin' with the wrong man.'

'No, that's one thing I won't be doing.'

'There are things I can do, little lady. There are some real bad things I can do. Trust me, bitch. Trust me.'

TWENTY-FOUR

His phone rang at two a.m. Like someone who knew he spent sleepless nights and would probably be awake, tossing and turning. They were correct. So if they knew him that well, he might as well take the call.

'Archer.'

'Q, it's Tom Lyons.'

'Two a.m. Tom?'

'It's three a.m. here. It's Detroit, *amigo*. Time difference, remember?'

'Oh, three a.m. Well, you're already at work then, right?'

'Funny, Archer. Listen. Sometimes it's easier to call when the rest of the world is fast asleep, you know?'

'I get that, Tom.'

'We've got Mercer on a cell phone talking to Jim Lasick, a drug cop.'

'You've got him? What does that mean?'

'Lasick has just been arrested. An hour ago. Two a.m. my time. He's a drug cop gone rogue. We set him up and made the bust square and fair. Jim Lasick offered coke to an undercover. He's been stealing from the evidence room. So, anyway, we've got his phone and there's a call – well, several calls – that tie him to Bobby Mercer. One of the calls was recorded. Mercer says . . . wait, let me read it verbatim. Mercer says, "Lasick. Archer has been ratting out blue. Now I don't know if Archer implicated you or not, but we're sending him a very strong message. Trust me, the son of a bitch won't be pushing his agenda much longer. Archer's wife won't know what hit her."'

Archer was quiet, hearing exactly what he'd suspected and understanding it meant absolutely nothing. He knew what hit her. A car driven by Bobby Mercer, and it robbed him of the most precious thing in his life. The message told it all, and yet it said nothing. The comment wasn't enough to bring charges, he was sure of that. No matter how damning it might sound.

'You heard me, Quentin?'

'Hey, Tom. Thanks. Damn, it's not easy to hear. But . . . maybe that and about twenty other pieces of evidence might clinch the case.'

'Buddy, we've got a prosecutor on our side. She wants to nail this guy as much as I do. She thinks this, added to other pieces, might cement the case.'

'I hope so, Tom. Damn, I hope so.'

'So you're still free to come up here, bring your phone and talk to our prosecutor? I think we're going to be calling you in the very near future.'

Cases piled on cases. The thrill kill murders possibly partially solved. More work than he'd ever had in Detroit.

'You need me, yes. Of course I'll be there. Denise is number one priority. You guys are great.'

'Lots of shit in the Crescent City?'

'I could use you and your entire crew. Things are really rough.'

'You working on the thrill kills?'

'What?'

'You know, the murders with the cans of gas?'

'You know about that? Yeah, I'm lead.'

'Oh, shit, it's been in the *Free Press* for a week. You're national, my friend.'

'Not the first time.' National news about the Detroit cop who turned on his fellow officers and his family. That had not been fun.

'Detective Lyons, I can't tell you what your support means. You and your crew. You knew Denise, you . . .'

'I did, Q. Of course. I thought the world of her. And you think I'd work this for just you? You are delusional, Quentin. I work it in the memory of your lovely wife, buddy.' He chuckled then was silent. Finally, 'I love you both. you know that.'

Archer felt tears welling up. He was silent. Maybe for too long. 'Q?'

'Yeah.' He took a slow breath. 'You're something else, Lyons. You tell the guys . . . well, you tell 'em, OK?'

'I will.'

TWENTY-FIVE

I t was early in the morning when Delroy Houston met up with Dushane White. They coordinated their rendezvous, hooking up at Krystal Burger on Bourbon Street across from the Hustler Club. Neon signs and cheap food. Choosing a corner table on the second of three floors, Houston poured cheap Kentucky bourbon from a silver flask into the two cups of black coffee in front of them. They each ordered four tiny burgers, juicy and the perfect meal for a long night on the street.

'Got to rethink the story to the reporter, Dushane.'

'Shit man, I told him we wanted to blow the cover on N.M. He's got that much already.'

'Can you shut him up? We called Case Blount's bluff and it worked. But maybe we took it too far.'

'Shut up a honky cracker reporter who thinks this gonna be his shot to glory? I hardly think so. You should have made this deal with Blount long ago, brother. You know, I'd just as soon pull some triggers and end this here and now.'

'Call the man, Paul What's-His-Name. Tell him you made it up.'

'He's not gonna believe it. I mentioned to him the names of a couple of spots. Hotel, restaurant, strip club.'

'Shut him up. We've got a thing right now.' Houston took a large bite from the small burger. Mustard, pickles, onion, tomato and lettuce. A burger salad so to speak. 'We get a cut, Dushane. We get a chance to call the shots. The story gets out and, my man, we are toast. Worse than toast. Burnt toast. Nasta Mafia ain't gonna go for negotiations if we're responsible for blowing their cover.'

'Shit, Delroy. Should have thought about that, my man. Now what do you propose that I do?' White absentmindedly stroked the long scar on his cheek.

'Shut down the report. Any means, you dig?'

'I can kill the reporter.'

'Except for that. Too much flack. No blood this time, bro. They dig into it, it comes up we had something to gain.'

'What do you think, Delroy?'

'I think, Dushane, maybe you tell him to shut up, drop the story, then issue a serious damn threat. One that tells him you are not fucking with him. There are serious consequences. He drops the story or—'

'OK, I'll work it out. But I'm telling you, killin' him is the easier solution. It sends a clear message, my friend.'

'No killing anyone. I need to break you of that bad habit, *my friend*. And take care of this soon.'

'Soon?'

'Next twenty-four.' Houston pulled a quarter from his pocket and spun it on the table. 'Heads, he gets the message.'

'Tails,' White said, a grim smile on his face, 'I get to kill the punk.'

Houston shook his head and cupped his hand over the coin.

'No. I'm telling you, Dushane. For the moment I promised Blount there'd be no more killings.'

'Let me see the coin, Delroy.'

'You hear me? No.'

'Let me see the coin.'

Houston lifted his hand.

The quarter lay tails side up.

Archer couldn't sleep. It was getting to be a ritual. No sleep, work his ass off, no sleep, work his ass off. He thought about taking a day off, but the time lost would just add to the problem. Tom Lyons was one of the good guys, an officer who sincerely believed that his participation mattered, that his job was to protect and serve and not get rich at the expense of those who hired him. The citizens of his city. Detroit, Michigan. Tom Lyons was waiting for the right moment. On his own, he was waiting for the right time to spring the trap and bring Bobby Mercer to justice.

And then he thought about Josh Levy, another cop he admired greatly. In the short time he'd gotten to know him, Levy had shown himself to be someone who showed passion, empathy and concern for the people he served. A detective with a heart. And like Lyons, Levy was one of the few officers he felt he could trust implicitly. He could do nothing but wait for Lyons and his team to get back to him. Meanwhile, he and Levy were waiting for lab tests on the knife. It seemed like all he did was wait.

Waiting was the worst part of his job. He'd waited for the photo of the killer. They'd finally figured it out. He'd waited through *how many* viewings of the varied camera recordings. Finally they'd seen the results when the perp buried the knife in the bush. Now he was waiting on the results from the knife. Fingerprints? Blood on the blade? He wanted TV results. *The crime solved at the end of the hour.* He imagined it was probably hard to sell advertising to a client for a show that was made up of hours, days, weeks and months of waiting. Just waiting.

Finally, Archer forced himself out of bed. Checking his phone, he saw a message from headquarters. Three overnight murders, including one of a tourist who ended up in the wrong end of town. The problem was, any part of the Crescent City could be the wrong end of town. You never knew.

Paul Girard had been expecting the call. The banger from Warhead Solja had promised him he'd be in touch. Girard just hadn't expected the contact at five a.m. on the following morning.

'Girard, I'm calling off the interview.'

Cold feet.

'I thought you wanted to bury your competition?'

'The story can't be told. Understand?'

Girard was silent for a moment.

'You there?'

'If you back out of the interview, then anything is fair game.'

'Meaning?'

'I promised you anonymity if you gave me the story. I wouldn't use your name, I wouldn't mention your gang. I was simply going to refer to you as an underground source.' Girard was somewhat surprised at his own bravado. This guy had threatened his life just yesterday.

'I'm not a source. The story was bogus. You don't write it, you don't print it. No story.'

Girard felt a tremor in his phone hand. He wasn't clear whether it was from fear or anger. Right now he felt a little of both.

'I'm going to write a story. Maybe not yours, but I am going to write about trafficking in New Orleans.'

'With or without me, you're going to write the story?'

Girard took a deep breath. 'I am.'

There was a long, uneasy silence on the other end of the call.

Finally, 'OK. I'll call you back later this evening. We'll set something up.'

It was too easy, thought Girard. The man backed down way too fast.

'I'll be waiting.'

'Don't tell anyone about this call.' The tone was threatening. 'Not a soul, you understand? We're still on, and you still play by the rules. You don't rat me out, and we'll talk later.'

'Understood,' Girard said.

He sat on the edge of his bed and rolled the conversation over in his head. First the man said he wanted to tell his story, then he said no. In a matter of seconds he was back on board. Without the gangster's insight, without his details on how the trafficking ring worked, the story didn't have legs. Senator LeJeune's background information wasn't enough. He needed strong information from the inside. That's what he'd pitched to *The New Yorker*, for God's sake. He'd bluffed his way back into the interview. And this could be the most important story he'd ever written.

Rising, he went to the bathroom to splash cold water on his face. He checked his watch. He was taking Kathy to lunch at Phillips Restaurant and Bar to see Marcia LeJeune in just a few hours. Almost seven hours. Damn, he could go back to bed but he wouldn't sleep. He decided on coffee and a review of his notes. And then he'd figure something else to do for the next six.

She woke up in a cold sweat, shivering. The wine bottle next to her bed was empty and the young voodoo lady realized she'd probably had one glass too many. It was six in the morning, a morning that could have been hers to enjoy. She was only obligated to the dementia center from noon till four today. As a volunteer, she could call her own hours. Kathy Bavely, a trained professional, was salaried and worked the regular nine to five. But today was her friend's off day, and she was attending a talk by Senator LeJeune with Paul Girard. Solange shivered again inside the thin tee, thinking of Kathy. She felt certain that her friend hadn't followed her instructions. Soak a paper in rum, burn it and scatter the ashes. It sounded ridiculous even to her. And yet it was exactly what she should have done. If she hadn't, bad things might happen to her.

Unplugging her cell phone from its charger, she called Bavely. The phone rang six times and went to voicemail. She called again with the same result. She was still in bed, or taking an early jog. Maybe taking a shower.

Solange stripped off the T-shirt and walked naked to her shower. Turning the handle and adjusting the water to warm, she let the sharp spray beat on her skin. This and a strong cup of chicory coffee would do a lot toward recharging her system. She would go in early to see Ma. If Kathy was right that the old woman waited by her door, anticipating her daughter's arrival, she didn't want to disappoint her.

TWENTY-SIX

Phillips Restaurant and Bar was tucked back off St Charles Avenue in Midtown. From the charming outdoor courtyard bar the waitstaff served glasses of champagne and Bloody Marys to the invited guests, 120 strong. Dressed in mostly business casual mode, they sat around tables decorated with red-and-white-checkered cloths. Heating lamps were placed around discreetly, taking the chill off the afternoon air.

Servers presented crispy unleavened bread topped with marinated grape tomatoes, black pepper, garlic, scallions and fresh basil. Serving plates of spicy pulled pork with barbecue sauce over toasted flatbread with crunchy Asian coleslaw were introduced to each table.

'Better than food at the center,' Kathy said.

'Wait for the main course.' Her date smiled at her as he took a bite of a brochette. 'Filet, garden salad and eggplant fries in a spicy aioli.'

'What does something like this cost?'

'One hundred twenty-five per plate. For us, nothing. I told them I'd write a piece for some local publications and blog sites. No reason to pay.'

'Kind of like singing for your supper?' Kathy asked.

'There she is.' He pointed toward the canopied bar as a tall, statuesque woman in a gold knee-length dress and dark jacket made her entrance. A scarlet scarf fluttered around her neck. Immediately the sponsors of the event rushed to greet her. She shook hands like the politician she was, her animated gestures highlighted by the swaying of her shoulder-length auburn hair.

'Very stylish,' Kathy said.

'You look pretty good yourself.' Paul let his eyes look her up and down. A yellow dress topped by a blue sweater draped over her shoulders.

'She does know you're here?'

Just then the senator glanced at their table and worked her way through a group of well-wishers.

'Paul, so glad you could be here. We have things to talk about.'

'Senator LeJeune, this is Kathy Bavely. Kathy is a caregiver at a dementia center on the river.'

'Water's Edge Care Center, am I right?'

Kathy broke into a big smile. 'So you've heard of us?'

'I have several projects that are important to me. Today human trafficking, but I have spoken out for years on Alzheimer's disease. Research is so important.'

'We look forward to your talk,' Bavely said.

'Thank you. I just hope we raise the money we need for the shelter.'

'I'm sure you will.'

The senator nodded to Paul. 'We'll talk afterwards.' She turned and hugged an older woman who approached her.

It wasn't a question or request. She obviously was used to telling people how it would be.

Girard turned his attention back to Kathy.

'Pretty impressive lady.'

'She really is.'

Thirty minutes later, Senator Marcia LeJeune was introduced and made her way to the podium.

'I have a shocking announcement,' she said. 'Every one of you has promoted human trafficking. Every one of you.'

There was stone cold silence.

'If you bought a shirt, a blouse, made in China or Sri Lanka, you helped promote human trafficking. If you bought a fishing rod or a bicycle made in Bangladesh, India, Brazil, or any third-world country, you helped promote human trafficking. If you own a smart phone, some of the components, the materials used to build that phone were mined using slave labor. Because human trafficking is rampant in this world. Billions and billions of dollars are made on the backs of people who are basically held as slaves. By a very conservative estimate – very conservative – there are twenty-five million people in this world who are held in an industry, a trade that they want nothing to do with. Twenty-five million people. A staggering number. They work fifteen, twenty hours a day, some are forced to work twenty-four-hour shifts. They are starved, forced to work long shifts and made to wear adult diapers because they are denied restroom breaks. Eighty percent of these people are women, and the majority of *them* are not in manufacturing or mining. *They* are in the sex trade.'

She studied the crowd, pausing, letting her opening remarks sink in.

'Not the greatest opening for a lunch time talk that you'll ever hear,' she said.

There was a tittering of laughter, but very brief.

'You're saying, "Come on, Senator, people have free will." They do, they do. Unless they are underage and trust an unscrupulous adult who is taking advantage of them. Until their family is threatened with violence or death. Until they are tortured to make them do what they are told. Until they have their passports and visas taken away from them. Until they come under the influence of and become dependent on drugs. Then,' she paused, 'they have no free will. Did you hear me? They have *no* free will.'

'She's going to get the money she wants,' Paul whispered to Kathy. 'She's really good at this.'

'And you're saying, "But Senator LeJeune, not here. Surely it's not happening here. Not in Louisiana, not in New Orleans."' She stepped away from the podium, her high heels clicking on the red brick patio, and she pointed to her right, her left, behind her and in front of her.

'Oh hell yes,' she said. 'Here in Louisiana, right here in New Orleans. Restaurant workers,' she hesitated. 'Not at Phillips. God no. That I can assure you. I know the owners of this fine establishment and you won't find it here, but there are other restaurants.'

There was a slight buzz in the courtyard, people talking, speculating.

'Yes, other restaurants, my friends. Hotel workers just a couple of blocks from here, yes. Food-processing companies within a few miles. I've had that verified. Agriculture facilities, farms and the sex trade.' She raised her index finger in the air. 'Let's talk about the sex trade for a moment.'

There was a murmur from the crowd.

'Right now, at the peak of Mardi Gras, the fun, carefree spirited celebration that we cherish, there's a young girl, fourteen, fifteen years old, servicing ten, fifteen, twenty men a day in a hotel room in this city. There's another one, and another one. They are controlled by a pimp, who is controlled by an organization, and this practice has to stop. It happens every year, people. Is this the kind of thing you want going on in your city? Well? Is it?'

Using vague terms, never mentioning specific locations, but with fervor and passion, the senator pressed the message that a shelter for these victims was critical in saving lives.

Thirty minutes later the lady brushed back her auburn hair, and made her final comments.

'I need fifty thousand dollars,' she said. 'You'll find envelopes with forms at all the tables, and credit cards and checks are welcome.'

Around the courtyard were some gasps but mostly nods. They had been invited because they were well heeled. Five hundred a head was not that much.

'And I'm going to match that fifty thousand dollars,' she said.

Now there was a loud gasp as diners looked at each other with surprised expressions on their faces.

'Our shelter needs expansion, maintenance, more staffing and transportation. We need to protect the people who have escaped slavery. We need to make more efforts to find these people who are enslaved. Let's be honest, people, you didn't know how prevalent trafficking was before this speech. And when there is no outcry, when there are no complaints, then law enforcement does not get involved. They turn a blind eye. They're overworked and they choose not to go looking for trouble.' She paused for effect and let her gaze pass over the crowd.

'By some accounts, New Orleans is short by five hundred officers. Five hundred law enforcement agents. There's no money, and the salary that is paid is paltry. So only when trouble comes to them, only when the police are directly contacted do they get involved.' She paused for emphasis. 'Can you fathom that?' This time even a longer pause.

'Ladies and gentlemen, we *want* trouble to come to them. With your generous donations, we will bring trouble to them, to the law enforcement agencies, and they will have to react. They will have to get involved. Law enforcement will help stop this crime.'

'She is going to match fifty thousand dollars?' Kathy Bavely was squeezing Girard's hand. 'Where does she come up with those kinds of dollars?'

'She makes pretty good money as a senator, but Adrien LeJeune, her husband owns a transportation company. They've got a number of busses, a company called America Travel, and they bring tourists from Mexico into the States. Budget vacations with four or five stops along the way. He does pretty well. I think the matching fifty thousand is pocket change for someone like Marcia.'

'Paul, are you going to contribute?'

He studied her for a moment, paying close attention to the low-cut yellow dress and the cleavage from her ample bust.

'No. I'm writing the story, not contributing. I look at it as maybe a conflict of interest and I—'

'Really? A conflict of interest? You listened to her talk and you're not even contributing to the solution?' She pulled out two twenty dollar bills from her wallet. As the plates passed by she dropped the forty dollars in. 'I look at it as being cheap. Seriously cheap. After everything she said, I can't believe you don't have any interest in helping,' she said. 'You're a hypocrite.'

'I'll do more good with my story than any five-hundred-dollar donation will do. The power of the pen—'

'Good luck with that story,' she said, feeling a blush of heat rising from her neck to her face. She stood up, walking toward the exit.

'Really?' He yelled after her. 'Because I'm not contributing money you're walking out on me?'

She turned and nodded. 'Really.'

She'd have to flag down a taxi, it was a long way from where she lived. But she had a credit card and she had an Uber app so with all that she would get home in fine shape. It was just that Paul Girard, even with his connection to the senator, to Marcia LeJeune's causes, didn't really care. It was all about his writing, his career. The selfish bastard only cared about his future while thousands of people suffered. There was no question he could afford the money. He was cheap and selfish, and she needed to re-evaluate this relationship.

She walked a few feet from the restaurant and pulled a cell phone from her purse, clicking on the Uber app. She barely glanced up when she heard the squeal of brakes as a black sedan screeched to a stop next to her. Much too soon for a car she hadn't even ordered yet. The passenger door opened and a hooded man with broad shoulders stepped out, wrapping his arm around the surprised woman's throat and knocking the phone from her hand. Her purse fell to the ground and in a matter of seconds he'd wrestled her into the back seat of the car. As she struggled and screamed, the back of his hand caught her high on the cheekbone. She felt herself losing consciousness as the driver pulled away.

'No fingerprints on the handle, Detective. It appears he used a glove.'

'Damn. Like the O.J. case.'

'But that's just the handle. It gets better from here on out. There's a lot we did find. We've got a speck of blood mixed with dirt on the blade so we can compare the DNA with Trevor Parent, your vic. If there's something there, we'll find it. The lab is working on it right now.'

'It's a start,' Archer said.

'Better than a start,' the tech responded. 'We found two prints on the blade. He wore a glove for the handle but for some reason didn't wear a glove when he held the knife by the blade.'

'The blade? You could have led with that,' Archer said as he looked at the knife in the see-through plastic bag.

'You can see where we dusted. A partial right index there, and' – he turned the bag over – 'a full-blown thumb here. At some time, someone held the knife by the blade and we've got their prints.'

'That's good news, but it doesn't mean they're the prints of the man who did the stabbing.'

'No, but we got a positive ID and it's not some little old lady who only used the knife to peel carrots.'

'What's the name?'

'A banger named Dushane White. We brought him up and his list of priors is as long as your arm. You name it, he's done it.'

'Photo?'

'Right here, on the screen.'

Archer studied the image for a moment.

'The scar on his cheek?'

'Knife fight. He killed the other guy and got off on self-defense.'

'The scar, the knife, we've got our guy. Absolutely no question,' Archer said. 'This is the guy who killed Trevor Parent.'

TWENTY-SEVEN

He was waiting for her in the restaurant as she walked in from the courtyard and they sat in a corner by a window, sipping champagne.

'We raised over fifty thousand,' she said. 'With Adrien's and my contribution it's around one hundred ten thousand. It will go a long way toward what we need.'

'Congratulations. I knew you could do it.'

'Where's the cute blonde?'

'Had to leave early. Another obligation,' Girard said. 'But, she did leave a contribution for the shelter.'

'Paul' – she leaned in closer – 'I need to know. How is your interview going with the gang member?'

'I'll know more tonight.'

'I thought it was a done deal.'

'The guy was all for laying it out as long as I blamed a rival gang. Then for some reason he called me this morning and told me it was off.' He shrugged his shoulders and took a drink of champagne. 'I think he got cold feet. He said he'd been wrong and the information he'd given me wasn't accurate. He told me not to run the story.'

She took a sip of champagne and crossed her legs. As her skirt rose he glanced at her smooth tan thighs. She was very attractive, and someone who could do a lot to help his career.

'So you're not doing the story?'

'I called his bluff and told him I would write the story with or without his help. He immediately backed down and said he'd call me tonight. I hope he changed his mind. We'll see.'

'So,' she said, 'what do you *think* will happen?'

'I think he'll do the interview and I'll get a great article for *The New Yorker*. I'm very hopeful.'

'Paul, I'm going to ask you a big favor.'

'Anything I can do to help.'

'This is big.'

'Ask,' he said.

'Hold the story.'

Girard paused, then took a deep swallow of his sweet sparkling beverage, draining the glass.

'You're kidding me.'

'I'm serious.'

'Hold the story? Why?'

'I can't give you all the specifics, but there are much bigger players involved. If you do get an inside scoop and you have your story published, it will destroy the plan to put an end to all of this.'

He stared at her. 'There's a plan in place? So you're telling me that authorities are already working on these gangs and my releasing information could jeopardize their mission?'

'You're very insightful. I *am* telling you that. It's much deeper than you can imagine and I'm not at liberty to discuss all the details but—'

'Marcia, Senator, *The New Yorker* wants to run this story. *The freaking New Yorker*. That means a whole lot to my career.'

'Paul, we're talking about a reprehensible business that nets hundreds of millions of criminal dollars in this state alone. We're talking about the exploitation of thousands of—'

'Senator,' his voice getting louder, 'I heard your speech. You referred to the numbers over and over again. Listen, I've been prepping this story for months. Trust me, I know the damned statistics.' *The New Yorker* for Christ's sake. Was she going to take *that* away from him?

'Paul, strictly off the record, there are Federal authorities involved. This is taking a long time to come together so I'm asking you to do me this one favor. Will you hold the story? For a couple more months.'

'I'm talking to my contact tonight.'

They were quiet for a moment and Girard could hear the clicking of pool balls hitting each other in the next room. College kids playing for dollar bills. Glancing up on the wall behind her he saw a round mirror and the reflection of someone rapidly approaching their table.

'Excuse me,' the waitress set a purse in front of him. 'You were with a young lady out in the courtyard?'

'Yes. Is there a problem?'

'A Kathy Bavely?'

'What's going on?'

'We found her purse on the sidewalk and I believe this is her cell phone.'

The lady handed him the phone and a red leather wallet, open to show Kathy's photo on her driver's license.

'Where is she?'

'I'm sorry, sir, there was no sign of her. The phone and purse were on the walk. We were hoping you could get these back to her.' She shrugged her shoulders. 'No one else here seems to know her.'

'Sure, I—I'll swing by her apartment and—'

'Oh, and sir, just so you know, there was no money in the wallet. Obviously we would never . . . maybe she was robbed?'

'No, I don't think that was it. Thank you.' The only bills she'd had in that wallet were the two twenties she'd put in Senator LeJeune's collection plate.

Solange left early. She'd begged off her duties for the rest of the day. Ma hadn't been responsive and after a couple of hours with her, she was frustrated. She prayed, she did the work that she felt she must do and while she observed the successes of others that she helped, she saw no success of her own. There was no one to turn to, no one to commiserate with. As she did every day, she wished that the gift, if that was what it was, had never been given to her.

Dodging the pigeons, their shit, the beads and drink cups that littered the sidewalks and streets, and the hordes of people who crowded her path, she worked her way to the small shop, hoping for some peace and quiet. But there she found a homeless person huddled in her doorway, a sweater pulled tight across her shoulders, her head bowed low between her knees and Solange hoped that the woman hadn't thrown up. It happened often and cleaning up vomit was not on her list of favorite things to do.

Pausing twenty feet from the door, she wiped her brow. It was only sixty degrees but she broke into a sweat and closed her eyes for a moment. She knew. Kathy Bavely hadn't written a message on paper. She hadn't soaked it in rum, burned it and scattered

the ashes outside her door. Kathy Bavely had ignored her advice
and gone her own way. That was her choice, but there were
consequences. Now Kathy Bavely was sitting in the doorway of
Solange's shop.

She walked up to her and put her hand on her head. Slowly
her friend raised her eyes and Solange recoiled. Kathy's face was
swollen, bruised black and blue around the eyes, and her lower
lip was split. Dried blood coated her chin and upper lip where
the thick red liquid had run from her nose.

'I walked out on Paul.' She whispered the words.

'What?' Solange leaned back, in awe and denial. 'He did this
to you? No. No.' She didn't believe it. The guy was a slimeball,
but surely he would't overreact like that.'

'No. It wasn't Paul.'

The girl was crying, tears running down her cheeks, her sobs
louder than her words.

'Then who?'

'I don't know.' She was gasping for air. 'Honest to God,
Solange, I don't know who they were.'

Solange took her hand and helped her up. Unlocking the door,
Solange helped Kathy into the shop.'

'I need to get you to a hospital.'

'No,' she said emphatically.

'Kathy . . .'

'I need some time to compose myself. I'm sure I'll be fine,
but not right now, Solange.'

'Then tell me what happened. Please, don't leave anything
out.'

'They thought we'd be together.' She took a deep breath and
tried to control the sobbing.

'Together? You and Paul?'

'They wanted both of us, but of course . . . of course I had
left him. On my own. It was probably stupid on my part, but he
wouldn't contribute to the shelter. Cheap son of a bitch.'
Collecting herself, she took several deep breaths. 'It was all about
his career, not about the abused women and children.' She broke
down again, sobbing uncontrollably. Gasping for air, she said,
'It's not safe out there, Solange.'

'Why did they want you?' She knew.

'It was a warning. You told me. You warned me. How did you know this would happen?'

Solange shook her head. 'I don't know, Kathy. I never know. Not for sure.' She retreated to the room in the rear and returned with a warm, wet washcloth. Dabbing at the wounds, she cleaned some of the blood from her friend's face.

Kathy took deep breaths, calming some of her anxieties. 'I know what you're going to ask,' she said. 'The answer is no, Solange.' The tears started again as she sat at the table, 'I didn't write the words or burn the paper. I didn't scatter any ashes. You know that too, don't you.' She buried her head in her folded arms.

'What did they say? Your attackers.'

'They told me I had to tell him not to write the story. The biggest man, there were three, hit me three or four times. They said this story is much bigger than Paul, and he would be the next one to pay a price if he didn't shut it down.'

Solange took her hand. 'I know you think this is silly, not dignified. But do this for me, Kathy.'

'Anything,' she sobbed.

'Do this and never speak of it again. I will do my damnedest to protect you. Do you understand?'

The girl nodded.

Solange pulled a small hand held mirror from a drawer behind the countertop and laid it on the table face up. Reaching a shelf behind the counter, she pulled down a small jar of herbs.

'Mugwort,' she said. 'An aromatic plant, used in Japan, Korea, China as an herb. Used by me as a powerful tool to ward off spirits.'

'Honest to God, Solange, this is just so weird.'

'I know. I know.'

She sprinkled a pinch of the dried herb on the reflective glass, then putting her hand on top, she looked intensely into Kathy's eyes.

'Put your hand on mine. We must cover the mirror. Do it.'

Bavely place her hand on top of Solange's.

'Now, repeat after me. Say exactly what I say, do you understand?'

'Whatever you want me to say.'

'You cannot see me.'

As though hypnotized, Kathy said, 'You cannot see me.'

'You cannot hear me.'

'You cannot hear me.'

'You do not want me.'

'You do not want me.'

'Now let me be.'

The young girl almost shouted it out. 'Now let me be.'

The knock on the door startled them both.

Solange rose and answered the call, opening the door just a crack.

'Yes?'

'Are you open?'

'No,' she said.

'Please.' It was a young woman's voice.

Opening the door further and peering out onto the crowded street, Solange saw the two girls. Both held drink cups and wore skin-tight jeans with leather jackets. Deliver her from drunken college girls.

'What do you want?'

'A spell. A potion. That's what you do, right? You cast spells, make voodoo dolls, things like that?'

'Do you even know what you're talking about?' she asked. 'Tell me, do you know why you're here?'

'We need money,' the one girl spoke in a boozy drawl.

'We need boyfriends,' the other one laughed. 'Rich, hung, handsome boyfriends. Can you arrange that?'

'I need some peace and quiet,' Solange said. 'I put a spell on both of you that you will never again bother people with your trivial pursuits.'

She held up all ten fingers, then, making two fists she thrust them at the drunken girls who shrieked and ran.

'Will that work? Seriously?' Kathy Bavely had composed herself.

'No.' Solange smiled. 'I made it up on the spot, but hopefully they'll get sober and give it a rest.'

TWENTY-EIGHT

'**A**rcher,' he answered, not recognizing the number.

'Quentin, it's Solange Cordray.'

He stopped still. Her voice caused him to hold his breath for a moment. There was a cold, icy feeling in his chest.

'Miss Cordray.'

'We need to talk. Soon. Very soon.'

'Uh . . .' The urgency in her voice was undeniable. 'Is everything OK? Are you in some kind of trouble?'

'No, it's not me, Detective. There's something deeper than the can of gas and energy that we worked with. I believe I have some important information that may help you. Where can we meet?'

'Here? At my office?'

'No. Not acceptable. A neutral ground.'

'Tomorrow? We could meet for coffee.' He had a full agenda today.

'Today. In the next hour.'

Impossible. He didn't have enough hours in the day even to do what had to be done immediately. There was a massive amount of paperwork, an organizational nightmare trying to orchestrate the arrest warrant and capture of Dushane White, thorough background checks on every known member of Warhead Solja and there was an urgent call he'd missed from the stripper, Alexia Chantel, that he needed to return and . . . shit. Shit, shit, shit!

'OK, Miss Cordray, you name the—'

'Rita's Tequila House on Bourbon Street.'

'Really?' A bar in the Quarter. Hardly a spot where information should be traded. But then, this was New Orleans.

'They've got a courtyard that will be empty this time of day. We can talk outside and no one will bother us.'

'I can be there,' he said letting out a slow breath. Josh Levy and some other officers could start working on the warrant and finding White. They'd already ascertained that Warhead Solja hung out in Treme, so it was a matter of surveillance. Waiting. Waiting. A clerk could start filling out some of the basic paperwork and the rest could wait. He'd take it home and work late. Rita's Tequila House. Really? He didn't picture the voodoo guru as a tequila kind of lady.

'Be careful.'

'It's usually me who tells people to be careful,' he said.

'Not today, Detective. There's some bad energy going around and I don't want you to catch it.'

It was thirty minutes to the Quarter and he jumped off the streetcar and walked Bourbon Street to Rita's Tequila House. Alexia Chantel had tended bar here, infatuated or in love with a guitar player. Now, he was meeting with a young lady that *he* might be infatuated with. The feelings were bothering him. Archer took a lungful of cool air and braced himself.

She sat outside by a stone fireplace with an inviting blaze, the warmth a welcome relief from the chilly afternoon.

'Quentin, thank you for coming.' She sipped a margarita, salt glistening on the rim of the glass. The voodoo queen wore tight jeans and knee-high leather boots, and he gazed longer than he should have.

'You've got some information?'

She motioned him to sit.

'Would you like a drink? I felt like I needed one.'

Archer stared longingly at the glass.

'No. I'm on duty. But believe me I would join you if I could. I could do with a drink right now.

'Maybe someday when you are off duty.' The offer hung out there.

Archer clenched. For a second he considered an actual date, a drink, a casual flirtation with this lady.

'You've got some information?'

'I think I can shed some new light on your thrill kills.'

'Anything at this point would be helpful.'

Nodding, she pulled her silk jacket tight around her.

I know I told you this was urgent, and it is, but I need to give you some background. Be patient with me, OK?'

He nodded.

'My friend from the care center has a . . . has been seeing a guy, a writer, who has seemed to be interested in her, too.'

'And that impacts my investigation?'

'I really think it does.'

Archer nodded. 'OK, tell me the story.'

'I'm not sure where to begin.'

'Start at the beginning.' He smiled. 'And keep it on track. Stories that involve love and emotion tend to go off on tangents.' He'd dealt with dozens of killings regarding relationships gone wrong.

'Paul Girard is a writer.'

'Wait. Paul Girard?'

'The writer's name. Paul Girard is the writer who is sort of dating—'

'Damn,' Archer said. 'I know that name.'

'Maybe you've read some of his work?'

'No, someone told me about a piece he wrote several years ago about Sunshine laws. I'm trying to remember what he says in that column. It just recently came up in one of the thrill kill murders.'

'How is that?'

'One of the *victims* was a target of Paul Girard's article. The coroner knew this victim. Didn't like him at all. He was a city councilman and there were stories, rumors that he used city money to pay for work around his home. Landscaping, painting . . .'

'Our tax dollars hard at work,' Solange said.

'Yeah. According to Marsha— the coroner—your writer Girard also accused the victim, Blake Rains, of hiring illegal immigrants to remodel his home. I'm sure that was the guy.'

'Your recollection is more proof that I can help you,' she said.

'This councilman, Blake Rains, even had a Guatemalan maid that he grossly underpaid and possibly raped.' Archer kept going. 'Not a nice man. Sometimes it's hard to consider someone a vic, a *victim*, when they cause so many people pain.' He stopped, somewhat embarrassed by his rant.

Solange shook her head. 'Illegal immigrants? Forced sex?'

'I don't have proof,' he said. 'We've been trying to find the maid, but she may have gone back to her country. She's possibly a person of interest but . . . anyway, I'm sorry. Go on with your story. Now I really want to know how Paul Girard plays into the thrill kill solution.'

'You really should have a drink, Detective. I think my story may dovetail nicely with yours. Maybe we should celebrate.'

Despite being on duty, Archer ordered a beer and listened as Solange's story unfolded.

'Kathy's been beaten badly, Quentin, but she'll recover. She was at a luncheon fund-raiser for Senator LeJeune with Girard but they fought and she left him at the hotel. As she was trying to get an Uber she was grabbed and shoved into a car by two men. They beat her badly and left her with a warning to give to Girard. The message was that he needed to drop his story about human trafficking.'

'Where is she now?'

'Resting at my shop. She's safe. And very shook up. She's had some time by now to relax and maybe freshen up. It will be some time before the bruises heal but I feel certain they didn't break any bones.'

'Still, we've got to get her to a hospital, and if she's ready, let me talk to her.' He took a swallow of his Abita Amber and felt it warm his chest. 'Has she called Girard yet?'

'She hadn't when I left, but she's lost her cell phone. I'm not sure she wants to talk to him.'

'She may be pissed off at him and the guy may be a jerk and not her ideal match, but someone needs to warn him. These guys who beat her up are likely to do the same thing to him.'

TWENTY-NINE

The body shop was located on Carrollton Avenue in Mid-City. In the front garage, it fixed car bodies, pounding out the dents, painting and replacing the fenders and rear panels of whacked vehicles. A perfectly legitimate and respectable business. But in the back garage of Dusty's Carrossiers (some French name for auto-body workers), employees stripped down stolen vehicles and sold the parts till there was nothing left but a bare metal frame. And then they found a way to sell that too. It was your basic chop shop.

Case knew of the establishment but until now had never visited. This was not his territory. Not his line of work. This was neutral territory for the two gangs. Dusty's was run by a third gang who had no interest in human trafficking, being much more comfortable with inanimate objects like cars, trucks and vans. All in all a very lucrative business.

They sat in the back office and waited, Blount having been the first to arrive. The bald-headed William 'Gangsta Boy' Washington and a new kid named Leon straddled wooden chairs, caps on backwards, both with lit cigarettes hanging from their lips. Weapons were left at the door. The smoke in the room was thick.

'So, this is a three-way meeting, but only two of us show up. Your boy disrespects us already,' Washington said, taking a drag off his cigarette and blowing smoke toward Blount.

'Not disrespect,' Blount said. He waved the smoke from his face. 'He's hung up in traffic.'

'Not a good start, fat man.'

Almost immediately Houston walked in, nodding to Blount. 'Gangsta Boy, I understand your frustration and apologize for being late.'

Gangsta Boy smiled.

The sullen-faced Dushane White followed, hat sitting crooked on his head. Surveying the assembled group, he said, 'Nobody

got no guns, right? Nobody got no knives? I want to make sure
I'm not walking into some kind of trap.'

'They collected them all at the door, Dushane. This is a friendly
meeting. No need for weapons.' Blount spoke in an even tone,
ever the peacemaker. It was important, more than important, that
these two warring factions settled their disputes right now. At
this meeting.

'They get yours?' White asked, stroking the scar on his cheek.

'I don't pack, my friend.'

The faint sound of a radio could be heard in the shop, the
song 'Panda' by Designer playing. Something about broads in
Atlanta, dope and—

'Let's address the elephant in the room,' Houston said. 'No
reason to waste time with formalities. Let's get right to the point.
We all make money off this thing, am I telling the truth?'

Washington frowned. 'We do, but some more than others.'

'Hear my story,' Blount said. 'Let me break this down where
we all understand each other. Let's assume there's a bag of cash
in a secret location. Hundreds of thousands of dollars.'

'A metaphor,' Washington said.

'Yes, Mr Washington, a metaphor.'

'What happens to that bag of cash?'

'Excellent question. For two years, two people help themselves to an agreed upon amount every week. Two people. Like
clockwork. They use the cash to buy food, booze, drugs, to buy
cribs, women, vehicles, maybe one to support a family and
these two people live very well. Very well indeed. They obviously have a job to do, place people in different positions, do
a little legwork as far as organizing, but the work is minimal
compared to the large amounts of cash they draw. And believe
me, these two draw a large, let me emphasize, a large amount
of cash. OK?'

'So, they are comfortable?'

'Damn, I would think so,' Blount said. 'But they are jealous
motherfuckers. They think that the other party is taking more
than his share. They want equal shares. And they go to war.
They've been comfortable but now, because of petty jealousy,
they put that bag of cash in great jeopardy.'

'We're not some fucking nursery school where you have to

tell the story of the big bad wolf, Blount.' Washington took a drag on his cigarette and blew smoke toward the stained ceiling.

'Then, stay with me, William.' He pulled a flask from his inside jacket pocket and took a swallow.

Washington showed his disgust but nodded, signaling Blount to move forward with his story.

'They show up one day and the bag is gone. Disappeared. Absolutely no cash. Nothing. And the rent is due, and the bitches are screaming that they aren't able to buy bling and get a fix. Vehicles are being repossessed, the kids need formula and food and all of a sudden the Feds are breathing down their necks! Heavy shit. A little more serious than the big bad wolf, Mr Washington.'

'And the bag went where?'

'You see, the two guys argued over who got the bigger share. When there was no agreement, they went to war.'

The warring gang leaders glared at each other.

'The locals, the Feds decided they couldn't let it go any longer and they cracked down. There was no longer any cash to feed the bag. It had all disappeared. Now where the two gentlemen had some clout with their bag of hundreds of thousands of dollars, the feds had hundreds of millions of dollars and they shut, understand gentlemen, *shut* down the operation.'

There was silence in the room. Outside the room a rotary saw ground through metal, a high-whining electric driver drove in screws, a buffer polished damaged paint and Lil Wayne on the radio recited passionate lyrics about a girl named Tina thanking her 'for taking my breath from me.'

Blount breathed in the cloying, acrid odor of stale cigarette smoke buried in the walls and moldy carpet of the room. He smelled the sweet sour sweat from the assembled and he felt his stomach roil. Pulling a used handkerchief from his rear pocket he blew his nose, an obtrusive noise in the quiet space.

'Gentlemen, I believe I have a solution. An answer as to how we can keep the Feds off our backs and continue to make a lot of money. Let's let jealousy disappear. Let's let sanity rule.'

The new recruit, Leon, stubbed his cigarette out in a drink glass and stared dumbly in Blount's direction.

'What the fuck, we should take the whole fucking bag of fucking cash and the hell with the rest of you.'

'Shut up, Leon.' Washington turned to his companion and glared into his eyes. 'You have no idea what you are talking about. Just shut the fuck up. I am sorry I even invited your sorry ass. We need some kind of meeting of the minds. Blount is right. If we fuck this up, we lose major revenue. There are hundreds of thousands of dollars to be parceled out, my friends. Let's see what the fat man has in mind. I feel certain that we can all benefit from his ideas. Seriously.'

Blount hid a brief smile. If Gangsta Boy bought into his idea, they were home free and clear. Or at least until the next dust up. If not, the entire business would implode and there would be nothing left of it. And that wasn't an option.

It was late afternoon when the tour bus dropped off the Mexican tourists at the Hotel Monteleone on Royal. The hotel, dating from 1866 would be their home for the next three days. With its Carousel Bar, restaurant, spacious rooms and the fabulous French Quarter right outside the doors, it was all anyone could want. A dream vacation. The budget-minded tourists lined up for check-in, supported by the hotel's uniformed attendants. Good food, fun and maybe a little mischief in this decadent Disney World for adults.

The luggage was unloaded, the dozens of bags crowding the sidewalk outside the hotel as the bus pulled away.

Twenty minutes later that same bus pulled into Congo Square in Treme, behind the Sister Anne School of Divinity. The driver parked in a garage that went on for half a block, four similar busses parked in the same structure. A white panel van pulled up beside the bus, and three stocky men stepped out, immediately opening one of the luggage doors on the bottom half of the bus. Two climbed in, crawled to the back and opened a false bottom. They then lifted and shoved cardboard containers to the opening, twenty boxes in all.

The swarthy man on the outside lifted one of the cartons, slit it with a box-cutter and pulled out a plastic envelope. Opening it, he poured a small sample of the white powder into his palm and sniffed it. He leaned his head back and counted to fifteen. The feeling was euphoric. A high like no other.

'Columbian hell dust,' he said quietly. 'Good shit.'

THIRTY

'Tell me exactly what happened.'

Archer had made sure she was checked over at the hospital, explaining to the front desk that she'd been mugged and had no ID. They'd given her a couple of stitches above her left eye and cleaned up her lip. She was lucky. A lot of swelling, but nothing was broken. It looked worse than it was. Emotional stress aside, she'd recover OK.

'They beat me up. Slapped me, hit me. I think it's pretty evident.'

The three of them huddled at the oak table in Solange's shop, over steaming cups of hot elderberry tea. Archer could smell incense burning in the small altar, fighting the aroma of the herbal beverage.

'Miss Bavely, I am so sorry for what happened. I've been in this business for a long time and it doesn't seem to get any easier taking depositions from an assault victim. I know this isn't pleasant, but I just want to find the men who did this to you.'

'And I'm not sure I want to find them,' she said. 'Look, they didn't want me. I wasn't the target. They wanted Paul. But if you find them and arrest them, it's strictly because of *me*. And I know there are a lot more of them out there. You put three of them away and the rest will come looking for me.' Glancing at Solange, she said, 'I should have listened to you. From now on, I swear.'

'I get it.' Archer sat back in the wooden chair. 'But now Paul is in danger. And maybe Solange. Obviously these people know who your friends are. You know we have to find these guys. You've got to help me.'

Taking a sip of tea, she nodded.

'Did they take you somewhere?'

'No, they just did it in the car. When I came to, my lip was split and I could feel blood running into my left eye. I guess that's when they figured I'd had enough.'

'Were there any names mentioned? Did they refer to each other by name or some familiarity?'

'I don't think so. They referred to me as bitch and a couple of other words I'd rather not repeat.'

'What exactly did they say to you?'

'The guy who hit me said this was a message for Paul. Kept calling him *the writer*. "You tell the writer that he had better not tell the story. The writer had better not talk about gangs and trafficking." He said Paul would receive worse if he did.' She touched her stitches and winced.

'It's going to be sore for a while. How did you get here?' Archer asked.

'They dropped me off about two blocks from Dumaine Street. I'm not sure why. I walked from there. I don't know what I would have done if you hadn't shown up, Solange.'

'Miss Bavely, you said you lost consciousness at one time during the ordeal, but you heard the message. Do you have a physical description of the attackers?'

She held the teacup tight, shaking as it rattled on the table.

'The man who slapped me, hit me, he was a black man with a black knit hat on his head. Big, but I don't know how big. I weigh 112 pounds, so everyone is big to me.'

'Anything else distinguishing?'

'Yes. He had a long ugly scar on the side of his face, like he'd been in a knife fight or something.'

Archer closed his eyes for a moment. This guy, Dushane White, was everywhere. There was no question. It had to be him.

'Kathy, have you talked to Paul? Does he have any idea?' Solange leaned over the table.

'No. I don't actually care if I don't talk to the son of a bitch again the rest of my life. He's a narcissistic asshole, and I look like this because of him. I should have walked away long before this. You know that, Solange. Hell, you told me that several times. I really need to pay attention to you.'

'That may be true,' Solange said, 'but he's a narcissistic asshole who is going to be in a lot of trouble if he prints that story. So maybe you should warn him. Seriously, you need to connect.'

'But how do I even contact him? They took my purse, my cell phone, my ID. Detective Archer, how do I get any of that back?

I've got absolutely nothing. I don't even know where to start.' Tears formed in her eyes.

'We'll file a report and call Phillips,' Archer said. 'Hopefully someone found them outside the restaurant.'

'In the meantime' – Solange placed her cell phone on the table in front of Kathy – 'why don't you call Paul? I really feel he needs to know as soon as possible.' There was urgency in her voice.

Kathy slowly picked up the phone, studying the keypad. After punching in the numbers she held the instrument to her ear and heard it ring once, twice, three times and go to voicemail.

'He's not answering.'

She set the phone back on the table as it started vibrating. Solange answered and they all could hear the voice on the other end.

'This is Paul Girard. Someone from this number just called me.'

'This is Solange Cordray, Mr Girard.'

'Kathy's friend?'

'Yes.'

'Oh my God. Is she OK?'

'She's—'

'They found her purse, cell phone and wallet outside the restaurant. Obviously I couldn't call her and when I drove by her apartment—'

'Hold on, you need to talk to her, Mr Girard. Let me hand the phone to her. She's had a rather eventful night.'

Levy picked him up at the voodoo shop, handing him a paper cup of green tea and they made the short drive to Treme in fifteen minutes.

'Treme used to be a plantation,' he said. 'Of course a lot of places here used to be plantations.'

He parked his car across the street from Trixie's Pies, a pizza place on Claiborne. The fading hand-painted sign that hung from the front depicted a large slice of pizza pie with round pepperoni slices spelling the name.

'Hungry?' Archer asked.

'We've got undercover over there,' Levy said, pointing to a

parking lot half a block away. 'Trixie's one of three places that Warhead Solja hangs out.'

'And we've got surveillance on the other two?'

'We do,' Levy said.

Surveillance. There wasn't a cop who liked surveillance. It once again meant waiting, often times in vain. Coffee, tea, a fast sandwich, an occasional restroom break.

'So, if I'm right, Dushane White beat up Kathy Bavely to send a warning to her boyfriend. The boyfriend, Paul Girard, is writing a story about human trafficking. This White is a piece of work.'

'Now, this is the same guy, this White character, who buried the knife in the bush, right?' Levy asked.

'The same.'

'Damn, Q, this thing is fucked up. We've got a gang that calls for initiates to kill random individuals and leave a can of Chill. Nasty shit. But we have this same gang killing people who may be involved in human trafficking and leaving cans of Chill there too. They're trying to lead us in another direction. Am I right? Cover their tracks and confuse us?'

Archer watched the entrance to Trixie's. The chances of one of the gangbangers actually entering or exiting were minimal.

'Josh, the guy who got knifed during the parade. Trevor Parent. You think he was involved in trafficking?'

'Come on Q, I think we all had that thought. This amoral ass deals in bastard kids. He's an uppity high-end adoption attorney and that's legal. But then, when the kids are placed, he sells the mothers. And they're placed in hotels, maid services, massage parlors that house them in terrible living conditions and take all the money they earn. Not so legal. You've read the background on him. Nobody liked the guy and there's a good reason why. Now, we know that Dushane White is one of the murderers. We've pretty much got him dead to rights on video killing Parent. So Dushane White cut the heart out of this guy, this adoption attorney, and our Dushane White is *not* looking for initiation. Hell, the guy is already connected. He's an established gangbanger and pretty high up in the ranks. Yet, he leaves a can of Chill with Parent's body. Exactly like guys who are vying for membership in Warhead Solja.'

'You're right, Detective. He hopes we're confused, thinking—'

'To make it appear it's the same reason the janitor and the bank teller were killed. Random. We're supposed to assume that it's all by chance.'

'They're messing with us.'

'Damn straight they are,' Levy said. 'Big time. But if we're right, we've answered one of your whys.'

'So,' Archer continued, 'Parent is a bad-news guy. But why would Warhead Solja kill him?'

'Good question. He screwed them out of money? Most killings are because of money, Q. You know that.'

'True.' Archer watched the doorway of Trixie's and sipped his tea. 'But let's suppose that Kathy Bavely is right. Paul Girard is going to write a story that involves two gangs that are selling people. Parent sold not only kids, but their mothers. Low-life scum bag, but a very rich low-life scum bag, right?'

'It would appear.'

'Let's say he's selling the mothers to one of these gangs for massage parlors, strip clubs, to hotels, restaurants, maid services, and let's say he crosses the line.'

'What line is that?' Levy asked.

'What if he worked for *both* of these gangs. Solja *and* Mafia apparently place these women in strip clubs. I've got a . . .' He paused. Alexia Chantel *was* a stripper but calling her that cheapened the respect he'd developed for her. 'Anyway, I've got a source, a young lady who works in a strip club on Bourbon. She tells me that Warhead Solja and Nasta Mafia both work her club. They place girls and sell drugs. There may be some serious rivalry here. I remember in Detroit,' he said, 'where we had Seven Mile Hoods and Vice Nation. Serious competition. When they clashed, there was blood. Believe me, a lot of blood.'

Levy nodded. 'So, the thrill kill murders may be because of a gang initiation and a gang rivalry?'

'Blake Rains, the councilman we found dead in the old Six Flags park,' Archer said, 'the guy was accused of having illegals working on his house. He had a maid from Guatemala who he apparently underpaid and tried to rape. And,' he paused, drumming his fingers on the dash like a drum roll, 'and, guess who exposed all of this? Guess who was the reason this all came to a head?'

'Paul Girard, the infamous writer,' Levy said.

'Bingo. Rains was up in Little Woods meeting with Nasta Mafia, I'd bet anything on it, and either they killed him because he was also working with Warhead Solja, or Solja killed him, but I know why whoever killed him moved the body. They didn't want us looking at Hector Sanchez and Rains getting killed in the same neighborhood. We would have jumped to conclusions. We would have had our connection. And they didn't want us to find a connection.'

'And we would have been right. You checking on blood at the amusement park and having the soil tested on his shoes – good work, Detective.'

Archer paused for a moment. He'd had his share of successes. But he forced himself not to think about the one case he still had to solve. Denise's murder.

'We've got to bring in White. Even if he's reluctant to talk, we can learn enough to break this open.'

'OK, Q, we've answered one of your questions. We know why the can of Chill shows up in multiple murders.'

'Because of initiation into Warhead Solja and as a diversionary tactic,' he said. Archer's eyes caught two men walking into the restaurant. He couldn't make out their facial characteristics. 'How are your men going to identify any of these guys? We're too far away.'

'With luck, Q. With a little luck. Everyone has photos of four of the top members and team one has a high-powered telescope.'

'We know White was Parent's killer. We know he's handy with a knife. We know this scar-faced punk beat up Kathy Bavely. We know he's an enforcer for Warhead Solja. We're pretty sure he sells drugs and people. What don't we know about him?' Archer asked.

'Good question. We don't know where Dushane White lives. His last known address goes back two years ago when he had the knife fight. A rental unit. That house got torched shortly afterwards. I believe it was a message, a little revenge.'

'What else don't we know?'

'We don't know if he has a job other than being an enforcer for Warhead Solja. Could be a dishwasher at a fast-food joint.'

'Want to place bets?'

'We don't know of any known living relatives. Mother and father are deceased, and it appears he was an only child. According to reports he was turned out at an early age, like twelve or thirteen and lived on the street.'

'What else?'

'We don't know where he is right now. We don't know if he knows we've found the knife.'

'Damn, Josh. I'd hate to have this case depend on whether we see this guy enter a pizza place in Treme.'

The two men walked out of Trixie's, one carrying a six-pack, the other a large pizza box.

'We've got a lot of feelers out, my friend. Good detective work is sifting through leads. And leads come from the common folk.' He laughed. 'We've been short on those in this case.'

Archer nodded and swallowed more tea. Actually, Solange Cordray, Mike the bartender and Kathy Bavely had provided a lot of the information. They had some decent leads. He'd simply followed up on them. This was the way a case was solved. Good citizens report, good cops follow it up.

A souped-up maroon 1990 Cadillac DeVille pulled up in front of Trixie's, glasspack muffler roaring, and two men in black stocking caps stepped out. The late-afternoon light highlighted their faces as one of them leaned down and talked to the driver through his open window.

'Beats the hell out of the cars we drive,' Levy said. 'Cheap, run-down drug dealer cars and . . .'

'Pay attention to the passengers, Josh, not the car. That guy has a scar on his face. I'm not one hundred percent that it's him but I've been watching enough video of White to be reasonably sure.'

As the car pulled away the two men walked in the door.

'If that is him, he's not making any effort to disguise himself or stay out of view,' Levy said. 'Just hanging out.'

'This leads me to believe he doesn't know we've got the knife. And if he does, he doesn't think we can tie it back to him.'

'Are we going in?'

'No.' Archer watched the door. 'Do we have a black cop on surveillance?'

'Green's in the parking lot over there.'

'We don't know what we're walking into, and two white guys going in will spook the hell out of them. Let's have Green go in, order a slice and get a feel for the place. If it looks safe, then *we* go in. Personally I'd rather wait until they come out to grab him. In there, we don't know what to expect.'

Archer reached inside his jacket, feeling the Glock in the shoulder holster and he immediately thought of Denise. She hated the gun, hated the job, hated the fear of something happening to him. Was always afraid that she'd be working some night when they brought him into the hospital. When they'd grab dinner during a break, when he'd come home at night, the first thing she'd ask was, 'Did you use your gun today?' She hated the gun, yet she knew it was his only protection. These days, cops were targets. They needed something. Today, he probably *was* going to use his gun. Hopefully he wouldn't have to fire it.

'Let's call for some discreet backup and call Green. It's time to put this operation into gear.'

THIRTY-ONE

'We can make this happen, Dushane.' Delroy Houston cupped a shiny quarter in his palm. 'Damn, these boys are handing it to us.'

'No disrespect, Delroy, but this could be bullshit. You know what I mean? Nasta Mafia is going to let us walk on their territory and only take a percentage? Give me a break, man. They are not going to let this ride.'

They sat in a corner booth, staring at each other across a worn wooden table, Houston spinning his quarter on the rough surface.

'I listened, same as you, Dushane. Blount made some damned good points and I think Washington gets it. We outnumber him, we got more girls and we got a mainline on the dope. Now I'm no math wizard, understand, but zero percent of nothing, is nothing. We destroy each other and we start lookin' for a new line of work. No more job, no more income, my man. Me, I'm happy with the current job. Pussy, drugs and cash to blow. I just think, on a smaller scale, Gangsta Boy sees that too.'

'For two cents, I'd pop that fucker. Son of a bitch needs to be popped, Delroy. You know that.'

'Your answer to everything.'

'Nasta Mafia is gonna fuck us, Delroy. They ain't gonna settle for a percentage. They gonna go for the full amount. You mark my word. I'm not wrong about this. A full-scale battle is about to happen, my friend.'

A fat bald man with a red, stained apron brought a sixteen-inch pepperoni and sausage pie, sliding the hot aluminum pan onto their table.

'Another beer boys?'

'We're good, Pop.'

The aroma of seasoned tomato sauce, Italian sausage and crispy dough silenced them for a moment as both men reached for a slice, stretching thick strands of mozzarella from the thin crust.

Chewing slowly, White was the first to speak.

'This is temporary, plan on it, Delroy. Nasta Mafia is gonna bristle when they have to play by our rules. Those boys will not play nice. What you plan to do when that happens? Uh? Because from today, they're planning how to make a comeback and maybe take us out. I know that, you know that.'

'Just let it go, Dushane. Eat your damn pie. Drink your beer. Be happy for once in your miserable life. You got money, you got women, you get a taste whenever you want—'

'Back of my mind, Delroy. Be prepared.'

'Speaking of, we take delivery of some very special stuff tonight.'

'More girls?'

'That's coming tomorrow, Dushane. This is some premium Columbian, my friend. Excellent shit.'

They heard the door open before they saw the young dark man, squeaky hinges on a rusted frame giving him away. The old wooden floor groaned as he walked to the counter, studying the choices sketched out on a blackboard hanging from the ceiling.

'Do you sell by the slice?' he asked the fat man.

'You buy the whole pie, Mr'

'Then I'll take a twelve-inch pepperoni and whatever is on draft.'

The man behind the counter drew a NOLA Blond and pushed the plastic mug to his customer.

'About fifteen minutes,' he said.

The two in the corner studied him. No one else in the shop and this man was obviously a stranger. Pop didn't know him.

'You recognize him?' Houston had his back to the wall, White turning to view the customer.

'No.'

Houston pulled the knit cap a little lower on his forehead and reached inside his nylon jacket, stroking the handle of the Sig Sauer three-eighty pistol tucked into his wide leather belt. Taken off of a white boy who threatened him over a drink. A simple task. The boy left the bar gunless with a limp and a left eye shiner.

'You packin'?' he asked softly.

'What do you think?'

'What I think is he's got backup outside. We take him out, they'll be here in seconds. Am I right?'

'As much as I'd like to put him down, right there with his beer on the table, you're right.'

'OK,' Houston said. 'Back door, like I'm goin' to the john. Then you.'

'What do you think he wants?'

'Blount said he heard they'd found a knife.'

'*The* knife? I thought I hid that pretty well.'

Houston shook his head. 'I don't know but this can't be good. I'll hook up with you back in the Quarter.'

The customer sat at a table where he could easily see both men. He sipped his beer and appeared to be checking his cell phone.

Houston rose, flipped his shiny silver coin onto the table and looked squarely at White. He spoke in a quiet, easy voice, deep sounds resonating from his throat as he bent down close to the man's ear.

'No gun play, my friend. No knife play. Exit in two minutes, understood? Don't fuck this up, Dushane. Don't do anything stupid because our jobs and lives are on the line, mothahfuckah.'

He walked back a hallway to the restroom and rear door. Carefully opening it to minimize squeaking, he stepped outside, dodging two overflowing trash cans and a black rat that scurried behind one of the containers. Dushane was on his own. If the cop was smart, he would have had someone cover the back exit just in case. Peering around the corner of the building, he saw a man looking straight at him.

'Shit.' He whispered the word, ducking back for cover. The police did have someone covering the rear exit.

'You!' The man was yelling at him. 'Who the hell are you? What are you doing here?'

Houston stayed in position, planning his next move. The guy could be an undercover detective. A narc or a cop who was investigating the murder of Trevor Parent or the killing of Hector Sanchez. Or who knew what else they could pin on his gang. No matter what he told Blount, Warhead Solja was responsible for a whole lot of killings in the Big Easy.

Pulling the Sig Sauer from his belt, he risked another look, briefly sticking his head around the corner. His heart was racing and he realized if he used the gun, there could be three or four other cops who would be on him in seconds. In the cool after-noon, he felt sweat break out on his forehead.

He could go back inside, but it was possible the cop, if it was a cop, had already taken Dushane out. He could double back the other way, but if they covered one exit, they certainly covered the other. A large concrete building was directly behind him with no entrance or exit visible. So with his gun pointed in front of him, he pulled back the stainless-steel barrel slide and spun around the corner, two hands on the handle, finger on the trigger.

The stranger was pointing directly at him with his right hand, and Houston froze for a second. Was there a gun in that right hand? Once again he ducked behind the pizza store and took a deep breath. Come out blazing and run for it or surrender? He couldn't be tied to the knife. No way. Dushane White was the only one whose prints could be on that knife. They didn't have anything on him. Putting his hands up, gun in the air, Houston stepped around the corner for the third time.

The man was still standing there, still pointing. No gun, just his finger pointing accusingly. He carried a large package of some kind under his left arm. And then Houston realized. It was a bedroll. A frigging rolled-up sleeping bag. He saw them every single day, at one time or another in practically every doorway in the Quarter. The guy was homeless and probably slept behind the pizza restaurant, an easy place to grab a discarded meal from the garbage cans. This guy and the rats.

Dropping his arms and keeping the gun in his hand he stepped out from behind the building and kept on walking, the homeless man pointing and shouting obscenities after him. Following a stone path he passed behind three other businesses, then took a right up to Claiborne. When he turned he could see the pizza place, Trixie's, down the road.

Because there were no police covering the rear, Houston wondered if the customer at Trixie's really was a cop. Maybe he and Dushane walked out on one of Pop's really good pizzas for nothing. And those two beers. Damn. There was a lot of paranoia going around these days.

Archer checked his watch, wondering if backup had arrived. Should be two cars, parked close by. His phone rang and he remembered he hadn't called Alexia. She'd given him some good information and he didn't want to lose that contact.

'Archer.'

'This is Green, Detective. I'm almost positive it was him. Dushane White. I snapped a photo. Of both of them.'

'It *was* him? Was?'

'Past tense. I'm sorry, man. The two of them slipped out a back door. I thought they were going to the men's room. When I went back to check . . .'

'Damn.' Archer glanced at Levy. 'Back door. They're gone.'

'I'm pretty sure I recognized his partner,' Green said. 'Delroy Houston. Delroy runs Warhead Solja.'

'He'll be harder to find now. He could go anywhere.' Levy stared at the building shaking his head. 'We're not that big a city, Q. There are forty-nine cities with more people in this country, but still it's easy to get lost here. You only have to look at my unsolved caseload to see it.'

'We'll get him, Josh. We'll get him.'

'It's time to bring this thing to a screeching halt, Detective Archer.'

'I know. Green?'

'Detective?'

'Did Houston and White have pizza? Did they have any drinks? Utensils, napkins? Had they been served?'

'They had it all, Detective.'

'Bag it. Pay the waitress or whoever and bring everything on the table. Glasses, pizza, napkins, silverware. We'll try to get DNA and prints just to make sure.'

'You know this will get back to them,' was the response.

'Well, I don't want to barnstorm the place. Keep it fairly low key, but hey, cover is blown, Green. Makes no difference. The people at Trixie's know these guys, and these guys now know we're onto them. Let the chase begin.'

Levy called the other two teams, informing them that the operation was terminated. Once they were tipped off, the two gang members were not going to show up at another establishment in the same neighborhood. That was pretty clear.

THIRTY-TWO

'**A**lexia, I'm sorry I haven't called. I got tied up in a—'
'Detective Archer, I told you there was trouble in our club. Well, as far as my involvement goes, there is *big* trouble.'

'Is there something in the works? Are you OK?'

'Listen, I can't talk long. I'm in the dressing room at work, but I needed to tell you. I received a personal threat from a guy I consider the number one troublemaker in town.' She spoke in a hushed tone. 'Now, I can normally take care of myself but this time I'm not so sure. I'm a little concerned.'

'He threatened what?' Archer pictured her in a brief costume, the blonde extensions and her pert breasts. He tried to erase the image from his mind.

'That's why I hesitated to call. He threatened to make trouble, but he wasn't specific. He said he could make things rough for me and I basically told him to go fuck himself, because that bastard doesn't own me, Quentin. Nobody owns me. And believe it or not, that didn't go over so well.'

'I can understand that,' Archer responded. 'Telling him to go fuck himself . . . probably not a good idea.' If nothing else, she was feisty.

'I tend to have a mouth,' she whispered, 'and as much as it probably surprises you, I often do things without considering the consequences.'

Archer remembered the kiss in the restaurant.

'The man sells drugs inside our club. And, he sells girls *to* the club. He splits the earnings with management. Damn, can't someone do something?' Her voice was soft but insistent.

'Not until someone makes a formal complaint.'

'Can I do that?'

'Of course. Is it safe for you to come forward?'

'Probably not,' she said. 'I will lose my job for sure, but if it meant we could clean up some of this . . .'

'You'd lose your job? That's all?' She was being a little cavalier. 'It sounds like you might lose a lot more than that.'

'Listen, I shouldn't be talking here. I don't need any more trouble than I already have, but Jeb the club owner is in on it. I know that, you know that. The managers all buy into it. Gangs, girls and drugs, it's what makes this place run. I hate this, Q, but without it the place closes down. Delroy Houston and his gang have put a stranglehold on this club. And they won't let go.'

'Delroy Houston?' Archer was surprised to hear the name. A perfect player for this type of vice, but twice in one afternoon?

'The man who threatened me. He's the head banger from Warhead Solja. You are aware of him, right?'

'As a matter of fact . . .' He couldn't tell her that Houston had given him the slip just hours ago. 'I know him. Now, do you know a banger named Dushane White? He works for Houston.'

'White? He's an enforcer,' she said. 'He comes in here and scares everyone half to death. There are rumors that he's carved up a couple girls who used to work here. I think he's a psychopath. Seriously.'

'Yeah, you're dealing with some really dangerous people, Alexia. Sick, dangerous people.'

'I'm at a point,' she whispered, 'where I really don't think it's safe for me to be here. There's talk that they're bringing four or five new girls in tomorrow night. I can tell you that most or all of them have never stripped before and they're being threatened with their lives, their families' lives if they don't perform and earn. I've never met them, but it's the same pattern. And I'm willing to bet none of them are twenty-one. Fifteen, sixteen, eighteen tops.'

'When the girls show up, who brings them in?'

Her voice was even softer. 'If it's Nasta Mafia, it's usually a guy they call Gangsta Boy. Slimy bald fucker who actually struts like a peacock when he walks. The girls who work for him laugh behind his back. If it's Warhead Solja, Dushane White walks them in. Believe me, the girls don't laugh about him. I think he'd just as soon slit their throats if they did.'

Archer was quiet for a moment. The blonde stripper had to get out, but if she left she could be in more danger than if she stayed. Inside, she was still an employee. If she quit, they could go looking for her and leave her in a dumpster when they were finished. He knew very well what happened when you pissed off people who had a lot of power. You or someone close to you could get whacked.

'You could leave. Now. You can always get another job.'

'I can strip anywhere. But why doesn't someone just clean this mess up, Quentin? Why don't the good guys show up? Where the hell are the cops? The drug enforcement officers? These slimeballs are trafficking underage girls and drugs right in front of me, and no one seems to care. Where are you?'

'Are you safe through tomorrow?'

'I have no idea. I work the late shift tomorrow night. I assume this asshole won't bother me, but I can't be certain. There were veiled threats and I have no idea if he'll act on them or not.'

'OK, you're scheduled to work the late shift tomorrow. Am I right? And that's when the new girls come in?'

'That's the rumor.' She paused. 'You know, Detective, it's very shallow to say this considering these girls are innocents who are being used. Kidnapped as far as I know. Damn, I don't want to be someone who is always about me, but this is just more competition for dollars, and I don't need the competition.' There was a long sigh on her end of the call.

'Are you up for another meeting at Café du Monde?'

'When I get off?'

'Sure. Three a.m.'

'Is this a date?'

Archer paused, smiling. It was strange that she would leap from immediate danger to that option. A date? The last date he'd had was his first date with Denise. Before that, a football cheerleader named Chloe, after he'd scored the winning touchdown at Crocket High the last game his junior year. The storybook episode in an idyllic life. Not so idyllic after the fact.

'A date? That would be interesting but sadly no. It's about cleaning up the club and getting some of the bad guys out of there.'

'You're going to finally bust these guys for selling drugs and underage girls? Tell me I've finally gotten through.'

'No, probably not that.'

'Then what?' He sensed the frustration in the tone of her voice.

'If this works out, we'll bust them for murder. That tends to put people away for a long time.'

He considered the meeting. It was a long shot; but there was at least a fifty percent chance that scar-face would be the one delivering the girls tomorrow night. And if he was, if Dushane White was coming into the club, it was the perfect opportunity to grab him. Pushing number five on speed dial he listened intently to the rings. Josh Levy picked up on the third.

'Archer?'

'Josh, I told you about the young lady who works at Woody's?'

'The cute blonde.'

'The same. We've had an interesting conversation.'

'And I need to know this because . . .'

'The strip club is supposedly getting some new dancers tomorrow night. Five girls from South America.'

'We're clubbing tomorrow? We don't do human trafficking.'

'Dushane White may be the one who delivers the girls. Apparently he is the pimp of the evening. And if he is, I'd like to have a surprise party for him.'

'Q, I like this. But what do I have to bring to the table?'

'That's the part you're not going to like.'

'There's not much about this job I *do* like.'

'I'm meeting Alexia this morning at three a.m. at Café du Monde.'

'No. You don't want me to . . .'

'Yeah, I'd really like for you to be there.'

'Quentin, three a.m.?'

'I don't have a lot of time to plan this party, Josh.'

'Jesus. Do you work this late in Detroit?'

'Yeah, we do. Or, we did. Listen, I want to nail this son of a bitch, Josh. We missed him the last time and I don't want to lose him again.'

'Three a.m.?'

'I'm buying donuts and coffee, OK?'

THIRTY-THREE

He handed her the purse and phone, watching her expression. Her face bruised, the tears in her eyes telegraphing the sorrow.

'I am so sorry, Kathy. I shouldn't have let you leave. I feel like I'm responsible for, you know . . .'

'You feel like what?' She stared into the face of the blond haired man sitting by her side.

'You know, I feel like . . .'

'You *are* responsible, you asshole.'

Paul Girard leaned back in his chair.

'They told me the only reason I was being beaten up was to shut you up. But you, you were busy with the senator so I took the beating for you. Are you happy? You cheap self-absorbed son of a bitch, are you really sorry? Because I've got to deal with black and blue, I have to deal with a bloody lip and stitches. I have to deal with worrying if these thugs will come after me again, worry about—'

'Kathy.' Solange Cordray put her hand on her friend's shoulder and could feel the tremors. 'I think he understands.'

'He will never understand.' Tears streamed down her cheeks and the entire event was real again in her eyes.

'I would never have . . . ever have . . .'

'Oh, shut up, Paul. Shut up. You are such a piece of work.' She was sobbing, her body shaking.

'Marcia LeJeune,' Solange said. 'You had a meeting with her when Kathy was attacked?'

Visibly shaken, Girard looked up at Solange. 'What about her? She's the senator that's fighting to stop this corruption.'

'She is championing the fight against human trafficking.'

'Of course. It's one of her main focuses. She's passionate about rooting out the people responsible.'

'Go to her. Tell her that you've got the story and tell her about the threat on Kathy and your life.'

Girard pushed his chair back from the table.

'She's got a plan to bust this wide open and she asked me to hold off on any further stories.'

'Are you willing to wait? To see if these thugs, these murderous gangsters will back off on their attacks?'

'If I don't pose an immediate threat, if I don't write the article . . .'

'You are such a fool. And you've put other people in jeopardy.' Solange pointed her finger at him. 'Go to her. Tell her about the threats, the danger and see what her reaction is. What's next? They kill someone to keep this quiet? Actually, I think that may already have happened. It's got to stop, Paul.'

'I trust her,' Girard said. 'Marcia is a strong person. Whoever did this to Kathy, we'll figure it out. And it's not going to happen again. I won't let it happen.'

'Paul,' Bavely said, 'what can you possibly do? You're an idiot. Please leave. I'll take care of myself. The last thing I need is some self-centered asshole who is only involved in this for his own interest.'

He stood up, turned and walked to the door, turning around at the last second.

'Look, Kathy, I'm sorry you got involved, and I promise I won't bother you again. But just for the record, I'm on the tip of a very big breakthrough. If I get a chance to expose the depth of this problem and actually am responsible for stopping some of the suffering, then . . .'

'Are you listening to yourself?' Her voice rose. 'All that will happen is you can make another check mark on your blackboard. It's all about you, Paul. This has nothing to do with stopping human suffering. You simply want the credit and the glory. Good luck with your career.'

Girard walked out, the screen door slamming against the wooden frame.

The two ladies were silent, neither ready to speak.

'You should stay here tonight. I've got a sleeper sofa in the back room and you can spend the night.'

'Solange . . .'

'I will not take no for an answer,' her stern voice making the decision final. 'While I feel you are safe for the moment, I'd feel much better if you stayed here. It's been a traumatic afternoon and we should be cautious.'

The young voodoo lady locked the door. 'There's a toothbrush in the second drawer. T-shirts in the bottom, and you can just pull out the sofa.'

Bavely walked to the back room and Solange selected a Shango seven-day altar candle, struck a match and touched the wick. The flame was immediate, a spark of deep orange, and the girl smiled. A god who represented thunder and lightning. She could use a little of that right now.

Shango, a powerful Orisha, was the spirit to make a person strong in the face of danger. The legendary fourth king of the ancient kingdom of Oyo, he was a Herculean deity. She took a second Shango candle and lit this one as well. Again the wick burned strong, a steady constant almond-shaped flame. This was for Quentin Archer. She felt he was in grave danger at this very moment and she prayed she was wrong. She prayed to Shango that the man would stay strong through whatever trials he was given. And God knew, he'd been through so many already.

Archer shivered in the crisp brisk air, walking to his cottage and thinking about the rendezvous with Alexia Chantel in the early morning. A chance to see the sultry seductress. The soon-to-be *wealthy* seductress who claimed she could retire in her thirties. Wrapping his mind around her situation he almost missed the short stocky man who brushed by him. Archer turned and watched as the man lurched down the sidewalk. Then, focusing on his destination, he walked the two blocks to the Cat's Meow. As he reached the porch, he felt a cold chill travel down his spine.

Spinning around, he saw a man, twenty feet down the brick walkway. The same one who bumped him on Bourbon. A stocking cap pulled low on his forehead and a heavy quilted jacket on his portly frame.

The light was fading as he glanced at the face. The fact that the man didn't disguise his appearance meant that he didn't care if Archer recognized him or not. And when he recognized the man, he immediately wondered if he was there to kill him. In a second, Archer decided that wasn't going to happen.

'I can't believe you had the nerve to come down here.'

'And I can't believe that you're still pushing your agenda in Detroit.' The tone was menacing, the voice deep and husky.

'You killed my wife you asshole. What do you want?'

'Your demise. You see, Archer, if you are gone, the need to know diminishes greatly. As long as you are alive, there are a handful of cops who would do anything to burnish your reputation. You die, nobody gives a rat's ass. You're old news.'

Archer stood on the porch watching the Detroit cop's hands. If he went for a gun, if he went for a knife . . .

'Why didn't you send my brother? He likes to yank my chain then disappear. You deprived him of his pleasure.'

'Because I don't think it's good karma to have brother kill brother.'

'You actually have scruples? Since when? You killed Denise, so now you want to kill me.'

'No admission of guilt, Q. And I simply stated that I want your demise. I never said I was orchestrating it. Of course, if an accident should happen, it wouldn't exactly bring me any grief.'

'I can't believe you actually are here.'

'A little time off. R and R, Q.'

'I've wanted to get my hands on you for—'

'Here's your chance, Detective. Take your best shot. But I'm not armed and I haven't laid a hand on you. So I'd be very careful. Assault, battery, on an unarmed cop. That's not going to play well at all.'

'Get off the property.'

'You're not very hospitable, Archer, and it's not your property. Belongs to the club over there.'

'Mercer, if I killed you now, no jury in the world would convict me.'

The man chuckled. 'Then do it, Quentin. You haven't got the balls. You running down here proves it.'

Rage, frustration, anger coursed through his veins. Reaching into his jacket he touched his Glock, thinking how easy it would be to get revenge.

'And I do have a vest on, Archer, so go for a head shot if you're going to really do this.'

'I will get you, Mercer. I don't know why you're here, but I'm not working on impulse. Not tonight. I'll find a way to nail you and at the least I'll watch you rot in prison. I promise you that.'

Mercer nodded. 'Not if you go first, Archer. No threat . . . I'm just saying that accidents happen my friend. People get run over by a car every day. Probably every minute somewhere in the country. You just never know when it's going to be your turn.' Smiling, he turned and walked down the pathway.

Archer pulled his gun and aimed it at Bobby Mercer's back. He could finish it right now. But the son of a bitch had thrown the perfect counterpunch. And there was nothing he could do. Spinning around, he reached for the doorknob. Glancing up he saw that the tape had been torn. Someone had broken into his cottage.

THIRTY-FOUR

He was shaking. The man was on his turf and there was absolutely nothing he could do about it. The man who took his wife's life, who was responsible for alienating his entire family, had been twenty feet in front of him. Taunting him. Hurling threats. And Archer was helpless. Powerless. Vulnerable. And he realized that his nemesis had pulled a coup. He was in awe. The hits just kept on coming.

Cautiously turning the key and opening the door, he peered in. Everything seemed to be in place. If the cottage were booby-trapped, he'd have to go inside and look for it. It could be just a mind game Mercer was playing, breaking the tape so Archer would waste time looking for a surprise. The lock on the door didn't seem to be tampered with and a quick glance around seemed to verify the windows were all closed and locked. He stepped inside and took a deep breath. Gas. Expelling the air from his lungs, Archer walked to the stove. The gas was on, the flame was out. He quickly turned off the burners then threw the door open and raised the two windows, letting fresh air into the cottage.

Thank God for Mercaptan, the rotten-egg-smelling ingredient that was added to natural gas to help detect leaks. He'd been involved in a murder where gas had been the weapon and he'd been made aware of Mercaptan during the investigation.

Mercer had gotten in. And as a reminder that he could strike anywhere, anytime, he'd turned all the burners on. With no flame.

His cell rang and he answered immediately, hoping it was Tom Lyons. He needed to talk to someone about the situation.

'Detective Quentin Archer?'

He didn't recognize her voice. 'This is Archer.'

'This is Marcia LeJeune.'

'Senator LeJeune?'

'The same,' she said. 'The office gave me your phone number.'

'What can I do for you?' He stepped outside into the fresh air.

'Detective, I understand you are working on a string of murders.'

'It's what I do, Senator. I'm a homicide detective.'

'These murders involve the Chill cans. I believe the press has labeled the killings the thrill kills.'

'Yes. Of course.'

'Detective, there is a strong possibility that these killings revolve around people who are involved in human trafficking.'

He was quiet for a moment, trying to figure out how much to tell her. Finally he spoke.

'We may have come to that same conclusion, Senator. There seems to be a tie-in between the murders and victims who were involved in trafficking.'

'You may know,' she said, 'that I have a very strong campaign to bring trafficking to a halt.'

'I understand you had a fundraiser yesterday.'

'Yes. We raised money for the shelter, but what you may not know, I have enlisted the help of the FBI and local law enforcement officials to put a stop to this human slavery in New Orleans.'

'Local law enforcement?'

'We haven't gone public yet, Detective. It's a need-to-know situation at this moment, do you understand?'

He didn't.

'Detective Archer, I'm asking, and your department will be asking, you to step down. You now have a *need-to-know* status. I've talked to your police chief, I've talked to your lieutenant and I've spoken with your immediate, a Sergeant Chip Beeman, and tomorrow he will ask you to wait until we have our people in positions. We can have a much broader impact if this is a coordinated attack on these people.'

Archer held the cell phone away from his ear and studied it. He needed a moment of reflection. No one from his office had contacted him, and he heard from them on a regular basis. There was a priority on finding the killer or killers regarding the thrill kills. He was on a mission and had no intention of being distracted. Now, after listening to the senator, he was certain that he'd hear from Beeman or someone in the very near future, but to hear first-hand from this politician made no sense to him. No sense at all.

'Obviously I want to help the situation,' he said. 'I'll talk to Beeman in the morning. Not to be rude, but I normally don't take orders from a Washington politician. I'm sure we'll support you in any way we can, but understand, I've heard nothing from my command and until I do, I'm not stopping the process.'

'I'm hoping we can avoid any conflict, Detective Archer.'

'And I'm trying to solve a series of murders, Senator. Every day I don't act, someone else could be killed. As I said, it's my job to solve these crimes and until I'm relieved of duty, I intend to do that job to the best of my ability.'

What kind of chain of command was this? He shook his head and ended the call. If and when he heard from a superior, then he'd consider calling off the investigation. But they'd put far too much work into it at this point to turn it over to some federal bureaucracy. He'd worked a couple of cases with the FBI in Detroit and, yes, they were very professional, well trained, paid much better than Detroit cops, but to a large degree they were pompous assholes who took over and treated the local force like their hired help. He wasn't a fan.

Archer went back inside and sat on the bed, listening to the music bleeding into his apartment through the open door and windows. He dialed Lyons's number and immediately got a voicemail. He decided not to leave any message and instead lay back, determined to get a little sleep before he visited the Café du Monde.

His phone chirped and he grabbed it, hoping it was Lyons.

'Quentin, it's Solange Cordray.'

He smiled. Just the sound of her voice and her name.

'I hope it's not too late to call.'

'No. Never.'

'I don't know what this means, but it seems important. Paul Girard dropped off Kathy's personal items, her wallet, phone and purse.'

'Great.'

'He shared some information I thought you should be aware of.'

'And?' He didn't want this call to end.

'*And* he mentioned his conversation with Senator Marcia LeJeune. As you know they had a meeting at the restaurant.'

'What was said?' His interest piqued.

'She asked him to drop the story he's been working on. Delay any release. She told him there was a concentrated plan to close down the trafficking that involved local and federal agencies and she needed him to go silent for a couple months.'

'Damn.'

'Is there a problem?' she asked.

'I shouldn't tell you this.'

'Quentin, I lit a candle for you. Tonight, I feel you are in some serious trouble. I don't know what it is, but I am praying for you.'

'Thank you.' For some reason it calmed him. 'I may be in trouble. It wouldn't be the first time. The senator called me tonight.'

'LeJeune?'

Archer stopped for a moment. The information had not been sworn to secrecy and he wasn't obligated to suppress the story.

'Yes. She asked me to suspend the investigation of the thrill kills. She told me the same thing.'

'And what was your response?'

'I told her I don't take orders from senators in Washington DC.'

'Quentin, continue to pursue the case. You're on to something big.'

'You really think so?'

'I do. It's just an instinct but . . . By the way, Kathy Bavely says thank you for looking after her this afternoon.'

'Solange,' and he realized they were now calling each other by their first names, 'tomorrow night I'm planning a major event. The arrest of a murderer, the possible release of some kidnapped victims.'

'I wish you good luck, but what does that have to do with me? Why are you telling me this?'

'Can you,' he couldn't believe he was asking this question, 'can you tell me if I'm on the right track? Will this mission be successful?'

'I told you, I sincerely feel you are on to something big. But I can't at this moment tell you if an operation will be successful.'

They were silent for a moment. Archer couldn't seriously believe he had asked for her professional help. Lyons and company would call him batshit crazy. She was a voodoo lady, tarot cards and casting bones. Fantasy land. Mystic magic. It made no sense.

'I can probably tell you later. But not at this moment. It may take some time. Let me consult and I'll get back to you.'

'Again, I hate to ask for advice without paying for it.'

'Someday maybe you'll do me a favor,' she said. 'I think that time may come sooner than you think.'

'Thank you, Solange. I sincerely appreciate your interest.'

'I know you do. By the way, Kathy is staying here tonight. Maybe tomorrow. I know there's a lot of protection in the Quarter right now, but . . .'

'I'll get extra detail tonight to watch your place, OK? Someone will swing by every half hour or so.'

'Thanks, Quentin.'

'Goodnight.'

'Goodnight to you.'

They stayed on the phone, neither hanging up. Finally Archer disconnected and put the phone on the nightstand, like a schoolboy hoping she would call back.

THIRTY-FIVE

It was two in the morning when the phone chirped again. Archer shook the fog from his brain and answered.

'Q, they put an arrest warrant out on Mercer. The prosecutor thinks she's got enough to hold him on the murder.'

Archer sat on the edge of his iron-framed bed, stunned.

'You there, buddy?'

'Yeah. I'm here.'

'OK, we are going to need your phone. Don't lose it. Don't erase anything. The prosecutor will want to see all calls, text messages, the usual.'

'When do you need it?'

'After they bring him in. There's no rush. Maybe in a couple of days.'

'They haven't arrested him yet.'

'No. I just found out.'

'At two in the morning?'

'It's three here, partner. This is real time.'

'You guys don't sleep.'

'Crime doesn't sleep, Q. You know that. Most crime happens in the wee small hours, right?'

'I'm not sure how you're going to arrest him.'

'They're staking out his house, watching his vehicles, the usual.'

'You can call them off.'

'Yeah? Why's that?'

'He's down here, Tom. We had an interesting conversation earlier outside my place. I could have ended everything at that moment.'

It was Lyons's turn to be quiet.

'Said he was on vacation. Vague threat about wanting me to go away. He said if I were to have an accident, things would quiet down up north. I don't think he knows how close you are.'

'I'm not sure about that,' Lyons said. 'It sounds to me like he's skipped town and may not have any intention of coming back.'

'Yeah, there's that.'

'Nobody here knows he's gone, Q. Damn, be careful. If he thinks he's got nothing to lose . . .'

'My brother Jason has nothing to lose, but when he's shown up here all he does is threaten me.'

'Yeah, but he's your brother. Blood and all that.'

'Mercer did mention that. He said he came down personally to harass me and didn't want Jason to get involved because he didn't want brother killing brother.'

'He really said that?'

'Yeah.'

'We'll alert authorities down there. How hard will it be to find him?'

'A friend of mine says it's easy to get lost and stay lost in New Orleans.'

'Damn, be careful my friend. Please.'

'He wants me dead, Tom. And that's not going to happen.'

He was at a table when she walked in in her gray sweats, fresh-faced and dewy-eyed, and Levy was ten feet behind her.

Archer smiled. 'Alexia, I'm so glad you came.'

'I should have known this was the lovely lady we were meeting,' Levy said.

Rising, Archer introduced them. 'Alexia, meet the second best homicide detective in New Orleans, Josh Levy.'

'Gentlemen.' She raised her eyebrows and looked questioningly at Archer.

'I need his advice and I asked him to be a part of our meeting. I should have told you, but believe me, you can trust him. You can say anything.'

Levy pulled out a chair and she sat down.

'The last time I was with two cops,' she said, 'was in Miami. One was watching and one was participating. The older cop was paying me for a lap dance for his partner who was turning thirty.'

'No lap dances,' Archer said. 'I promise.'

'We do entertain members of your force from time to time.' She smiled. 'So what is this plan?'

Archer ordered three chicory coffees and three beignets.

'We've got a fifty percent chance that Dushane White will bring in some South American underage girls to Woody's tomorrow night.'

She nodded. 'That's the rumor.'

'You have to keep this totally quiet, Alexia.'

Levy glanced at him. 'Are you sure you want to go public with this, Q?'

'She's trustworthy, Josh. Trust me on this. She came to us. If she keeps it quiet, it's not public.'

He nodded and sipped his coffee.

'We have an arrest warrant for White. And we almost had him earlier yesterday. He broke surveillance and we have no idea where he is. If he shows up tomorrow at Woody's, we've got a good chance of getting him.'

'So what do you want me to do?'

'Tell me how this transfer of girls happens.'

'In the past, they've come in a rear entrance. There is a separate dressing room in the back and I think they give the girls a brief tutorial as to what's expected. They provide a costume, such as it is, and push them out onto the floor. They spend an hour or so watching the other girls and then they are forced onto the stage. From day one, they are responsible for a certain number of contacts each night, and the ones that actually last become a part of the team.'

'The ones that last?' Levy asked.

'Not many of them stay too long,' Alexia said. 'I'm guessing at a lot of this, but I've heard that the girls who don't live up to expectations get shipped off to massage parlors up in north New Orleans off Gentilly Road. No dancing required, you just have to rub and tug. If they don't perform there, there are worse jobs. Hotel grunt work, seafood packing, even working on farms. Full employment, you know? 100 percent. The girls have value. There are plenty of places who will pay an agency for their services but pay dirt wages or less once they start working.'

'Dushane comes in with them?'

'If he delivers, he definitely stays. I don't know what he threatens them with, but he'll sit at the bar and watch. Girls tend to perform much more enthusiastically when the pimp is in the house.'

'Jesus,' Levy took a bite of his beignet. 'This is such a . . .'

'Sordid business?'

He smiled. 'Good choice of words. And nothing personal.'

'It's what I do, Detective. I understand the implications.'

'What did you do before stripping?'

She hesitated. 'I'm a,' she hesitated, 'I *was* a pharmacist.'

'No kidding?'

'No kidding.'

'And you quit for this?'

'I didn't exactly quit,' she looked at the two detectives. 'I had a boyfriend who turned out not to be much of a friend. Let's just say he had leverage and threatened me if I didn't supply him with drugs. I'm not proud of what I did, hell, I'm not proud of what I do, but long story short, I don't sell drugs anymore.'

'Wow.' Archer shook his head. 'And the boyfriend?'

'Doing time, thank God. I promised myself I was going to take charge of my life and never again let a guy intimidate me.'

'That does explain a lot,' Archer said.

'And I was making a hundred plus a year. Pretty good money for legally dispensing drugs. But to these guys, that's chump change.' She took a swallow of the bitter beverage and closed her eyes for a moment as if to erase the memory. 'There are drug dealers then there are *drug dealers.*'

'So now,' Archer interrupted, 'you make two to three hundred thousand a year. A lot of it tax free.'

'You said that, Detective Archer. I would never admit in front of two law enforcement agents that I am cheating the Internal Revenue Service.'

'He sits at the bar? Dushane White?'

'He does. He'll nurse a drink for two or three hours and sometimes walk up and talk to a girl, explaining that she needs to try a little harder, I guess. There is fear in their eyes. In my eyes I've got a little humor, a little sarcasm, a little pity and a *lot* of boredom.' She stared at Archer with a dead serious look. 'These girls are scared to death.'

Archer turned to Levy. 'My thought, we grab him before he

goes in. We're in the alley with patrol car and two to four cops. When he shows up—'

'Probably in a van,' Alexia said. 'I've seen this white panel van out there when I leave my shift.'

'We take him there.'

'Problem is, Q,' Levy frowned, 'he's got four or five hostages if we can't separate them.'

'True.'

'What's the scene inside?' Levy looked at Alexia.

'What? Another strip club virgin? I don't believe it.' She shook her head. 'What did you do for fun in college? Half-naked girls are wandering around, trying to get a drink from a john, trying to get a lap dance, trying to get a guy into a private room, and some guys are game, and some want to be coaxed.'

'The bar?'

'Our bar crowd is made up of the voyeurs. They stay as far away from the stage as possible. They don't necessarily want close contact. They want to be on the outside looking in. Once in a while a guy at the bar is a player but not that often. And about every night some of the boyfriends sit there. I guess they get off on the fact that eventually they are going home with one of the dancers. After she's successfully gotten a bunch of strangers off. It's a fucked up world, Detective.'

'So,' Levy sipped at his now lukewarm coffee, 'this Dushane sits at the bar. He's not that social, he's nursing a drink and two customers that he doesn't know named Archer and Levy walk up, stick a gun in his ribs and lift him off his seat. That could happen, right. He has no immediate hostages and we haul him out either front door or back.' The detective laid his hands out on the table. 'Could that happen?'

'Oh, I've seen guns drawn in clubs before,' she said. 'With the terrorist threats, with the mass killings in theaters and nightclubs, it probably would freak a lot of people out. You understand?' She pushed her soft blonde hair back from her face. 'It would scare the hell out of me.'

'If we announce that we're police?'

'A lot of married guys are going to head for the exits, Quentin. That's the *last* thing they want to hear. And, some people fear the police as much as the terrorists, Detective Archer. I'm sure you are aware of that. And if you overplay your hand, we have customers who are packing. They may get involved. The quieter this whole thing is the better. We could have a remake of the shoot-out at the O.K. Corral.'

'Can you help us?' Archer asked.

'I don't see where I would fit in.'

'You would tell us what's going on.'

'Just how would that work?'

'We're just two customers. You flirt. Just like you did the other night. We'll buy you a drink, talk about other favors and you keep coming back to us when you know something. Like when Dushane shows up. Like if the girls are in the back dressing room. Like if he's coming out to sit at the bar, when the girls are entering the club.'

'I can probably do that. But, boys, I can't go down for this. If that gang got wind that I was feeding you information, I don't want to think what could happen to me. You've got to promise me.'

'And we'll keep you out of it. Tonight in the club, just do what you always do. I mean, whatever that might be.' Levy got a little red in the face.

'What is it you think I do, Detective? Since you've never been in a strip club, what do you imagine goes on?'

'I don't even want to know.'

'Final question,' Archer interjected. 'Is there a time frame when he shows up?'

'No. But we're open till six in the morning, so plan on possibly a long evening.'

'When do you leave? What time does your shift end?'

'Apparently not until you guys yell, "Police."'

'She's right. It could be a long night, Q.'

'Could be a long morning, Levy.'

THIRTY-SIX

'It's a crap shoot, Archer. We either put five girls at risk in a back alley or put a room full of dancers and pervs in danger. I don't know.'

'So you're not looking forward to it either?'

'Not so much, pal. Watching naked girls dancing is enticing, but I don't like the prospect of having firearms on display. That element frankly scares the hell out of me.'

'Then we get him when he leaves,' Archer suggested.

'Like we did at the pizza place?'

'That didn't work out so well, did it?'

'No.'

'This guy is a psychopath,' Archer said. 'No matter how we approach it, he's not going to care who he takes out. There may be casualties. But one thing is certain. If the opportunity arises . . .'

'We've got to take *him* out.'

They agreed to see each other at the office later in the morning to flesh out their plans. In about four hours. Archer nodded as they went their separate ways.

Archer had refrained from discussing the conversation he'd had with the senator. Until he heard from Beeman or some other superior, he wasn't about to make alternative plans. There was a possibility of stopping the thrill kills tonight or early tomorrow morning and that was priority. Number one priority. And if anybody in his department tried to rein him in he was going to fight like hell to get Dushane White.

His cell vibrated and he checked the number. Detroit, but he didn't know the number. Hesitating, he took the call.

'Detective Archer?'

'Yes.' He checked the time. Four a.m.

'I am so sorry to bother you at this hour, but I just found out that Bobby Mercer . . . this is Maurine Sheldon, a prosecutor in Detroit, and—'

'I know who you are. Thank you for your interest in the case.'

'Detective, I probably woke you from a sound sleep, but I just was made aware that you've had contact with Officer Bobby Mercer. We have a warrant for his arrest and had no idea he was in New Orleans. Are you in any danger?'

'Ma'am, I'm a homicide detective with the New Orleans Police Department. I'm a former detective with the DPD, and half of that force is out to get me for turning on Mercer and my two brothers. On both of those counts I'm not sure I could be in any more danger.'

She was quiet.

'Yes, Mercer was here this afternoon. Surprised me. I could have put a bullet in him but I didn't. And I have no idea what his intentions are, but I know he killed my wife and I hope you are on board with Tom Lyons and his team because I want that bastard to pay. Big time.'

'I think we can nail him, Detective. And I'm very concerned that you've had contact and he is in your town.'

'I am as well.'

'I'm in touch with Detective Lyons, and we are in touch with your New Orleans department. We'll find him. Sorry to wake you.'

'Thank you for the call. Believe it or not, I'm still up working on a case.'

'I guess we all are on call twenty-four/seven, Detective,' she said.

'A friend of mine recently reminded me that if crime is up at all hours, we've got to be available.'

'Detective Archer, I will leave you with this. It isn't my job to get personal in my cases.'

'I understand that.'

'I have to deal with the facts. I have to make sure that all the information I need is in hand. My feelings about a case have nothing to do with whether we agree to prosecute or not. You guys have to present enough information to make the case. You've been around long enough to realize that.'

'Of course.' He had no idea where she was going with this.

'Detective Archer, I don't know you. But between me and you, damn, I want this son of a bitch. I'll deny I ever told you this, but I would push for the death penalty.'

'Except,' Archer let go a long sigh, 'Michigan doesn't have the death penalty.'

'In this case, it's a pity. But, Detective Archer, we can get this guy for life. If and when we catch him.'

'I want him more than you do.'

'I'm sure you do. I lost a son ten years ago. A victim of a drug-related drive-by shooting. It's a violent world we live in, Detective Archer. I try every day to gain some ground. Again, sorry for the early call.'

The early morning chill sent shivers down his spine and he pulled his jacket tightly around him, turning up the collar and shoving his hands in his pockets.

THIRTY-SEVEN

One block from the Cat's Meow he sensed he was being followed. Ducking into a doorway he waited. The dull roar of bass-driven music echoed down the street and he strained to hear the sound of footsteps. He waited thirty seconds before he stuck his head out from the hiding place and glanced down the street. Nothing. Archer's heart was racing as he stepped out and retraced his steps. Two, three, four doors down and it was the same. He saw nothing. He wasn't crazy. Someone was following him. He knew it. A couple of drunks in dark suits stumbled down the middle of Bourbon and passed him without a look.

Closing his eyes for a moment he pictured a car, coming up the street and veering onto the sidewalk, heading straight for him. Imagination was a funny thing. His own New Orleans force had been alerted to Bobby Mercer, but he was the only one in danger. Mercer had threatened him and there were no cops in sight right now that could help him.

Archer walked slowly back toward his cottage, wondering where his stalker was. There was someone back there. A block before the club he heard the thumping bass and some off-key wailer singing a Creedence Clearwater Revival version of 'Rolling on the River'. 'Left a good job in the city.' Well, it hadn't been that good a job. But it sure followed him wherever he went.

Spinning around he saw the man, a dark jacket, collar turned up and a black stocking cap pulled low on his forehead. Reaching for his Glock he pulled it from his holster. *Don't ever go for your gun unless you plan on using it. Don't ever shoot unless you plan on killing someone.* The credo of the force. But this was justified defense. He had no intention of using it, no intention of killing someone. He just hoped it would scare off his attacker. The man kept coming.

'Don't come any closer, friend.'

His finger rested outside the trigger guard. Too many cops

killing too many people, unarmed, not threatening. Too many officers fearing for their own life, caught up in the moment, working off an adrenaline rush. Pointing his gun at the thug, he measured the steps. How close would the man get before he would call his bluff?

The arm around his neck took him by surprise. Someone was behind him, the stalker now running toward him. *Damn, two of them.* No visible weapon from either attacker, only an arm around his neck from the person in the rear. If he shot the man running at him, it would be a case of an unarmed assailant gunned down by a bullying police officer. As if the New Orleans PD needed another black eye. But if he didn't do something soon, he was going to be assaulted front and rear. Feeling the squeeze, the pressure on his windpipe, and gasping for breath, Archer pulled the trigger wide, the deafening explosion bouncing off the walls of buildings for several blocks. Chips and dust flew from the stone facade of the wall next to him. He felt the arm around his neck release its grip and he watched the first attacker stop dead in his tracks, not sure what had just happened.

Spinning around, Archer hit the man behind him with his Glock, breaking his nose, blood spraying from his face. He landed on the ground, his hand covering the broken cartilage. Immediately Archer turned and the other attacker was half a block up Bourbon, running as if his life depended on it. The detective clenched his teeth. It did.

When he turned back, his assailant had struggled to a standing position. The man's hands were in the air.

'Don't shoot, man. Don't shoot.'

'Do you have a problem with me? You put your arm around my neck and try to choke me?' A small crowd gathered on the other side of the street.

'Absolutely not, my brother. Don't know you, don't know anything about you. I was paid to put you down.' Blood dripped from his chin, but he kept his hands up.

'Kill me? Honestly, you were going to kill me?'

'No, no. There was no killing from my end. Give you a scare. That was all. My partner and me . . .'

Holding the pistol on him, Archer called for backup on his cell. He studied the young man for a moment, a purple hoodie with LSU embroidered on the front, ball cap with the New Orleans Saints logo and LeBron James Nike shoes. Like the kid was going to the big game, just not sure which one.

'Who paid you?'

'Cash transaction. I don't know him.' He sniffed, finally rubbing his hand over the bloody mess on his face.

'Bobby Mercer? Short, stocky guy?'

'Maybe. A short stocky guy but I didn't get his name.'

'Are you carrying?'

The man nodded. 'In my belt.'

Archer removed a Raven MP-25 from the man's waist, then cuffed him with a disposable hand restraint. The wood grip gun, a Saturday night special, was available on the street for probably twenty-five bucks. Not that accurate with a tendency to jam, but with enough power to kill a man. Archer knew the gun and was sure of that. And he was pretty sure the guy *had* been sent to kill him. Probably with that small pistol.

A squad car pulled up to the curb and a uniform shoved the man into the back seat. Archer handed him the weapon.

'Someone said they heard gunfire, Detective? Was a firearm discharged?'

'Not to my knowledge, officer.' He was required to report it, but it was his word against theirs. 'Take good care of the prisoner and I'll file paperwork in the morning.' And morning was fast approaching.

A white cargo van pulled into the large garage in Treme, parking next to a luxury tour bus. Two men stepped out, the skinny one opening the luggage doors and climbing in. Crawling on his stomach to the rear he started pushing the corrugated cartons to the opening, his partner picking them up and carefully placing them in the rear of the van. Opening the third carton, the partner pulled out an envelope, slitting it open with his pocketknife. He sprinkled the white dust into his palm and licked it like a kid licking raw sugar. It only took a moment. Closing his eyes and rocking back and forth on his heels, he knew it was the real stuff.

'It's pure, Jimmy.'

'Save a taste,' he shouted from inside.

'One of the perks, my man.'

A souped-up Buick pulled into the garage and three men with surgical masks jumped out, guns drawn.

'Keep loading,' the lead man said.

'Hey, pal. You don't want to mess with this. Seriously, this is—'

The one loading the van pulled a Smith and Wesson 9mm from his belt and fired, the bullet hitting wide of its intended target. The three men opened fire, eight shots hitting the man's body as it twisted and turned. The dying man took an involuntary step backwards, slamming against the white van, his blood spattering the paint job with a grisly pattern.

'Come on out,' one of them called to the man named Jimmy.

'Don't shoot. Don't shoot.'

'Out. Now.'

'Please, man. I'm a family guy. Got a little kid. My woman's got another one on the way. For Christ's sake, I'm no problem. Just let me go.' The voice from inside the luggage compartment.

'I'll come in there and gut shoot you if you don't get out of there.'

His head breached the opening, a pleading look on his dark face.

'All the way out, and keep your hands where I can see them.'

He crawled out, swinging his body over the edge and finally standing up.

'How many cartons?'

'Fifty,' he said. 'Take them.'

The masked man laughed. 'Oh, we will. We're not working on a percentage. We're taking everything you've got.'

'I'll walk out of here like this never happened.'

'It did happen, my friend. Over by the van.'

Slowly he walked to the vehicle, stepping in sticky pools of blood.

'Do you want to tell your friends at Solja Warhead that this isn't over? Would you do that for us?'

'I'll get the word out,' Jimmy said, a tremor in his voice. 'I promise I'll do that. No problem.'

'I think they'll get the message anyway, don't you?'

'Please, I—'

The man turned and nodded to the other two. 'Don't want to mess up the van any worse than we did, brothers.'

They walked over to Jimmy, lifting him up by his arms,

and forced him to the ground next to the bloodied remains of his friend.

'You want to fuck with us, this is what happens.'

The three men unloaded their weapons, standing back so the blood didn't spatter on them. The explosions were deafening, as Jimmy's skinny body jerked on the cold concrete floor.

Thirteen shots went through the soft tissue, destroying bones and organs, and when the last shot finished resonating through the building, they stood there admiring their work. Blood, guts and gore, the carnage was everywhere. The metallic smell of fresh blood, the putrid odor of human waste and gunsmoke permeated the air.

'Alexander, get in there and drag out the rest of the boxes.'

Ten minutes later the last of the cartons were loaded. Two of the men climbed into the van, backing out of the spacious garage. The third backed the Buick out and rolled down the window. Reaching into the passenger seat, he picked up a blue-and-white aerosol can and tossed it at the two bodies. Let someone figure *that* one out. The two vehicles disappeared into the night.

THIRTY-EIGHT

'Archer, you look like you drank your night away. Eyes bloodshot, dragging your ass into work.' Chip Beeman leaned over Archer's desk, looking him in the eye. 'Seriously, you look rough.'

'It wasn't alcohol, Sergeant. Levy and I had a late-night meeting with a source, and I've got a guy in lockup who tried to kill me when I returned home. All in all, an eventful evening.'

Beeman shook his head. 'But you're still alive, and there are more problems. Maybe you've heard.'

'The senator?'

'About that,' Beeman said. 'She's trying to pull rank that I'm not sure she has.'

'What's going on, Sergeant?'

'This lady has brought in the Feds. She wants to single-handedly control the human-trafficking issue in New Orleans.'

'She called me.'

'Honest to God? She called *you*?'

'Very emphatic that we stay out of her way.'

'Well, she called everyone else as well. Very sure of herself. We're supposed to back off. From the top down, they're saying we need to let it go for the moment and see where this is heading.'

'And I agree,' Archer said.

'You do?' Beeman took a step backwards. 'That's not exactly what I expected from you.'

'Sergeant,' he looked up from his desk, feeling the weariness and anxiety from a sleepless night, 'we don't deal in human trafficking. I have no problem staying away from that. We do deal with murders. Let her have what she wants. I've got a suspect in the thrill kills, and that's my entire focus. If trafficking overlaps, I can't help that. But let me pursue my investigation and we can put a stop to these killings. I think we can arrest one suspect tonight.'

Beeman nodded. 'I thought the same thing. There's a loophole there. If she's not specific, then we go about our business. And, Detective, our priority is to stop these killings. If you think you can make an arrest tonight . . .'

'So we're clear on this?' Archer looked up at him.

'No. Not at all.'

'We're safer if there is mass confusion?'

'Off the record, Archer, yes. And, off the record, do you want to tell me how you are going to capture this suspect?'

'No. I think, due to the message from the Feds, it's better that you don't know. We will need patrol backup tonight, but I'll arrange it.'

'From upstairs, Detective Q, it's official. Hands off on anything regarding human trafficking.'

'From downstairs, Sergeant Beeman, I'm just doing my job. No interest in the trafficking element.'

'I'm glad we had this conversation, Archer.'

'I was a little foggy this morning, sir. If I missed something, I'm sorry.' He gave Beeman a tired smile.

'Be careful. I'd hate to have something happen to you.'

'I'd hate for that as well, sir.'

Archer had the early-morning thug brought into an interrogation room. Jazeel Jefferson stuck to his story. He didn't know who had paid him, and he was never introduced to his partner, the second attacker. Yes, the man who hired him was short and stocky. No, the man had not instructed Jefferson to kill the detective, just rough him up a little. Archer tried but couldn't shake his story so he sent him back to lockup. Once the paperwork was filled out, charges would be filed. For now, simple assault. Archer felt certain there would be more to follow.

He and Levy grabbed an early lunch at Lil Dizzy's on Esplanade at the top of the Quarter. Fried chicken and a trip to the salad bar. When they returned to the table, their plates full of healthy greens and fruits to compensate for the greasy fried chicken, she was sitting there.

Archer paused for a moment, always surprised at how taken he was with her. She'd added a touch of color to her cheeks and a hint of lipstick, giving her a more grown-up appearance.

Her dark eyes looked up at him and he felt a slight jolt in his chest.

Recovering, he asked, 'How's Kathy?'

'She's fine, Quentin. I'll tell her you asked. Took a day off from work, but I think it's more a mental thing than physical. She'll probably stay at her place this evening.'

Solange smiled at Levy as he sat across from her. 'Detective, so good to see you again.'

He nodded. 'As you know, I'm here because of you, Ms Cordray. The last time we met, you saved my life.'

'And I appreciated the thoughtful note and flowers.'

'You seem to have an uncanny way of showing up at opportune times,' Levy said. She'd pulled a weapon and fired a shot, taking out a gunman who was threatening Levy.

'If your life is in jeopardy again, I hope I can be there.'

'And I'm hoping my life won't be in jeopardy again.'

'Solange,' Archer interrupted, sitting down next to her, 'can we buy you lunch?'

'No. I wanted to talk to you personally. Both of you actually.'

The waitress poured coffee and there was an awkward silence as the two men each took a forkful of lettuce and sliced tomato.

'How did you find us?'

'Look around, Quentin. There must be five tables of officers. It's a police hangout. I had a hunch.'

He smiled. 'Your hunches are unbelievably accurate. So what do you want to tell us?'

'You asked me if your project would be successful.'

Glancing at Levy, Archer nodded. 'I did.'

'What project are we discussing here, Q?' Levy shifted his attention, gazing at both of them.

'Our project tonight, or early tomorrow morning. She tends to have good instinct, Josh.'

'So she knows?'

'No. I simply told her it was a project. No details.'

Levy shook his head. 'The entire town is going to know soon.'

'I can't tell you if it will be successful or not,' she interjected. 'I know that Detective Levy is involved and I can tell you that people will get hurt. If you proceed with this plan, some may be killed.'

'You believe that?'

'Pappa Esplan Ghede believes that. He stands at the crossroads of life and death and ushers passed souls to the spirit world.'

Levy shook his head. 'Ms Cordray, while I am in awe of your sense of timing and thankful for you stepping in to save my life, I'm not sure I can buy into some guy named Pappa who is a death god.'

She smiled. 'And I don't expect you to. I often feel somewhat foolish when I make a prediction, but it's what I see. It's what I know. And all the candles, gris-gris bags and spells will not stop tonight from happening.'

'You're sure of this?' Archer asked.

'There is a good chance there will be casualties. Whatever you are planning, people may die.'

'Ours?'

'I can't say, Detective Levy. I pray that won't happen.'

The coffee was cold, the chicken no longer appetizing.

'Do you drink, Detective Levy? Alcoholic beverages?'

'Occasionally. Why?'

'Pappa drinks. The reputation of the spirit god and his consumption is huge. Ghede means tipsy, due to his love of fermented grass spirits. The two of you would get along well.'

'Why do you say that?'

'White rum is his beverage of choice.' She gave him a wry smile.

Levy stared accusingly at Archer.

Archer put his hands up. 'Hey, I've never been drinking with you, Detective Levy. I have no idea.'

'Gentlemen, be very careful tonight. Please, don't take any unnecessary chances.' She turned to Archer. 'I really want to see you again. In a less stressful situation.'

He nodded, not sure how to respond.

'Detective Archer, if you want to minimize the danger and the chance that people may die . . .' She paused.

'Yes?'

'Cancel the project. It's the best advice I can give you.'

She stood and without any hesitation walked to the door.

'What the hell was that all about, Q? She warns us about dying tonight, then makes a date with you?'

'Do you drink white rum, Josh?'

'Yeah. Mojitos. Every time. How the hell did she know?'

'I think it's more than parlor games and Ouija boards with her.'

'But a drunken god named Pappa who takes you to the other side?'

'We won't know until we get there, will we?'

'I can wait. I've got plenty of time,' Levy said.

Archer's phone buzzed and he took the call. After thirty seconds, he closed his eyes and took a deep cleansing breath. A minute later he ended the call.

'What? Something about Detroit?' Levy said.

'Two bangers, they're pretty sure they are from Warhead Solja, in a warehouse garage in Treme. Blown away, literally. Multiple gunshot wounds. But there are several twists.'

'What twists?'

'First of all,' Archer said, 'there's a packet of Columbian powder sliced open next to the bodies. Two sets of tire tracks in the blood. A tour bus from South America with the luggage doors open and . . .' He paused.

'And what? That's enough to keep us going for a week.'

'When Warhead Solja makes a hit, they tend to leave a can of, I'm sure you will remember, Chill.' He frowned.

'I'm well aware, Archer.'

'These are Solja soldiers. Dead *Solja* soldiers. Someone left the identical calling card with their remains.'

'Damn, it just gets stranger and stranger. Fifteen minutes tops from here. Let's drive over.'

Archer dropped the cash and a tip and they walked out the door.

THIRTY-NINE

'I paid you half up front. So don't give me this shit about how two of you couldn't take this guy. And you aren't even in jail. Your dumbass partner is. Christ, I expected two of you to be able to pull this off. You were recommended, man. Somebody thought you were the ideal team. I mean, we average a murder almost every other day in this town. And you can't pull off *one*?'

'Look, fucker.' The voice on the other end was strained. 'I don't care what you offered Jazeel. I just want another thousand to keep it quiet.'

'Other than a phone number, you've got no ties to me. You don't even know my name. So go fuck yourself. You're lucky you got away with your life, you fucking bottom feeder. Don't call here again or I swear to you I will track you down and carve my name in your forehead.' He'd never dream of it, but he knew people who would. He knew people who could. He knew people who had.

Sitting at his desk he pulled out the flask and took a long swallow. He speed dialed Delroy Houston.

'What you want, Blount?'

'Those two boys I hired . . . your recommendation? They screwed it up big time. One is in jail on assault and the other one had the nerve to call and threaten me. Listen, I want him out of my hair and—'

'I haven't got time for this shit.'

'Oh? We're trying to get rid of an obstacle and you don't have time to deal with that? You tell me what else is so damned important and—'

'Apparently your ear isn't to the ground, Case. We've got some serious shit going on, in *case* you haven't heard.'

'What's that?'

'A little turf war. Nasta Mafia just wasted two of our boys and stole about five hundred thousand in Columbian powder.

Apparently your little pep talk didn't have traction, my man. There's some serious shit coming down, Blount. We're going after those mothahfuckahs and it's going to be a bloodbath. Believe that, my friend. You might think about relocating and starting over.'

They pulled into the garage, two spots down from the bus and the blood.

'That's some nasty shit, Q.'

'One or two shots should have done the trick. These guys were obviously sending a message.'

The crime lab staff was dusting the luggage area on the bus and scouring the concrete floor for any clues.

'What's the deal with the bus?'

'Tour bus,' one of the uniforms said. 'Company called America Travel.' He handed Archer a plastic bag with the Chill can inside. 'Thought you'd appreciate that. It was on top of body number two.'

'They're messing with us, Q.'

'They've been messing with us since the beginning. What do we know about America Travel?'

'Not on the radar. I'll do a quick search,' Levy said.

Archer walked the perimeter. The two bloodied bodies, the inhumanity in the killings. They hadn't wanted him to see Denise after the accident. Her body had been destroyed, crushed and he was OK with their decision. He wanted to remember the sweet smile, the soft shoulders and trim waist. He thought fondly of the sweet smell when he nuzzled her neck, the swell of her hips and her breasts. To see all of that after she'd been run over, it would have been devastating. Tom Lyons had actually been the one to identify the body.

Archer steeled himself for the sight of dead bodies. It was part of his job. Especially when they had met gruesome endings. These guys, laid out on the cold concrete floor, had been seriously wasted.

The one banger's body was destroyed beyond recognition. Multiple shots entering and exiting. Four or five shots to the face had made identification impossible. The other looked like maybe six or seven bullets had done the job. An ambulance was on the property as the attendants looked for his approval to put the corpses in body bags. The wallets with IDs had been secured so he nodded. They were pretty sure who these guys were. No recognizable scars on the faces, although it would have been hard to tell. But according to identification it wasn't Dushane White and Delroy Houston. Those two were apparently safe. For now.

'Detective,' Levy walked over, showing him his iPhone screen. 'I think you're going to find this interesting.'

The image opened with the headline, *America Travel*. The screen showed a panoramic view of some romantic highway scene, all blue sky and sunshine. Under the banner the script painted a picturesque adventure with landscapes, quaint towns and cities where restaurants, cafés, shops and historic landmarks dotted the map. The dream trip of a lifetime.

'OK, so it's a tour bus,' Archer said. 'Maybe a little too idyllic, because it's not all roses and rainbows, but—'

'Yeah. Tourists from South America, Central America and Mexico travel to the United States, and it's pretty pricy. Here's a trip to LA, one to New York, Miami, just about anywhere on a first-class bus.'

'And I see New Orleans is on the list. But what's this bus doing in Treme? My guess is Treme isn't one of those garden spots in the brochure. I sincerely doubt that tourists are staying on this side of the Quarter.'

'I suppose,' Levy said, 'they brought a busload of tourists to New Orleans. They put them up in some fancy hotel, and they sit here for four or five days until it's time to pick them up. And you've got to park somewhere. The rent here in Treme is probably cheap. But the idea that a drug deal may have gone down here, and the luggage doors of the bus are open . . .'

'What are you suggesting?'

'Obviously that will come out when the lab reports their findings. But what a novel way to transport drugs to the States. Think about it, Q. What if you've got a bunch of high-rolling foreigners who stow their tony Louis Vuitton and Fendi luggage right next to a shipment of pure cocaine? And they have no idea. Maybe border patrol and customs goes through a couple of suitcases and just gives them a pass and—'

'Louis who?'

'Vuitton. Louis Vuitton. You don't know these guys?'

'Levy, I've got one banged up Samsonite from fifteen years ago.'

'They're luggage designers, Archer. My ex was obsessed with designer fashions. It's still costing me an arm and a leg every paycheck.'

'And we've got to wait. Wait until the lab decides if there's any drug residue on the bus. Damn, damn, damn.'

Waiting. It was the bane of his existence.

'Look here.' Levy scrolled down the screen. 'This next line will definitely interest you.'

And there it was. At the very bottom of the page. *An Adrien LeJeune Enterprise.*

'You don't think . . .'

'I do think,' Levy said.

'Damn. If that's any relation to the senator . . .'

'I ran a search on that as well. It's her husband.'

'Girls are coming in tonight, right?' Blount asked.

'They are.'

'Any chance we can delay that transaction?'

'Money's already been paid, Blount. People are expecting the merchandise. This is a fucking business, understood?'

'We've got a little escalation in the gang war, Manny.'

'Tamp it down.'

'One group just took the Columbian dust, killed a couple of . . .'

'I don't care. You're paid to deal with it.'

'Well, we talked about shutting down soon anyway. Maybe now is a good time before it gets out of control.'

'The exit strategy hasn't been put in place yet, Case. Sure, we can move it to another city. God, we can go anywhere and set this up, but it's not ready. There needs to be certain precautions. And as you know, there are some people who are at greater risk than others.'

'Manny, am I safe here?'

'Keep a lid on this thing, Blount. You're integral, but it's up to you to stop this problem before it gets any bigger.'

'They stole the powder, they killed two gang members. What the hell do you expect me to do?'

'Give them more money, equal billing, whatever you've got to do. We're depending on you.'

The line went dead.

Blount put his head on the wooden desk and gently banged it, five times. Two violent gangs, a South American cartel, a well-connected hierarchy. And one employment counselor. Who was expendable? He was afraid of the answer.

Manuel made the call to the States.

'We may have to pull the plug a lot sooner than we thought.'

'The senator is setting up the takedown. She's got the FBI involved and local law enforcement. When and if they hit, it will take everyone by surprise. She is going to destroy a lot of businesses, expose a lot of corruption and get accolades that should keep her in office for years.'

'Well, that all depends.'

'I'm telling you she's on a roll.'

'And I'm telling you that all depends.'

'On what?'

'The next forty-eight hours.'

'And what exactly is going to happen in forty-eight hours?'

'One gang stole half a million in dust from a bus. Two guys died execution style during that exchange. The other gang is bringing in new girls tonight. There's a question how that's going to go over.'

'Shit.'

'I thought Blount had it handled but that didn't pan out. How fast can someone muster the militia?'

'I'll get back to you, but not by tonight, that's for damned sure.'

'I'm safe,' Manny said confidently. 'No one is coming to Ecuador any time soon to have it out with me. You, you're questionable, and I hope you have a solid backup on this drug problem. This thing with Case Blount and the two gangs, they are toast. So I'll leave it up to you.'

'Employment agencies and gangs are a dime a dozen. Within a week we pull up stakes and move the operation.'

'A week may be too long, my friend,' Manuel said. 'You'd better make some decisions and make them damned fast.'

FORTY

A chilly breeze ruffled the feathers on a Big Bird costume. The man wearing the yellow outfit flapped his wings as he weaved down Bourbon.

Archer took the call as he walked down the street to Woody's.

'Detective, we've concluded the residue in the bus is a product known as *bone white*. It's a very pure form of cocaine. The traces were faint, but if it was in the hold and packaged well, there wouldn't be much evidence. We've got just enough to be sure that's what it is. And' – the lady paused as if to spring the surprise – 'it's the same product that was in the slit envelope. That powder was bone white as well.'

There was no doubt, the killing had been over a drug transaction. And the assumption was that it was Nasta Mafia who won this round. Two Warhead Solja members gunned down. Archer was pretty sure there would be retaliation.

The crowd in the club was thin this early in the evening but around nine or ten there would be an ocean of people, half of them watching, half of them putting on the show. The show he was going to see tonight was somewhat more secluded than those on the streets during Mardi Gras, but the shouts would be the same. 'Show us your tits!'

With the carnival in full swing there should be a big crowd at the club and he just prayed that the souls who worked there and played there would be safe. If there even was any danger. But then, Solange Cordray said there would be, and he had found doubting her was a big mistake in most instances.

The outside greasy-haired bouncer weighed about 350 and was wearing a sport coat about one size too small. Archer figured he was probably packing. One of those guys who could handle himself size-wise but the idea of having a concealed permit made him even more of a badass.

'Guaranteed good time,' he said, pointing his thumb to the

exterior door as Archer approached. 'Best looking girls in the business.'

Nodding, Archer made the turn and walked into the club. Smiling at the bored hostess, he laid down his ten dollars. He was almost becoming a regular. There was no sign of Alexia or Levy. Archer briefly entertained the thought that she might be in a back room with the detective and actually laughed out loud. Taking this business seriously was tough to do until you realized that some of the workers were here against their will. Some of them were hopeless drug addicts, and their pimps and boyfriends sat on the periphery, watching every move. The amount of dollars changing hands every minute during the evening hours was amazing. It was nothing for a visitor from out of town to stop in and blow a thousand plus dollars on drinks and lap dances. A bachelor party, thousands of dollars. This was a big business, a cutthroat business, a sadistic business where guys like Dushane White and Delroy Houston ran stables of girls up and down Bourbon Street, and up north into the massage parlors.

He sat in view of the door, wanting to catch Levy's attention when he entered. Ordering a diet cola from a young girl in fishnets and a bustier, she surprised him by whispering in his ear.

'Mixed drinks, beer same price as a Coke,' she said. 'Why not have a little fun? Order some alcohol.'

From habit he said, 'I'm working.'

'*This* is work? What are you, a cop?'

He quickly ordered a beer with the Coke and smiled at the girl. 'Wouldn't want to be a cop in *this* city.'

'No,' she responded, 'I would think not.'

A girl on the pole glittered with sparkles, her legs wrapped around the brass rod as she slid down fireman style. Her brief costume wedged between her legs, giving the appearance of total nudity. Archer didn't find it that sexy, but again thought about Alexia, the blonde-haired Sexy Lexy. He might find her interesting up on that stage, and tonight he might be presented with that image.

The music throbbed, a song called 'Rack City' by Tyga. He was pretty sure that was the name of the song since the rapper repeated the phrase about one hundred times in four minutes.

The lyrics he could pick out were certainly ones that never played on the radio. The tamer chorus simply repeated *Rack city, bitch, rack rack city, bitch,* over and over. Archer didn't think he'd be humming it after he left Woody's.

'Come here often?'

She was behind him and he turned, smiling and nodding.

'Buy a girl a drink?'

'You, young lady, are going to bankrupt me. Every time I come in here you want a drink.'

'It's my job.' She laughed and pulled out a chair.

Archer tried to keep his gaze off the sheer top and thong bottoms. Her golden hair was longer, fuller and her eyelashes almost an inch long. Not the sweatsuit-wearing minimalist girl he'd seen the last time.

'Something tells me with the two of you tonight,' she said, 'I'm not going to make much money.'

'I would guess, between Levy and me, you could make as much as twenty bucks before the night is over.'

'I stand corrected,' she said. 'I'll notify my financial advisor.'

'You have one?'

'Of course. Remember, if I can stay alive, I'm not too far from retirement. And I make a lot more than you do.'

Fishnets brought his Coke and beer and he ordered Alexia the champagne cocktail. Ten cents worth of Sprite.

'So it's early, but I don't want to miss this guy. We've got two undercover cars outside and if they see the white van, they're going to call us. We make a decision then. Take him outside, inside or when he finally leaves.'

'Quentin, if you pull that in here, it could be a disaster. You must know that.'

'I do. And out on the street, it's going to be as crowded as it will be in here. The streets will be packed.'

'You can't arrest him somewhere else?'

'Alexia, we can't *find* him somewhere else. Believe me, we've looked. And as you pointed out, he may not show up here tonight. This might be a delivery from Nasta Mafia.'

'Or, and understand I'm working off of sketchy information, these girls may not show up at all. No promises, Detective.'

'I get it.'

'Well, now I feel a whole lot safer,' she said.

'Hey, we're going to arrest this guy but there is no way we're putting any bystanders in harm's way.'

'Bullshit,' she said as the girl in fishnet hose brought her cheap lemon-lime drink. Archer dropped fifteen on the table.

'We're simply trying to take a homicidal maniac off the street.'

'Please, Detective, do it quietly and safely. While this may not be the most seemly group of people, these customers and employees are *my* people. I can bitch and moan about conditions and personalities, about devils and angels, but they are all a part of my life. Be very careful tonight where you tread.'

Archer took a sip of his Coke and looked the girl in her eyes.

'Can I be brutally honest?'

'Of course.'

'You are well above your station.'

She smiled. 'A sincere compliment. But you already know my medical background, so . . .'

'Oh, I think you've figured it out beyond your education. You're bright, witty, very insightful, and yet you've got a plan few people have. I don't intend to screw that up. But . . .'

'But what, Detective?'

'I've got a murder suspect I have to arrest. It's part of my job, Alexia, as much as this' – he threw his arms out as if encompassing the room – 'as much as this is a part of your job.'

'I will help you as much as I can. But right now prepare yourself, because it's my turn on stage,' she said.

'I bought you a drink,' Archer said. 'I'm hoping you don't expect one dollar bills in the G-string in addition.'

'No.' She stood up, her near-perfect body on display for the entire club. 'I expect you to do your job with no casualties. That's what I expect.'

FORTY-ONE

t was almost seven when Levy walked in.

'Got caught up in a case, Q. Sorry. It was a drive-by shooting, what a mess.'

There were few murders that weren't a mess. Archer shook his head.

'What did I miss?'

'You missed Alexia topless,' Archer said. 'I seriously felt like a peeping Tom. It was like spying on your sister.'

'More information than I need to know. And I don't have a sister.' Levy glanced around the room. Men sat at tables and congregated at seats around the stage. Girls served drinks, talking to groups, and everyone was pretty much behaving themselves. 'This is not what I expected.'

'What did you expect?'

'Something more sordid. This place seems pretty sterile.'

'Lots of rooms, corners, lounges where the other stuff happens,' Archer said. He'd been in this place before. One time. Now, he was an expert.

'What's the plan?'

'It's up in the air,' Archer said. 'The girl is afraid we're going to instigate a free-for-all. I think, if it's just Dushane White, we put a gun in his ribs, walk him out and that's it. If he puts up a struggle of any kind—'

'Shoot him?'

'I didn't say that.'

'Then *what*?'

'That's the problem, Detective Levy. If it weren't for the whats and the whys we'd have this thing solved.'

'In the meantime,' Levy glanced at a half empty cup of Coke and a full bottle of beer, 'we sit here and pretend we're on a stakeout.'

'Good point, Detective. We are on a stakeout.'

'Gentlemen, would either of you like a lap dance? Satisfaction

guaranteed.' She was high-school age, her almost naked body
skinny and underdeveloped. Archer was embarrassed at her
approach, but he wasn't here to bust underage prostitutes. Not
tonight. Tall, somewhat gawky, a short bob, a sprinkling of acne
on her cheeks and an adolescent smile. They both shook their
heads. She moved on. Time was money.

'Like Disneyland for adults,' Levy watched her little ass swing,
most of it on display as she walked away. 'I mean, this is a
playground, right?'

'Except' – Archer motioned to the bar where a strange
assortment of characters congregated – 'those are the guardians.
The caretakers. It's hard to make a case that the kids are in good
hands.'

'Point made, Detective.'

Levy ordered a beer and Coke, learning from the wisdom of
the older soldier.

'So, we could be here . . .?'

'For ten, twelve hours,' Archer answered the question.

'We can spell each other,' Levy said. 'I mean, I'll go play a
video game in the car and . . .' He turned his attention to the
stage and watched a voluptuous blonde reveal her 38D breasts.
'Never mind.' He stared at the girl. 'There's probably enough to
keep us entertained right here.'

Archer's phone buzzed as Alexia approached their table. He had
an idea that the messages were going to be the same.

'The van just pulled in and he's apparently got six girls with
him.' She glanced back to the rear of the club.

The call was from a patrol car. 'Archer, there are two of them.
And they've got six girls. Do you want us to try and make the
arrest?'

'No. Let's get them separated from the girls. Stay in place
because we may need you.'

'It could be an hour or two before he brings them out,'
Alexia said.

'An hour or two?' Levy's eyes stayed focused on the girl's
face. Archer knew that was difficult. He remembered the first
time he'd seen her in her work clothes. Quite a shock.

'Orientation,' she explained. 'Some of these girls have never been naked in front of a man. We've got virgins coming in tonight, Detective Levy, and they are expected to produce immediately. Believe me, it's a shock. And they are doing this under duress, threats against their family and themselves, and a quick fix of heroin. So the guys need time to get these girls prepared. They never are. Prepared, that is. But whoever is with them will lay down the law for the next couple of hours.'

'I can't believe this really goes on.'

'You're about to witness it.'

'This is human trafficking, Q.'

'No. We're not touching that right now. It's off limits, Levy. This is about bringing in a suspect in a murder case. That's all it's about. We need to get this guy off the street. That's our priority.'

'But if it happens we slow down the trafficking problem . . .'

'So be it,' Archer said.

It actually became boring. One girl followed by another, one offer after another at their table. The faces were different, bodies were different, but the overall style was the same. If you didn't have money, they moved on. And there were the men at the bar, acting nonchalant, as if they couldn't care less what was happening on the stage, on the floor, but Archer caught them watching, intently at times, making sure their girls were performing, making money. And there were several boyfriends who apparently got a kick out of watching their girlfriends teasing other men.

'We could go down to this dressing room,' Levy said. 'Walk in and surprise them. It might work.'

'He's got six hostages.'

'I'm just nervous about calling him out here.'

'We can only play it by ear, Josh.'

The tables were full, the bar almost full and seats around two stages were all taken, the men thrusting dollar bills into the strippers' G-strings, trying to touch a little more than was legal.

'Did you bring one dollar bills?'

'No, I didn't plan on tipping the dancers,' Archer said. 'But the waitress brought back eight ones with my change.'

'We can always play liar's poker.'

Archer nodded, pulled out a bill and studied the serial numbers.

'Two nines,' he said.

Levy pulled a dollar from his wallet and said, 'Two tens.'

She was restless and closed the shop early. Dealing with drunken tourists and selling cheap gris-gris bags and voodoo dolls was a way to make quick money. It was not at the top end of her profession and she felt her serious calling was more important at the moment. She needed a clear head, an open mind. There was something coming down and she needed some control.

Putting on a lightweight jacket and wrapping a shawl around her shoulders she locked up the building and walked out, embracing the brisk evening. Seven men carrying a large Gay Pride banner marched in lock step down the middle of the street, and a group of screaming girls wearing matching T-shirts ran by her on the narrow sidewalk. A bachelorette party in serious need of sobering up.

Woody's Gentleman's Club with the extended balcony above was dead ahead, across the street. She'd seen it since she was a young girl but tonight the building tugged at her. A heavy-set man in an ill-fitting sport coat paced outside, motioning men to come inside. Solange walked another block, working off nervous energy, then crossed the street and headed back the other way. When she got to the club she stopped, confronting the big man with the slicked back hair.

'Inside, women are taking off their clothes for the amusement of men, right?'

The big man dodged her and kept on walking.

'Wait.' She followed him. 'There are hundreds of girls out here on Bourbon who bare their breasts for free every night. And the alcohol at any of these bars is probably a whole lot cheaper than inside your club. So what do you have to offer that guys can't get out here?' She needed to know. There was some reason this club, this nefarious establishment was suddenly important to her.

He stopped and spun around. 'Lady, I will give you a free pass if you want to look inside. I would wager that, just lookin' at you, you could be a top earner in there. Girls like you are the reason men come in. If you watched the girls out here on the street who as you said "bare their breasts", then you'd understand. Some of these mamas shakin' their titties, often times it's not a pretty sight. You want a look inside? Be my guest. No charge.'

She wanted to. Felt compelled to. Something was going on in that club that she was intimately involved in. And it suddenly hit her. Archer, Bavely, Levy . . . this was where it was all going down. A strip club. It made no sense, and made all the sense in the world. And there was nothing she could do about it. Even if she entered, even if she mustered whatever power, control, she had, she couldn't stop what was about to happen.

It was inevitable. Taking a deep breath and saying a short prayer, she walked away, asking any spirit to intervene and stop any death and destruction. The man shouted after her.

'Hey, girl, I'm not messin' wich you. I get paid if I turn someone like you. I'm askin' real nice, come on in and take a look. Girl like you could make some serious jack.'

FORTY-TWO

'I just came out of our dressing room, and there's some commotion out back.' Alexia smiled, apparently flirting with the two men. 'I think they're making their grand entrance.' Patting Archer on his head, she said, 'Sorry, but I can't do much more for you guys.'

'Hey, you've done a lot all ready. If you can take off . . .'

'I should. I really should. But I want to see how this plays out. And by the way, Delroy Houston, the guy who threatened me, he's here too. Any chance you can take him with you?'

Archer shook his head. 'I wish we could.'

'Maybe he'll stay his distance tonight,' she said.

Over the loudspeaker system the gravel voiced announcer shouted out, 'Hey-ohhhh! Gentleman, we have a real treat for you tonight. Six beautiful young ladies from South America are debuting for the first time in the United States. Ladies, if you would take the center stage so everyone can get a look.'

Slowly the girls walked into the room and one by one they stepped on stage, wearing tiny bras and thong bikinis. They appeared to be somewhat uncomfortable and glances to the right, to the left and over their shoulders said they might bolt at any minute, but expressionless faces and a slow cadence made Archer believe they'd been drugged. Probably with heroin.

Turning his attention to the bar he saw the two black men sit down, one of them speaking to a patron who immediately gave up his seat.

'By the seat of our pants, partner,' Levy said. 'How do you want to play this?'

'I hadn't figured there would be two of them. Both packing I'm sure.'

'We grab one, the other can be a problem.'

'We can't bring uniforms in,' Archer said. 'Freak the whole place out.'

'You take one, I'll take the other one. A gun in their gut, we escort them out the door and—'

'They use the outdoor crowd as cover and split. Or worse,' Archer continued, 'they use the crowd as hostages.'

'We're taking a big chance no matter how this plays out.'

They watched the girls step off the stage as the announcer asked for applause. 'Hey-ohhhh.'

After a smattering of claps, he continued.

'Gentlemen, please be generous with our new talent. They may not speak English very well, but then we don't pay them for conversation, do we? As always, private rooms are available and the lounge is only twenty-five dollars, tips appreciated.'

'Now it's getting nasty,' Levy said.

'Let's take him now.' Archer turned his attention to the bar. 'Houston seems to have vacated his seat, maybe for a restroom break.'

'You walk up like you're ordering a drink, I'll put the gun in his gut and you show your support. If Houston comes back, he's yours. Does that work?'

'Let's hope and pray,' Archer said.

He stood up from the velvet swivel chair and casually walked up to the bar. No one paid any attention to him.

'What do you need?' the lady behind the bar asked.

'Dixie beer,' he answered. He glanced at the door as two muscular black men walked in, pausing for a moment to scope the club, then their eyes rested on the man with the scar on his face.

'Hey, Dushane White. What it is, brother?' The bald man yelled over the music, Lil Wayne doing 'Lollipop'. *She lick me like a lollipop, she lick me like a lollipop, she lick me . . .* over and over again.

Out of the corner of his eye Archer saw Levy approaching, hand under his jacket, ready to draw the Glock. And the two new guys just kept coming.

White tensed, glanced toward the rear of the club as if anticipating something or someone.

'Easy, big man,' one of the men said. 'We just want to—'

'End this shit,' the other one finished the sentence.

They were now in close proximity and the music, while still thumping repetitively, was more background.

'Fuck this shit about percentages, Dushane.'

The man drew a Smith and Wesson 9mm and keeping it close to his chest he aimed it at White. Archer between the two of them, just asking for a beer.

He took the beer, glancing at Levy and giving him a brief nod, then swung the bottle around, hitting the gunman hard in the face. The tall man staggered a step back, surprised at the action, his free hand up stroking his bruised jaw. Archer reached for the pistol, yanking it from his grip and striking him again in the face as the gunman fell to the ground.

Now in control of the 9mm pistol, he swung around and shoved it into Dushane White's stomach.

'Seat of our pants, Levy,' he said. 'You're under arrest, Dushane White, for the murder of Trevor Parent.'

Levy pulled his Glock, training it on the man who was still standing, warily watching the bald man on the floor as Delroy Houston came barreling out of the restroom in the back of Woody's, his gun in his hand.

Archer saw him coming, and briefly debated whether to just pull the trigger and damn the consequences. Couldn't do it.

Girls were screaming, running out the front door, charging into the dressing room. Two men jumped up from their seats, dumping the young ladies in their lap to the floor. The crowd surged for the doorway, people going down and several being trampled. When the man standing pulled a gun from his jacket pocket, Delroy Houston fired his Sig Sauer, the explosion rocketing through the room. That's when dozens of men and girls came pouring out of the private rooms and down the stairs, some pulling up their pants as they hobbled to the exit, girls running into the street completely naked.

Confusion reigned as the mob became a mad crush, exiting the club being their only purpose and the man who remained standing still held a gun in his limp right hand, blood running down his arm from where Houston's bullet had gone through his shoulder.

Archer kept the 9mm in White's stomach, determined not to lose him this time. Levy held his gun steady on the two newcomers as sirens outside cut through the noise and confusion and four uniformed officers pushed their way inside, guns drawn. Dushane

White put his hands in the air. The bald man on the floor, grabbed a stool and lifted himself up.

'You wanna kill me, Gangsta Boy?' White glared at the young man. 'You best stand in line. You may have taken out a couple of our boys in the garage, but you got a long way to go before you get me. See this scar? Messed up my face for a long time. But the other guy, pushin' up daisies, my man.'

Levy disarmed the other man, Leon Jefferson, according to his driver license. And as they handcuffed and shepherded the men to patrol cars it became very apparent that White's partner, Delroy Houston, had disappeared. As crazy as things got, Archer was surprised they were as successful as they had been. They'd get Houston. It was a matter of time.

Picking up his cell phone he dialed a number. A girl's voice simply said, 'Leave a message.'

'Brooke, this is Detective Quentin Archer. You wanted a story. I've got a story for you.'

The Cadillac picked the two of them up three blocks from the club. Houston had the gun burrowed into the small of her back.

'One funny move, Lexy, and I'll blow a hole right through that sexy body of yours, do you understand?'

She nodded as he pushed her into the back seat. Dressed in her gray sweats, her hair tied back in a ponytail she looked nothing like the stripper named Sexy Lexy.

'Drive up Magazine Street and drop me,' Houston said.

The driver headed up Canal and then right on Magazine.

'Right here,' Houston said. 'We'll be fine.'

He shoved her from the car, and they walked a few short blocks to Crescent Employment. He had her cell phone in his pocket and was totally in control of the moment.

'Friend of mine does business here,' he said. 'This hour of the morning he won't be doin' business and we need a place to hang. Maybe I'll tap a little of this while we wait. What do you think?' He patted her rear.

'I've got teeth down there. I think I'd probably bite it off.'

He laughed, a throaty chuckle. 'You might just like it, you know. Strange fruit and all that.'

'You know they're going to find you.'

'You'd be surprised,' he said as he stuck a key in the lock.
Opening the door he escorted her in with a push. 'People can
hide in this town, no one finds 'em. True enough.'

'They found you tonight. And your scar-faced friend.'

'We were stupid.'

'Yes, you were.'

He smiled, then hit her across the face with the barrel of his
gun, tearing skin and bringing tears to her eyes.

'I can say that, you can't. Now you settle down because ain't
no man wants a lap dance from a hooker with a fucked-up face.
You understand?'

She nodded.

They walked up the stairs and sat in a small lounge off Blount's
office. He got her tissues to wipe up the blood. It hadn't been
sixty seconds, the big man with his arm around her neck when
they heard someone opening the door downstairs.

'The fuck?' Houston lifted his arm and stood up. 'You stay
put, bitch. You move one inch, I will fill your ass with lead.'

Walking to the head of the stairs he peered down in the dim
light. *Two in the morning, what are the chances that Blount
decides to work?*

'Adrien, I'm clearing out tonight. Shit, the bus got busted.
Woody's was a rout. Listen to me, man, it's over.'

Blount's voice on his cell phone.

'No, no, I'm not fucking covering for you. They found powder
in the bus. How are you and your lovely wife going to explain
that? And nobody is going to tie me to that. Nobody.'

He was coming up the stairs. Houston took a couple steps
back.

'Hey, the two gangs? They are expendable. I'm letting both
of them take the fall. Me, I just load a couple of boxes and move
on down the road. These other guys, let them rot in hell.'

Another moment of silence.

'You don't want to fuck with me, Adrien. Anything I've done
under the table has been in cash. No record. I can be out of here
in an hour and set up shop in another town, another country.
Leave me alone and I won't make trouble for you. But I can't
deal with your misfortune.'

As he crested the top of the stairs, Houston reached out and grabbed the cell phone from his hand. Blount stood frozen, not believing what he saw, the tall powerful black man with a gun in one hand, a cell phone in the other.

'Adrien,' he used his most menacing voice, 'this is Delroy Houston. One of the gang members that is expendable. One of the bangers who will rot in hell. I always wanted to meet you, the man behind the curtain. Listen, I'm going to take care of weasel dick here, but I want some assurances from you.'

Blount spun around poised to run down the stairs as Houston wrapped his thick right arm around the fat man's throat.

'I've got the mother in a chokehold. I'm holding a gun. He's going nowhere. Now listen, mothahfuckah, here's what I need from you.'

FORTY-THREE

'**N**asta Mafia drew first, Q. The kid, William Washington, was going to shoot Dushane. We didn't make a single move before that. Would have been disastrous. These two guys got in the way. And if you hadn't taken him out with the beer bottle, it could have been a lot of people getting shot. It's all going in my report.'

'No one was killed, Levy. Some injuries, a couple serious, but we are blessed, my friend. And we got White.'

'Seriously, maybe we were blessed. Not a mark on us.'

Archer nodded. 'It could have been . . . should have been a lot worse.'

She was on the sidewalk, just outside the circle where a crowd had gathered hoping to see inside the strip club. There was nothing left to see.

'Quentin, you survived.' She sounded almost surprised.

'Where did you come from?'

'I had a feeling.' She shivered inside her jacket. 'I know . . . you don't want to hear that. It was as if I had an Egun experience. Where the soul of an ancestor went in and protected you. I'm so happy you and Detective Levy are safe.'

'Did you save my life again?' Levy looked down at her, smiling. 'If you were responsible . . .'

'I'm never sure, Detective. But I think there is one more life to save.'

'We've got Dushane White. We've got two members of Nasta Mafia. Whose life do we need to save?' Archer asked.

'I followed two people on my Honda,' she said, motioning to the motorcycle parked on the sidewalk. 'They escaped from the club. One was running from you out the front door, and one I believe was running back to you. All I know is that they ended up together, probably not a good mix. I know where they are.'

'Who?'

'The gangbanger who goes by the name of Houston and the blonde.'

'Shit.'

'Detective Archer, I seriously believe she is in a lot of trouble. You need to come with me.'

Archer motioned to a squad car.

'We can take that. How far away are they?'

'Ten minutes, tops. Assuming they're still there. I have the address.'

Archer gave it to the uniform and slid into the passenger seat as Solange stepped into the back.

'Levy, you handle it here.'

'Careful, Archer. I'll call for backup.'

'Let's go.'

'What's the game plan, Detective?' the uniformed officer asked. 'Maybe we should wait for reinforcements.'

'Seat of our pants, Officer. I think there's a girl who might be in a lot of trouble and I don't want anyone dying tonight.'

Alexia sat next to the fat man on the leather couch, packing tape wrapped around their hands and legs.

'I've made some calls. They've secured the tour bus, Blount. Crime scene tape on all the doors. But, the school bus that brought the girls from Ecuador,' he said, 'that's clean. They haven't figured that one out yet. So, we've got a driver who is headed south. He picks the three of us up in ten minutes. Your friend Mr LeJeune, he puts two hundred fifty thousand in a suitcase for me, and we're off to the races.'

'Where are we going?'

Houston flipped a quarter, catching it and studying the results.

'Me, I'll decide when I get there. Always wanted to visit Guadalajara, Mexico. Mariachi bands, tequila and lots of *coño*. I hear a pimp can do very well in Guadalajara. You? I may just decide to kill you. Or you two just might end up in Ecuador. I would think that Manuel would be happy to see you. You who kind of screwed this whole business up.'

'And how did I do that?'

'Easy-peasy, Blount. All you had to do was turn it all over to us. Instead you couldn't divorce Nasta Mafia. Your downfall, my

friend. The downfall of Adrien and the senator as well. Man what
a story that's gonna be.'

'You really think you're going to jump off a bus and disappear?
My guess is that Dushane White is going to rat you out to save
his skin. I think that every boy in your gang is going to lay blame
squarely on you for the thrill kills. They're your boys, Delroy.
They do what you tell them to do. Once the cops get a taste of
what you've done . . .'

'I've got a stash, I've got two hundred fifty Gs from our friend
Adrien and his lovely wife. I'm gonna disappear and do just fine,
Blount. It's you who needs to worry.'

Blount shook his head, smiling.

'It's all cash, Delroy. You know that. There's no evidence, no
proof that I had anything to do with . . .'

'I kept a diary, Blount. A little black book. Every ounce of
powder, every girl who came into New Orleans is in that book.
If we put out-of-work mammas to work in the fields, or in a
seafood plant, if we had to oversee the workforce, I documented
it. If you gave me twenty workers for maid service, or workin'
in the bowels of some restaurant, I wrote it down. Put your name
down on every transaction, asshole. Every stripper and every
hand-job artist in the massage parlors, Hundreds of drug ship-
ments, several thousand placements. People you pimped out for
Manny, for the LeJeunes and who knows who else.'

Alexia spoke up. 'You're seriously telling me that Senator
LeJeune is a part of the trafficking problem in New Orleans?'

'Oh,' Delroy said sarcastically, 'you are so perceptive. Part
of? I'd say the senator and her husband *are* the problem. Probably
a lot of other places too, Lexy. Lots of money to be made, right,
Case? You just can't trust anyone, can you?'

He heard the knock at the door downstairs.

'The bus is here. I could finish you both right now, but I like
having some human shields. It's been a rough night. I'm going
to cut your legs free, you're going to walk down the stairs and
get on that bus. No problem. Do you understand?'

They nodded as he sliced the tape with a box-cutter.

'Hands stay taped.'

He ushered them down the stairs and opened the door. The
driver, a swarthy Latin American, glanced at his passengers and

shook his head. He'd apparently transported a lot of passengers under duress.

He walked them to a Bluebird 71 yellow school bus, *St Anne School Of Divinity* stenciled on the side. The vehicle was parked streetside half a block up. Houston kept his gun trained on them as the two boarded the bus.

'You're going back to Ecuador, am I right?'

The driver nodded.

'I'll probably be getting off somewhere in Mexico, maybe before that. The two inside, no passports, so we'll probably dispose of them before you drive into Mexico.'

'Sir,' a thick Spanish accent, 'I am getting mixed signals. I have a suitcase for you from Senior LeJeune.'

'Perfect.' The man had followed the plan.

'And orders to drive you wherever you want to go.'

'Even better. We should leave now.'

'But I have recently received other orders.'

Archer rounded the rear of the bus, his gun trained on Houston.

'Shit.'

Pointing his Sig Sauer, Houston fired and grabbed the bus door, ducking behind the metal and glass.

Archer hit the ground, a bullet passing through his left thigh.

'Come on out, Delroy. I've got backup here in two minutes.'

'I can be gone in two minutes.'

He'd never been shot and the wound stung. He tried to stand, but the leg wouldn't support him.

'Throw your gun out and come out with your hands in the air.'

'Fucking cops. You'll shoot me.'

'No.'

'You're down, man. You throw your gun away, I'll have the driver take us away and we're good.'

Houston stepped out from behind the door, his pistol pointed at Archer, who was laying on the ground. He took one more step, his right foot catching in a break in the pavement. Lurching forward he pulled the trigger for the third time that evening and Archer fired from the ground. The bullet caught Delroy Houston in the chest. The man went down where he stood, the gun clattering onto the street.

'Solange, I asked you to stay with the bike.'

The young black girl stood over him. 'He tripped on the sidewalk. Thank God he tripped. We walk on the bones of our ancestors, Quentin. Often they look out for us.' She knelt down, putting his hand in hers. 'In this case, I think someone's ancestor was looking out for you. And maybe for the blonde girl.'

FORTY-FOUR

The headline was bold.

Senator Marcia LeJeune Blindsided by Husband's Business

Archer read the story. The tale of an unfortunate woman who championed the fight against human trafficking only to find that her husband's business thrived on the very same trafficking. And thrived on the smuggling of drugs.

'He works in Mexico,' she was quoted as saying. 'I see him infrequently and am seldom in contact with him. These accusations come as a total shock.'

His leg was healing, but he was on four weeks' leave. He needed an activity. One day off was more than he could normally stand. Distractions like the occasional phone call were welcome.

'Q, they haven't found Mercer. I know the US Marshall's task force is following up a lot of leads, but no luck so far. What's your thought? Is he still down there?'

'I told you, they say it's easy to get lost down here.'

'Be safe, my friend.'

'I have no choice. I'm off duty.'

'I heard. Are you healing?'

'Four weeks. I hope so.'

'You got headlines up here. Big hero. Some of the guys think you went down there just to get press.'

'Tell them they can go—'

'Quentin. We find that asshole, we will close the case. We know he ran her down. And you have some tremendous support here, my friend. Believe that.'

Solange stopped by the next afternoon, Fat Tuesday.

'It's the big day, Quentin.'

He smiled, still lying on his bed with his thigh bandaged.

'Tonight, they parade Bourbon Street, then clean up the slop and supposedly close down the bars.'

'If I remember last year, that never happens.'

'No. Nobody closes the bars in New Orleans. It's one of our many endearing qualities.'

'Any good news?'

'Kathy is healing nicely. She's back at work and done with Paul. Although,' she added, 'the son of a bitch has taken the story about her misfortune and yours and sold the story to *The New Yorker*. He finds a way to turn tragedy into a profit.'

Archer brushed his hair back, swinging out of his bed. Grabbing a cane by his side, he struggled and stood up.

'If you need something I can—'

'No. I need to walk. Get some exercise.'

'It's still a little chilly outside.'

'Tell me about Alexia.'

Solange hesitated.

'She had some stitches. I think she's taking a short break from her job.'

'She'll be all right?'

'Yes. Can I ask you a question? Personal?'

'You can ask. Do I have to answer?'

'No. Of course not.'

'What's the question?'

'The girl, Alexia, I have this . . . feeling, and you don't like it when I do that but I just had this sense that . . .'

'I like her. She's full of spunk, she's cute, she calls it as she sees it.'

'OK, that's what I was going for.'

'Solange, I don't think I'm ready to seriously be attracted to someone right now. But, can I say this without being too forward? If I was, it wouldn't be her.'

'And how is that forward?'

'You're a smart girl, you'll figure it out.'

She stood up and offered her hand.

'The senator, she's clean on this trafficking thing?'

'Detective Archer, you are helping put her husband behind bars. What do you think?'

He hesitated. 'I never want to believe anyone could be responsible for torturing other people. So in my heart, I don't believe she had any involvement. That said, in my training as a law enforcement officer, I sincerely believe she and her husband were knee deep in this. We just haven't been able to prove anything. I believe that her husband, Adrien, is not going to rat her out. It's better to have a wife in the senate in Washington than in some federal prison.'

'The press is giving her a clean slate.'

'We don't always get all the bad guys, but in this case, we got quite a few.'